"[A] serious, **wonderful** work of litera...
—Caro...

"**Sly wit** . . . Morton's is a more shaded and compassionate voice than many of those in contemporary American fiction. He may be to Sally's generation what Ann Beattie is to those a decade older—not the most flattering chronicler, but one of the truest."

—*Philadelphia Inquirer*

"What makes Morton's novels seem like gifts is that they're grounded in the recognizable, banal world of coffee shops and bus stops and hospitals and offices, and are alive to the possibilities that world offers for beauty and human connection. At first they seem to be all grace notes, until you hit a passage where the emotion is well-deep, and you realize everything else has been preparing you for that moment. There may be young novelists who are more daring, or work on a larger scale. I can't think of one who combines brains with tenderness the way Brian Morton does."

—Charles Taylor, *Newsday*

"This is a deceptively ambitious novel. I don't know of a comparable example—an American male first novelist writing with such confidence from the point of view of a woman."

—E. L. Doctorow

"Morton describes Sally's confusions as well as her yearnings with delicacy and insight. His characters are never reduced to caricature . . . He regularly exhibits what might be called a friendliness toward his characters that is both clear-eyed and unsentimental—an attitude reflected in the informal, unpretentious, but emotionally accurate quality of his writing."

—Robert Towers, *New York Review of Books*

continued on next page . . .

"Brian Morton's tender, droll, deceptively placid *Dylanist* is **full of acute observations** of the sweetness and pain of growing up into the peculiar weightlessness of recent American middle-class existence. It's a lovely, distinctive novel and I enjoyed it immensely." —Todd Gitlin

"**A lovely novel**, at once tender and amusing. I found the story of Sally Burke, a young woman struggling to find a path in life, deeply touching. Especially impressive is the portrait of her father, Burke the 'union man,' a figure of great moral complexity and strength. The whole thing is finely done, honest, and artful." —Irving Howe

PRAISE FOR BRIAN MORTON'S
Starting Out in the Evening:

"**Such a pleasure to read** . . . nothing less than a triumph." —William H. Pritchard, *New York Times Book Review*

"**Wonderful** . . . this is what a novel is supposed to be." —*Newsday*

"**Brian Morton's *Starting Out in the Evening* is that rare event:** a finely tuned serious novel that conjures a fully formed and vibrant sense of life in all its complexity and eccentric character. Leonard Schiller, an Upper West Side writer of some repute, is courted in the twilight of his life by Heather, a 'little miniskirted biographer' who wants to write her master's thesis on his novels. Ariel, an aerobics teacher uncharitably viewed by Heather as 'another boring forty-year-old obsessed with her biological clock,' is sweetly befuddled by life, looking for love and a father for a much-longed-for child, not necessarily in that order. These three characters seem so organic and real, their emotions and actions so natural, that the reader slips instantly into intimacy with them. Schiller, Heather, and Ariel lean on and pull on one another with delicately drawn lines of vulnerability and need, gently manipulated by a sensitive creator, who has elegantly accomplished what Leonard Schiller devoted his life to: He has 'through art [brought] a little more beauty, a little more tolerance, a little more coherence into the world.'" —*Elle*

"Subtle, tender, and moving."

—*Publishers Weekly* (starred review)

"Morton demonstrates an **astonishingly sensitive** appreciation for his characters."

—*Library Journal* (starred review)

"A **captivating and lovingly rendered** story about the value and costs of a life devoted to literature . . . [a] winningly unconventional hero."

—*Time Out New York*

"*Starting Out in the Evening* is the story of an artist's struggle, a writer's life, but it fans out to encompass the heroic struggle of life itself that *becomes* art."

—*USA Today*

"*Starting Out in the Evening* never sinks under the weight of its own probing ideas, for Morton stays rooted in the humanity of his characters and their diverse quests . . . **stirring.**"

—*San Francisco Chronicle*

"A pleasure . . . deliciously complex."

—*The Dallas Morning News*

"Brian Morton's novel is **cause for celebration** . . . gorgeous . . . it deserves an enormous success."

—*Palm Beach Post*

"[A] memorable hero."

—*The Wall Street Journal*

"Wonderful . . . gentle and wise."

—*Detroit Free Press*

"**Elegant** . . . rich with language and ideas, an impassioned look at the life of an unfashionable but tenacious old writer."

—*Forward*

Berkley Books by Brian Morton

STARTING OUT IN THE EVENING
THE DYLANIST

THE DYLANIST

BRIAN MORTON

BERKLEY BOOKS, NEW YORK

THE DYLANIST

A Berkley Book / published by arrangement with the author

PRINTING HISTORY
HarperCollins edition published 1991
Berkley trade paperback edition / March 2000

The Penguin Putnam Inc. World Wide Web site address is
http://www.penguinputnam.com

ISBN: 0-425-17226-0

To my mother, Tasha Morton,
To my sister, Melinda Morton Illingworth,
and to the memory of my father, Richard Morton

PART ONE

1

She was a romantic about love, a cynic about everything else. Sally Burke, seven years old, consented to go to the World's Fair for only one reason: she thought she might meet her future husband there.

Both of her parents had attended the last New York World's Fair, in 1939, although they hadn't met until ten years later. She sat in the backseat, next to her brother, trying to imagine a world in which her parents had not yet met.

At the 1939 World's Fair, had they noticed each other? She imagined it as a scene from a movie: her mother, no more than a girl, catches a glimpse of a handsome young man in the crowd. Suddenly, it's as if the two of them are alone, and everything is utterly silent.

And then the crowd swallows him up and the noises return. And the girl, her mother, shakes her head, wondering whether she'd only imagined it all.

Or maybe it was nothing like that. Maybe they saw each other and felt nothing. Could that be?

Sally vowed to be on the alert. If she saw her future husband, she'd know.

"This is hardly a real World's Fair," Burke said. They were walking near the Fountain of the Planets. "It's a pet project of Robert Moses."

"Who's Robert Moses?" Sally said.

Burke began to tell her about Moses, the man who'd built half of New York. He spoke to her, as always, in a considered, level voice.

Her mother, on the other hand, could barely restrain her own excitement. "We're about to see the future!" Walking between her children, Hannah gave each of them a squeeze on the arm. "I may not have seen your father at the last World's Fair, but I saw something even better: I saw television, for the very first time in my life."

The fair claimed to be a window on tomorrow. The smooth clean silent monorail floated overhead, and you were supposed to believe that someday you'd travel through the cities like this. Sally knew it wasn't true.

But as the day went on, she found herself loving the fair. One exhibition featured a scale model of New York. The tiny streetlights blinked; the skinny little rivers shimmered. If she could lie across this city, she could rest her feet in Central Park and lower her head into the water just south of the George Washington Bridge. The city is like a body, she thought. She didn't know what she meant by this.

In another part of the fair, a guide to population trends: a map of the country studded with tiny lights. When a red light flashed, someone was born. When a black light, someone was dying.

She tried to imagine the lives behind each light.

"The Land of the Dinosaurs." They bundled into a sort of floating cup and they drifted, high in the air, through a dense green jungle where dinosaurs grazed, munching the tender topmost leaves of the trees.

"Watch out there, Sarah," Burke said. "One of those creatures is likely to take a nip at your finger."

She knew, of course, that he was only teasing. She knew the dinosaurs weren't real. But even if they were real, she thought, she wouldn't be afraid. The dinosaurs were a noble race: stately, placid, humble. They seemed so awkward, so ill-equipped to survive . . . it must have been obvious even to them that they were doomed to extinction.

At the Illinois exhibit, you went into a dark auditorium, where a robot version of Abraham Lincoln sat on stage, saying wise things about preserving the union.

Sally sat on the aisle, next to her father. Listening to the labor of his breath. He smoked three packs a day; every breath was an exertion.

He stretched his arm along the top of her seat. In the darkness, she hitched herself up a little, so she could smell his hand. He had a special scent: tobacco mixed with another odor, an odor all his own. Heavy, a little sweet. Baked bread.

After the show they went to buy hot dogs and look at the souvenirs.

"You didn't seem too interested in Honest Abe there, Sally," Hannah said.

"Sarah is a revisionist," Burke said, lighting a cigarette. "She believes that Lincoln was essentially a tool of the industrial capitalist class."

Hannah went to the hot-dog stand and Burke browsed over the trinkets being sold to glorify the State of Illinois.

Daniel was moping because John Wilkes Booth hadn't popped out of the wings. "I was ready for him," he said to Sally. "I was ready to wrassle him down to the ground."

"What the hell is *this*?"

Burke was looking with disgust at the souvenir table.

"That's the rebel flag, my friend." The guy who was working the stand glided over, hands in pockets. "The fightin' flag of Jefferson Davis and Robert E. Lee. One dollar."

"Thanks, pal, but I don't want one. I want to know why an exhibition in honor of the man who signed the Emancipation Proclamation is selling the flag of the Confederacy."

Before he said this, Sally hadn't really been listening. But when her father used the phrase "the flag of the Confederacy," she snapped to attention. When he was angry his voice became clipped, his vocabulary precise.

The guy behind the table, nametagged "Brad," was young, lean, pockmarked. He seemed lazily, complacently amused. "Hey. It's a part of history."

Burke raised his eyebrows and drew his head back slightly, as if he needed distance to examine properly this interesting new species of idiot.

"The fuckin' swastika's a part of history too, pal, but I don't expect to find 'em on sale at the Jewish Museum."

This logic didn't seem to mean much to Brad. "Free enterprise," he said contentedly. "If you don't like it, move to Russia." People actually used to say this.

"Is there a manager I can talk to here?"

"You're lookin' at him. Talk."

Burke stepped back; he looked at his shoes; he was deep in contemplation.

He nodded, as if he'd finally understood the problem he'd been considering. He seemed calm. He stepped forward, dipped down at the knees, placed his hands beneath the table on which the flags were displayed, picked it up, and smashed it against the wall.

After Burke had released the table, but before it slammed against the wall; while one or two of the flags were in the air and the others, defying gravity, still rested on the tabletop; while Burke still wore his look of violent effort and Brad, for some reason, was covering his head, as if he was afraid that someone was about to strike him from behind—Sally held this moment in midair. She savored it. She saved it. She knew what the rebel flag was; she thought she understood her father's passion. She didn't know why it was a beautiful moment to her; but it was.

2

If Sally Burke became a kind of radical, this was because of President Johnson's ears.

In 1964, Lyndon Johnson campaigned for the presidency as a peace candidate. His opponent, Barry Goldwater, aimed to bomb Vietnam back into the Stone Age.

"If Goldwater gets elected," Hannah said, "we should think of moving to Canada."

"He doesn't have a chance," Burke said. "And you know how cold it is in Canada? You'd lose all circulation in your feets."

"Canada is the home of the walrus, the polar bear, and the otter," Daniel said.

Hannah always feared that the Dark Ages were just around the corner. Fascism was always waiting in the wings. She was terrified of Goldwater, and she didn't trust the polls.

"Those bastards . . . it's probably a setup. Everyone who wants Johnson will just stay home . . . only the bastards'll vote."

Sally was terrified of Goldwater too. She had no wish to live among the walrus, the polar bear, and the otter.

Like her mother, she was sure that Goldwater would win. On the main street of Teaneck a huge Goldwater billboard went up one day. His face, dreamily spiritual and twenty feet high, above the caption: In your heart, you know he's right.

The words stuck in her mind. She thought about them all through dinner. Lying in bed that night, she thought about them still.

Do I? Do I know he's right, in my heart?

Goldwater claimed to know her better than anyone else did. He was saying that beneath her apparent agreement with her mother, beneath her conviction that peace is better than war, she secretly had to admit that war was better.

If she were old enough to vote, would she tell her mother she was voting for Johnson and then pull the lever for Goldwater? Yes. Maybe. Wasn't there a part of her that knew that her parents, always saying peace was right, always saying that white people and Negroes can get along with each other—didn't she know, deep down, that this was only wishful thinking? When a liberal and a conservative debated on TV, the liberal always had a high-pitched voice; when he crossed his legs you saw a patch of flesh above his sock. The conservative was always relaxed and smooth, with a little smile of aggressive confidence. In his heart, he knew he was right. And the liberal, in his heart, must know he was wrong.

Maybe.

She lay in bed, wondering if she agreed with Goldwater instead of her parents. It was true that there was a place inside her where she felt no loyalty to anyone. . . . She tried to imagine what life would be like if her parents and Daniel died. She didn't think it would be that different.

She pictured his big face on the billboard, the look of calm, saintly mission. The calm saintly mission to bomb them back to the Stone Age.

In your heart you know he's right.

She searched her heart, but in vain.

Johnson was elected handily, and quickly set out to bomb them back to the Stone Age. Hannah, who was always ready to walk with her brimming cup of trust toward any politician who came out in favor of peace, was crushed. She lay flopped on the couch declaiming against Johnson, "that lying bastard."

Burke, more cynical, was merely amused. "Shall we move up to Canada, honey? With the otter, the seal, and the antelope? Should we pack our bags?"

Sally was eight when Johnson started to bomb North Vietnam. For the next three years, she endured, with clocklike regularity, the huge, expressionless, doglike face of Lyndon Baines Johnson, appearing on TV every three months, and announcing, in his stupefying drawl, that his deep desire for a negotiated settlement left him no choice but to increase the bombing.

By the time Sally was nine, it was obvious to her that the intellectual victory had gone to the antiwar movement. She no longer feared in her heart that he was right. Daniel, at thirteen, had entered into a debate in the letters column with the leading conservative pundit of the local paper, and after three exchanges had reduced him to the argument that "despite the clever arguments of people like my young correspondent, we can rest assured that the president has access to information that the rest of us lack."

At school, the war was debated at least once a week.

"If the Communists take over Vietnam, pretty soon they'll take over the world. Pretty soon you'll have to say the Pledge of Allegiance to the Russian flag."

"If Hitler tried to take over Vietnam, wouldn't you fight him?"

"If somebody broke into your house and beat up your grandmother, wouldn't you fight back?"

Only three people in class were against the war: Sally, another girl, and a boy. And Sally and the other girl were afraid to talk.

She went with her family to a big peace march in New York. Some of the other marchers got splattered with eggs. The hecklers were telling the marchers to go back to Russia. "The bastards," Hannah was saying. In Hannah's mind the world was divided between a tiny flock of the righteous and the enormous and omnipotent legions of "the bastards."

Two men on the sidewalk screamed till their faces were throbbing. Sally would have found them terrifying if her father hadn't been so unperturbed. He seemed to take a kind of pleasure in the sight. "What a piece of work is man," he said.

She felt as though her family was part of a tiny group of sane people in a world ruled by the mad. She realized that she didn't know too many facts about the war—but the people who were for it didn't seem to know any either. How could you think it was good that your country was murdering people when you didn't know *why* it was murdering them?

It wasn't just the men who threw eggs who were mad. Madness was in power. Every three months, the massive face, the deep voice, lying, lying, lying. She wanted to grab him by his stupid ears and scream. There was nothing she could do to make him stop the killing. His droning voice drove her mad; his long, doglike face drove her mad; but worst, worst of all were those massive ears. This is what the government came to mean to her: the president murdering thousands of people and lying about the reasons; those enormous ears, ears so huge they belonged on a basset hound, but deaf to reason.

Years later, when gentle liberals took to walking about with buttons that said Question Authority, the slogan filled Sally with disgust. Spit in authority's face.

3

The family spent a week at a motel in the mountains; playing outside, Sally and Daniel saw a boy playing alone, but they ignored him. Later in the day, someone closing a car door nearby told the driver to "Watch your fingers"; the boy looked mischievously at Daniel and Sally, rubbed his hands together, and said, "Wash your fingers." Both of them thought this an example of a rare wit, and for the rest of the week they played with him every day, interrupting their play from time to time with cries of "Wash your fingers!"

At the end of the week they played with Sam for the last time. When their parents came to pick them up, Daniel and Sally, for the last time, told him to wash his fingers, and ran to the car.

As Sally was getting in, Daniel put his hands on her shoulders and turned her around. Sam was by himself in the courtyard, going at the earth with a stick. Daniel brought his mouth next to Sally's ear, and in a calm, clear, serious voice, he said: "Think about this. We'll never see him again, for as long as we live. Never."

Sam trotted toward the gift shop. Sally was amazed. He

seemed to have an aura about him, a glow. He was glowing with the mystery of time.

Sally Burke was a philosopher. Pondering the nature of the universe: this was her passion and her task.

What she lived for was simply to wonder. Giggling in bed with her friend Jodie on a sleepover. Wondering what it would be to lie in bed with a boy. Would there be as much giggling? As much *fun?*

When she was five her mother went to work, teaching in another town. Sally had a half-day of kindergarten; Daniel had a full day of third grade; she couldn't be home alone. So Hannah arranged with Susan Baker's mother that Sally would go home with Susan after school.

When she spent her first day at Susan's house, she thought she was there because the two of them had the same initials. She was too young to realize that this could be coincidence.

But she soon realized that Susan was different. Susan swore: she said "Mother fucker." Sally knew that fucker was a bad word; she didn't know what mother had to do with it. She thought the phrase was just a combination of unrelated words, words linked only because of their sound.

One day they were coming home and Susan felt sick, and she threw up in the snow, and didn't even mention it to her mother.

Life with Susan Baker. Susan Baker kicking her dog, St. Elmo. One day St. Elmo was whining and Susan Baker hauled off and kicked him. Two days later St. Elmo died. Susan Baker didn't seem to care. She seemed to regard it as all in a day's work.

After two months Sally switched to an all-day kindergarten and didn't have to go to Susan's anymore. On her last day there she took the opportunity to denounce Susan Baker and all her ways. Susan Baker's mother was there, and Sally assumed that Mrs. Baker would agree with every word she said: she assumed that she herself was the daughter of every mother's dreams. To her astonishment, she found that Mrs. Baker saw it all differently: she said that Sally had broken half of Susan's toys and hogged the other half. Now it was true that Sally had broken a lot of Susan's toys, but she'd broken them by accident. And they were stupid toys anyway. But she didn't even mind it that Mrs. Baker was shouting at her. As Mrs. Baker shouted, Sally's thoughts were on other matters. She was marveling at the sheer strangeness of this: that someone else's sense of things could be so different from her own.

Broken toys. On a humid afternoon just before her tenth birthday, she rooted around in the dimness of the attic. The land of broken toys. The attic was to the rest of the house as dreams are to waking life. Dark, filled with treasure, and governed by laws of its own. No one ever went there except Sally, but every time she went there, she found that everything had moved.

It was like a sinister museum. Dresses and dolls that she had loved turned up in the attic years later, transformed, hostile, strange.

A dress her mother had bought her almost two years ago, when she was in third grade. She remembered the first time she'd worn it. Elsa Kaplan's party. Robert Berger was there. She had wanted him to notice her. And he had. They'd even kissed. Then he moved to Leonia.

"Did you love him?" her friend Jodie asked gravely one day.

She didn't even know what she answered. What she answered was less important than the fact that she had entered a life in which questions like this were asked.

A humid, threatening Sunday at the tail end of June. The

air was so sticky it was like you were making your way through cobwebs. Hannah and Daniel were off somewhere; Burke moved through the house two floors below. She heard him dimly through the vents. Burke in his natural loneliness, muttering to himself.

Ancient messages. She sat looking through the boxes and boxes of postcards, from a Mrs. Kathleen Scully to Great-Great-Grandma Burke. She had died giving birth to Sally's great-grandmother. No one on earth remembered her. The postcards said things like "See you on the 25th." There were hundreds of them. It was astonishing that so many pieces of paper could say so little. And this was all that was left of Mrs. Scully and Great-Great-Grandma Burke. If not for these post-cards it would be as if they'd never existed.

Me too someday. My children, their children, their children. I'll have disappeared.

Life was full of holes you could fall into and never be heard from again.

What she lived for was simply to wonder. She walked home from school, pondering the nature of time. Her father had been born in the same year as President Kennedy. She'd always thought of her father as old: he was older than other fathers. But whenever they talked about President Kennedy now, they remembered him as a young man. He was frozen in an eternal youth, and her father was aging.

Complaining about a bully who had pulled her hair in school. Her father told her that that kind of person was known as a left-handed monkey wrench. Once he had been named, classified, she felt better. She felt less afraid of him.

In the deepest nether regions of the attic were several car-tons of books. They were all in good condition, and years ago, when she was little, she'd tried to do her parents a favor by bringing them downstairs. Hannah carried them back to the attic. Why? "When you're older," Hannah said.

When she was a little older, it occurred to her that they were dirty books. The simplicity of this explanation struck her as beautiful.

She went upstairs to look at the dirty books. But she was disappointed. They had titles like *History and Reality*. If there was anything more boring than history, it was reality.

There was one that she always thought should be interesting. It had a nice title: *The Wind in the Olive Trees*. She thought it would be about ancient Greece: Pallas Athena, the goddess of wisdom, the patron of the olive tree. But it wasn't. It was about some war.

She went up to the attic every few months, and every time she went there she looked at *The Wind in the Olive Trees*, expecting to be old enough to understand why it had to be kept hidden like this. But she never was.

Burke was just beneath her now, in the bedroom. Still talking to himself.

She crouched in the cobwebby heat, holding her breath, to listen.

When he thought he was alone, he unburdened himself. Sometimes he told himself the punch lines of private jokes. You'd hear him saying—in an Irish brogue you never heard from him in normal life: "There's a new era of cooperation with the bosses." And then chuckling madly.

Sometimes you heard him repeating his favorite axioms, to reaffirm his sense of life. "If you want something done right, you better do it yourself." The beginning and the end of wisdom.

But today he was in the mood she liked best, the dreamy mood. "Hannah?" In a gentle, dreamy, faraway voice, he called his wife's name. Sally never heard him speak her name so tenderly in her presence. Maybe when the two of them were alone? She doubted it. It was as if he could be closest to people when they weren't there.

The attic was hot, the air was inert. She could almost smell the wind from the olive trees, the humid skin of the olives. From where she was crouching she could see the dress she had worn to impress Robert Berger.

"I think that when you've loved someone, you never stop loving him," Jodie once said. The wisest thing she'd ever said. The most generous. The most human. When she'd said it she was eight.

Endless talks about boys with Jodie. Boys were natives of a foreign land. They were next to you in class every day, but they might as well live on the other side of the river: you could see them, but you couldn't really talk to them, and you couldn't know what they were like. Sometimes she wondered why she and Jodie talked about boys so much. They talked about boys in a way she found slightly unpleasant. They talked in some language Jodie had invented or learned, a language that implied that boys had to be tricked into liking you. That wasn't what Sally really thought. She never spoke about it, but she dreamed of a kind of boy she wouldn't want to talk about with Jodie. Around Jodie she had to be clever and sarcastic. She had no doubt that the boy of her dreams existed and that she'd find him someday. Usually when she thought of her future husband, he was in suspended animation. But now it occurred to her that even if she didn't meet him for another fifteen years, he was alive *now*. The crazy thing was that if she met him in fifteen years and asked him what he was doing on this date in history, June 17, 1967, he wouldn't remember. While she was sitting here, holding him in her mind.

"Joan?" Burke said, from the bedroom.

Burke didn't realize that Sally was still in the house. Her father had a fond but distant regard for her, as if he observed her through a telescope. Sometimes when she slept over at Jodie's she'd call home, and if her father answered she'd ask for herself. She wouldn't even have to disguise her voice. He'd say that Sarah wouldn't be back until tomorrow. She would hang up, delighted with her trick, but also full of pity for him. It was a trick she never could have pulled on her mother. If you changed your underwear in the middle of the day, Hannah would somehow know you had new underwear on. If Sally asked her father how old she was, she wasn't sure he'd know. He'd have to guess.

Burke was at a slight angle to the rest of the family. Once he came into the living room and saw Hannah and Daniel lying on the couches, Sally lying on the floor. "The Jews are a horizontal people," he observed mildly, and left the room.

At a slight angle to the world. His name was Francis Xavier Burke, but no one called him Francis, no one called him Frank. He had only one name. He was Burke.

He never called Sally Sally. He always called her Sarah: the name she was born with.

She liked this. His formality, somehow, felt like intimacy, like a secret the two of them shared.

"Joan?" he said. "You wanna get the . . . you wanna get the paper?"

Sometimes, when he thought he was alone, he talked to his sister. Joan Burke, Sally's aunt, had died when Sally was seven. Sally didn't remember her very well. But she did remember the tales of her death. She'd had a cancer that had gone into her brain. She called out for her cat, Pinochle. She thought the doctors were waiting for Pinochle to arrive, to make his diagnosis.

This was because of brain damage. Sally, the summer after third grade, had gone to brain-damage camp. Hannah had a job there, as a counselor for the "neurologically impaired." She taught the brain-damaged children, and brought her own children along.

It was a hellish summer. Retardation, water on the brain, borderline impairment, everything that could happen to make you less than fully human. They pull on your head when you're coming out of the womb. Up till then you were perfect, and you could have stayed perfect, but the doctor squeezed your head too hard, impressing his fingerprints into your soft skull, and you're brain-damaged for the rest of your life.

Along with dinner the campers were served their medicine, in little paper cups. Even with the medicine people were always "pulling a seizure." There was always some jerky kid racing around yelling, "Packy's pullin' a seizure down by the swings!"

All summer long the air was thick with cruising wasps. Big fat retarded boys quivered in fear when they went outside. A wasp landed on Sally's wrist; she'd been told not to provoke them with sudden actions; so she sat there, unmoving, watching the wasp, as it patiently and precisely inserted its stinger into her wrist.

Sally made friends with a girl named Liz. Sly-eyed, sharp of movement, witty and intelligent. A little too witty: she could never stop the jokes, they poured from her mouth. She was one of the smartest people Sally had ever met. Hannah said she wasn't brain-damaged, just hyperactive.

They had relay races. When Liz ran, she was the most beautiful creature Sally had ever seen.

At dinner Liz ate everything, but she wouldn't touch her milk. One night the counselor at her table, in a surly mood, told her to drink it up. She said no. The counselor told her that she couldn't leave the table till she drank her milk. Liz folded her arms across her chest and didn't say anything. The counselor looked with a mute appeal at Mrs. Ravitch, who ran the camp. Mrs. Ravitch, in tennis shoes, came gliding up silently, with her air of calm, unhurried menace. "I'm sure you'd really like to drink that milk, wouldn't you, Liz?" Liz didn't speak; she didn't look at her.

Sally knew that she was going to lose.

Mrs. Ravitch picked up the glass. Liz sealed her lips. Mrs. Ravitch brought the glass forward.

But why? Why not just skip the stupid milk, if the milk makes her—

Liz knocked the glass in the air, spilling milk on everything, tried to turn the table over but it was too heavy, lashed out with a few wild flailings, catching Mrs. Ravitch on the lip, tearing her lip with her ring—

During free time a week earlier Sally and Liz had gone to the edge of the camp area to look at the mountains, and Liz had shown her the ring, which was a present from her grandma who died.

Mrs. Ravitch and the counselor grabbed her and dragged her toward the door, Liz kicking and screaming and trying to grab anything she could grab—a chair, a table, a hand. She reached for Sally's hand as she was being dragged past.

Sally pulled her hand away.

Liz looked her in the eye. And then she was dragged out the door.

Sally never saw her again.

She hadn't meant to pull her hand away. It was instinctual—she was scared. But why was *that* her instinct? Why wasn't it her instinct to grab her hand? Why did she have the wrong instinct?

She never forgot that moment. She lay in bed, months later, living it over, wishing she could live it over differently.

"I have no guts." One of her parents' friends said this, at the end of dinner. He'd told a long story about having done something he was ashamed of. Sally hadn't been listening, but this stark sentence woke her up.

A heavy, red-faced young man—he'd worked with Burke for a while. After he made his confession, she looked at him more carefully. He looked as if he wanted to be punished.

But Burke wouldn't punish him. "It's not a case of having

guts or not having guts," he said. "Nobody's *born* with guts. You just weren't prepared. You made a mistake—what you have to do now is learn from it."

"Maybe the only thing to learn from it," the man said, "is that I have no guts."

"That's crap," Burke said. "That's self-indulgent. You can beat yourself up for the rest of your life, if that's what you want to do. Or you can pick yourself up and do better. There's nobody alive who hasn't made mistakes, bad ones. The question is, what do you do *after* you've made your mistake? That's when you find out who you are."

As she listened to this, she was proud: he was so commanding, so assured. When she saw tough-guy detectives on TV, they reminded her of her father.

There were times when he wasn't so commanding. He was a terrible driver: a trip to the local candy store with him could be an experiment in terror. Once when someone commented on the fact that it was Hannah who always drove, Burke said, "She's funny that way. She gets carsick if anybody else is behind the wheel." Burke, who wasn't afraid of anything, was afraid to admit that he couldn't drive.

Sometimes he seemed . . . helpless. Lying in bed one night, she heard Hannah ask him to make sure she was asleep. She didn't want them to know she was awake, but when he opened her door, for some reason, she decided not to close her eyes. She didn't speak, she didn't give him any other sign that she was awake; but she lay there in bed with her eyes open, staring at him. He stood in the doorway peering into the dark room. Then he closed the door and she heard him saying to Hannah, "She's out like a light."

He simply couldn't see her eyes in the dark—she understood that. But all the same, it disturbed her. It made her wish that she could protect him . . . it made her feel that he needed to be protected.

"Sarah?" he said.

He was downstairs, just below her. It was as if he'd heard her thinking about him. She was startled, but she stayed where she was, crouching near the attic door.

"Sarah?" he said.

He hadn't heard her thinking about him. He didn't know she was in the house. He was calling her name for reasons of his own . . . it was doubtful that he really understood them himself. If she were to come downstairs and show herself, he wouldn't know what to say.

4

Sometimes you read of entire populations that history passed by. "The discovery of the sea-lanes between China and Western Europe facilitated the transport of jewels and spices from the East; and the towns along the now-obsolete land route, once thriving centers of trade and culture, lapsed gradually into somnolence and decay." The traders and scholars in the decaying towns, it may be, didn't have a clear idea of what was happening to them, of why their way of life was lapsing into decline. They carried on bravely their rearguard existence, refusing to believe that there was nothing they could do to maintain or revive it.

Yes. If you read history, you read about this sort of thing often enough. But it probably doesn't occur to you that similar descriptions might apply to your loved ones—or even to you.

During much of Sally's childhood, her father was a man without a country. The locomotive of history takes many sharp turns, said Lenin, and those who can't hang on are thrown on their ass. Francis Xavier Burke had been thrown on his ass.

His past, his origins, were a mystery to his daughter. He would reminisce for hours, but somehow it all remained vague. He'd tell about his athletic triumphs at Flushing High School; about the gentlemanly ex-cons his father brought home to tea; about his break with the Catholic Church, at the age of eight.

"What happened, Burke?" Hannah said. "You saw Father Flanagan pay a little visit to the local cathouse?"

"Like hell I did. I didn't need any revelations. As soon as they told me that dry little cracker was the body of Jaysus, I knew it was all a bunch of horseshit, and after that I never looked back."

He talked a lot about his youth, but Sally always felt the way you feel when you're reading a book of stories translated from the Hungarian. If a man in one of these stories, visiting his boyhood village, kisses his aunt on both cheeks, you don't know if he's bewildering her with an unfamiliar gesture or touchingly honoring the customs of the region he's left behind. Hannah's stories of her youth were immediately understandable—her mother, the seamstress; her father, the painter and actor. Burke's were stories of a strange country, with strange ways.

Once when Sally was little, she and her mother took a plane trip somewhere, and they passed over Chicago in the dark. And sometimes, after this, when she thought about her father's life, she thought it was like Chicago, observed from the air. You could see the lights clearly—but what each light signified, what lay in the dark spaces between them, you had no idea.

One day Jodie and Sally and a few other friends were playing in the house; Jodie was explaining how they could set up the chairs into a playhouse; and when Burke said, with crisp admiration, "She's a real organizer," Sally was as jealous as she'd ever been in her life.

For the first fifteen years of his working life, Burke had worked as an organizer for the Office Workers' union. His work was his devotion; he was fulfilled. Organize, to him, was the most important word in the language.

He talked lovingly of the years he'd spent organizing: in Moline, East Moline, Davenport, and Rock Island ("You never heard of the Quad Cities, Sarah?"), in Baton Rouge, New Orleans, Philadelphia, East Lansing. He tramped around places that were as strange to Sally as the cities of the moon; hung around the factory gates to see where people went at the end of the day; hung around the bars they went to; for nine years he lived out of a suitcase; "That's how I got these flat feet, Sarah, from trudging around the Quad Cities"; he would come into the city unnoticed, leave unnoticed when the job was done; winning sometimes, losing more often, for that was the nature of things; persistent, endlessly persistent, he worked against what he called the boss class with the patience of a man who knew himself to be playing a small but necessary part in a struggle that was many generations old.

Then something happened. The locomotive of history got shunted onto the wrong track.

What happened was this. It was discovered that the labor movement was infested with dangerous radicals: card-carrying members of the Communist party. Eleven infested unions were purged from the Congress of Industrial Organizations; most of these unions soon fell apart, and the people who'd worked for them were shut out of the labor movement. It didn't matter whether you were a Communist or not: the mentality of the day encouraged guilt by association.

This was not relevant in Burke's case, for Burke *was* a Communist, body and soul. He was dedicated, body and soul, to the overthrow of the capitalist order.

But let's not get carried away here. He was a guy from Flushing. He loved Abraham Lincoln. He loved DiMaggio. At the union office he read the *Daily Mirror*—a tabloid with a great sports section. He kept it hidden inside a copy of the *Daily Worker,* because the more pious of the comrades would have disapproved.

So he found a job as a plater in the Ford factory in Mahwah, and he and Hannah had children, and the two of them retired into themselves, for history was on the wrong track, and all they could do now was to live private lives.

He worked the lobster shift, three to eleven; he didn't get home until long after Sally had gone to bed. But sometimes she woke up and heard her parents talking in the kitchen. Hannah fixed him a snack of cream cheese and chives on Ritz crackers, night after night, for twelve years, and the two of them sat at the kitchen table talking as he ate his midnight snack. Sometimes Sally heard their laughter through her half-opened door.

He was home during the day, when Sally was too little to go to school. Home to prepare gourmet breakfasts of toast and cocoa. He'd put the toast on the table and say, "Take it away, Angelo"—she never knew why. She dipped the toast in the cocoa: the buttery chocolate, the sweet bread. Home to give her a midday bath, to lift her from the water with his tobacco-scented hands. She liked to stay in the bath as long as she could—as long as she could fool him. "I'm still *soapy,* Dad." "Then get back in there and unsoap yourself." He fell for all her stratagems: he was easily fooled.

Burke and Hannah eventually drifted away from the party, which had less and less meaning for their lives; but they remained loyal to a sort of dream communism, a communism of the imagination. There wasn't any single moment when

Sally learned about their politics. It came gradually. Her parents would have their friends over—they had a small group of old, steady friends—and they'd talk politics, which bored Sally to death, she tuned it all out. At the end of such conversations her father would rise and scratch his head and say: "I'm aware that Marx and Engels were infallible, but frankly I think if they were around today they wouldn't know their ass from their elbow either."

One couple, the Levines, used to come over and spend the night arguing with everybody else. Sally gathered that the Levines had been Socialists. Apparently Socialists and Communists were different.

She asked her father what the difference was. "Oh, just a little disagreement about democracy," he said. "The Levines believe that you can make an omelette without breaking any eggs."

She didn't know what communism meant to her parents, but she could tell it meant different things. Burke was dry about it, cynical, matter-of-fact. For him it was something hard.

For Hannah, whatever else it meant, communism meant her father, the star of the Yiddish theater, carrying her on his shoulder in the May Day parade; it meant Saturday night socials with the other Young Pioneers, making lemonade, singing folk songs, and making prank phone calls, in a spirit of youthful mischief, to people chosen at random from the phone book. It was a sentimental relation. One night when they had their friends over Hannah said, "We didn't leave the party. The party left us." She sounded mournful.

Communism was a word she spoke with fear and reverence: as if it were the sacred word of a persecuted religion. "Don't ever tell anybody that we used to be Communists, Sally. Anybody."

For Sally, communism was strange. It was an idea with too

many sides: an idea that couldn't be thought. Khrushchev pounded his shoe on a table; Khrushchev said, "Ve vill bury you." But Benny Sherman was a Communist, and Benny Sherman was gentle, and Benny Sherman had been buried himself. Hannah told stories about the long-lost Benny Sherman; she'd been sweet on him when she was a girl. He tried to cultivate a mustache; he smoked a pipe. When she talked about him her voice changed. Hardly more than a boy himself, Benny Sherman went to Spain to fight for democracy, and now he lies buried in the Spanish countryside, under a green hill.

Don't ever say the word outside the house. Hannah lived in fear that people would find out . . . but find out what? What was the terrible secret? That she had loved Benny Sherman? That the Young Pioneers made phony phone calls? Sally didn't understand a thing.

5

What could be more horrible than a trip to Grandma's? Sally sat with Daniel in the backseat, sweltering. They were on their way to Flushing. Even the name of the place where she lived was horrible. The land of the flushing of toilets.

They rang the doorbell and waited for the buzzer to buzz. Burke didn't have a key to his mother's apartment.

They walked through the dark, potato-smelling halls. Grandma Burke was waiting at her door—skeletal, white as mist. She gave Sally a kiss. "Look how beautiful you're gettin'." Her kiss was bony, light, and dry. Preferable in its way to Grandma Salmon's, which was a big wet lip-smacking extravaganza, a kiss that had you wiping your face for the next half-hour.

Having offered up her cheek for the kiss, Sally had fulfilled her responsibilities for the day. Grandma Burke liked her, but she lacked the energy to pay attention to her for long. So she was free.

But she wasn't free to do much. The TV reception was bad in Flushing, and she'd forgotten her book. Daniel was absorbed in *From Here to Eternity;* he didn't want to play. He never wanted to play anymore. The era in which they'd spent whole afternoons inventing scenes from the life of Lord Booby, genius, polygamist, and madman, was long gone.

She looked at her grandmother's bookshelves. She knew them by heart. There were a lot of fat books there: they used to be Joan's. They were too grown-up for Sally, but it was nice just to have them there to look at. She took down the one with the strangest title. *How to Read a Book*.

"So how've you been, Mom?" Burke said. He settled into a chair and took out a cigarette. He had his absentee smile on. A smile that was meant to show good will—but that also showed that he didn't expect you to say anything interesting. Sally sat on the floor, contemplating her father's smile. He might as well have carried around a smiling mask.

Grandma Burke went off into a long story about Mary Fussell, a slightly younger woman in the building who was the chief source of drama in her life. Burke smiled with boredom and Hannah knit, moving her lips as she counted stitches.

Sally wandered off to the bathroom, for comic relief. There was an old weather-beaten poster on the wall: an illustration of a smiling black boy standing naked in a tub of blackish water. The caption: "How Ink Is Made."

The sight of this always amazed her. It was so foreign from anything her father would find amusing. How could he be Grandma Burke's son?

Grandma Burke lived in an alien world. She never came out to New Jersey. Sally didn't believe she *could* come out to Jersey. Flushing was an ancient land; the furniture, the odors, the shadows in her apartment were from the nineteen-teens; if you brought her to New Jersey, she would turn to dust.

On the bedroom wall, Jesus was pinned to the cross. He looked down at her sorrowfully.

She much preferred to visit her mother's parents. True, Grandma Salmon could be annoying—she was always squeezing you and pinching your ribs and accusing you of being a "skinny little chicken"—but she always had strange and delicious things to eat: gefilte fish, potato latkes, matzoh brei. The food was so good it made up for the grief she gave you when you ate it. As she served you she would denigrate the food—she'd overcooked it, she hadn't used enough salt, she hadn't had the proper spices; but if you tried to reassure her by saying the food was good, she would glare at you in outrage: "It's only *good?*"

The reason Sally liked to visit them was Grandpa. Grandpa was more fun than any other grown-up Sally knew. He was full of jokes, stories, word games; he was never too tired to play; and if he went downtown, even for half an hour, he was sure to return with a little present—a brush, a mirror, a doll.

Grandpa was an artist. His paintings were all over the house in Teaneck, and Sally assumed—there was no reason to doubt it—that he was one of the greatest painters who'd ever lived. He'd been an actor in the Yiddish theater when Hannah was a girl, and now he was the director of the Milwaukee Jewish Center's theater company.

Because they lived so far away, she saw them only a few times a year. She often wished that they could change places with Grandma Burke. Once, when she was six, she had suggested this, but her father had not been happy about the suggestion; from then on she kept that daydream to herself.

She waved goodbye to Jesus, came back to the living room, and sat cross-legged on the rug. "Don't sit on the floor, you loon," Hannah said. "There's room for all." But it was important to sit on the floor. It was important to stay away from the green chair. Grandma Burke's green chair waited in the corner: ageless, brooding, patient, and filled with evil purposes. It had a lumpy back that hurt your head. It had tight little coils of fabric that went through your dress like steel wool. She tried to keep a safe distance between herself and the green chair, but somehow, by the end of every visit, the green chair had trapped her again.

For dinner Grandma Burke served various kinds of burnt food, on dishes with the dried flecks of meals past. Dinner did have a bright spot: Grandma Burke always made potatoes, which she referred to as "padaydas," which always caused Sally and Daniel to commune in secret mirth.

They visited Grandma Burke about once a month. An afternoon in Flushing—how can that be so bad? But it never ended. Grandma Burke, insubstantial, thin as mist, never had a thing to say—never an observation, never a joke. Hannah would knit, biding her time; Daniel would sit reading or listening to a ball game. Burke would talk to his mother, though not much; mostly they just sat there, not saying anything. A smell of mealy potatoes in the air, the chair of sorrows, the airless apartment, the martyred Jesus pining on the wall, How Ink Is Made, and Burke sitting there, with his mask of friendliness on, and what kind of man was he anyway?, because it was impossible to tell whether he was here because he loved his mother or because this is what you have to do. By the time they left Sally usually had a headache. On the ride home she would lie in the backseat, exhausted, looking up through the rear window, watching the dark trees shoot past.

Sometimes she wondered whether she herself would be a lonely old grandmother someday, making some young girl miserable simply by being alive.

6

Daniel read at the dinner table; he read in the car; he read as he brushed his teeth. He read in bed and never bothered to put the books aside before turning out the light, so every night he slept with three or four books beside him. His books stood crookedly on his bookshelf, bulged out of shape from soap and ketchup and root beer and rain and the weight of his body.

He was shy from the start, and as he grew older he grew shyer. Sometimes Sally sensed in him a certain fear of life. It puzzled her. She thought of her brother as something of a god; she couldn't understand what he had to fear.

When he was in the eighth grade, he made it to the finals of the statewide spelling bee. Sally sat with her parents in the audience. His rivals were eliminated one by one. Daniel was the youngest kid on stage. And yet he seemed the least concerned. The others were all biting their lips with nervousness. Daniel looked as if he was sitting at a bus stop on a Saturday morning, waiting for a ride to the beach.

Sally sat between her parents. Hannah was knitting furiously; even Burke seemed uneasy, stepping out of the auditorium once in a while for a smoke. But Sally was calm, luxuriating in her sense of destiny. Daniel was unconquerable.

Daniel and two others were left. He stepped up to the podium to start a new round, looking bored. The moderator pronounced the word, which Sally had never heard before. Daniel repeated it. Then he repeated it again.

She sat forward.

"E-l-e-e-m-o-s-i-n-a-r-y."

"No, I'm sorry. Miss Perkins?"

Miss Perkins, a fifteen-year-old who resembled the last of the woolly mammoths, stepped forward with a cunning and confident air, and spelled eleemosynary.

Daniel sat in his chair, rubbing his thumb over the nail of his other thumb, giving the process the minutest attention.

On the way home Hannah tried to comfort him. "It's just a spelling bee. Who cares about a stupid spelling bee, anyway? And what a word. What a nerve, to ask you to spell a word like that. I wonder who *chooses* those words. I wonder how that Perkins girl knew that word was going to be asked. You could tell she knew. You know, I bet my bottom dollar there's something fishy going on there. I have some contacts in the state Board of Ed. I'm going to have this looked into . . ."

Burke didn't say much. But later in the day he told a story, apropos of nothing, of how the great DiMaggio had been struck out in the ninth inning by Bob Feller in a crucial game at the end of the year, and the Yankees had lost the game and the pennant race. And how the next year, in an equally important game, Feller tried to throw the same pitch he'd beaten DiMaggio with the year before—and DiMaggio had belted it deep into the left-field seats.

"I seen a lot of long home runs—Ruth, Kiner, Jimmy Foxx, Hank Greenberg. But that was the most tremendous shot I ever saw."

7

Burke spoke in parables. He never told you large general truths about how to live. He told you about DiMaggio.

He liked to talk about the day Ted Williams hit a huge fly ball to the monuments in center field. Running flat-out with his back to the infield, DiMaggio made an over-the-shoulder catch. The next batter hit a dinky little pop-up just behind second base; Burke, following the flight of the ball, expected to see it drop in—but DiMaggio, playing the hitter perfectly, was already there. He didn't even have to move.

Burke never drew any morals, but Sally thought of this as his lesson in the value of being prepared.

The tale closest to Burke's heart, and therefore to Sally's, was about the way DiMaggio retired. One of the many ways he set an example was in how he gave up the game. Unlike the greats who hang on after their talents are spent, muddying the memory of their greatness, DiMaggio retired at the peak of his form. He was hitting as well as ever; he seemed to be as fast as ever; and it seemed he'd be able to keep it up for years. But DiMaggio knew that he'd lost a step; he knew his swing was a fraction of a second slow. It wasn't reflected in the box score yet, but in a year or two, it would be. So

DiMaggio allowed those who loved him to remember him as he was in his prime: he had one more championship season, and then he retired.

One effect of these stories was to turn Sally into a baseball fan. Baseball was a language she needed to know, because it was a language in which her father revealed himself.

"I hope I go out like that myself, when it's time to go," Burke once said. "Joltin' Joe."

8

Sally celebrated her eleventh birthday in the summer of 1968. For the next few years, she ceased to exist.

After dinner there was chocolate cake. Sally blew out the candles, wishing for the affections of a certain Peter Arnold.

Later she went to her room. On her night table was a beautiful, adorable, shiny, tiny TV.

Hannah was behind her, grinning. "Isn't it cute?"

She had seen it on sale and "couldn't resist." She'd grown up in the thirties, and she was incorrigibly frugal: if Sally left a bit of meat on the bone at dinner Hannah was sure to lecture her on her wastefulness and display her own shiny bone as proof of the lessons of the Depression. But the reward for all this was that she allowed herself an occasional touch of extravagance.

Sally took out a subscription to *TV Guide*. It was waiting in the mailbox every Friday. Every Friday she walked home from school with a reverent step, seeing it very clearly in her mind. She brought it upstairs and laid it reverently on her bed. The *TV God*. Without hurrying, she changed her clothes, and then, in the hour before dinner, alone, with no duties, with the weekend stretching out before her, ah, the weekend, she did her devotions: she sharpened her red pencil and, lovingly and carefully, she underlined the important shows.

Later she would turn her attention to her other sacred text, Leonard Maltin's *TV Movies*. She saw the movie *Fahrenheit 451*, about a world where books are illegal and a colony of dissidents, each of whom learns a book by heart. If she lived in that world, she decided, she'd memorize Leonard Maltin's *TV Movies*. She had it half-memorized already. Movies she hadn't seen, movies she didn't intend to: *Bus Riley's Back in Town*, for instance, two and a half stars, sounded mediocre; but if you mentioned it she could tell you instantly that it starred Michael Parks and Ann-Margret, a "muddled William Inge script of folksy people in the Midwest," redeemed by memorable cameos.

She could remember the night it all started—the night her TV devoured her. She'd had it for about a month; she was sitting in her room after dinner watching a rerun of "I Love Lucy." She realized that she hated Lucy. Lucy had found lipstick on a shirt she thought was Ricky's—it was really Ethel Mertz's lipstick and Fred Mertz's shirt—and Ricky had seen Lucy leaving the apartment dressed as Charlie Chaplin, but he didn't realize it was Lucy, he thought it was Another Man . . . typical stupid "I Love Lucy" mix-ups, where you want to press your nose against the TV and scream, "IT WAS LUCY DRESSED AS CHAPLIN! IT WAS FRED MERTZ'S SHIRT!"

There was no reason to be watching this. It didn't bring pleasure. It brought pain. She'd been reading the philosophy entries in the encyclopedia lately, and she learned that man is a rational animal: he flees from that which causes pain. She could turn off the TV. Nothing was stopping her. In a moment she'd get up and turn it off. She'd turn it off right after this commercial. A mother was smilingly informing her daughter about "the long-distance deodorant." The loneliness of the long-distance deodorant. Why was she waiting until the end of a stupid commercial before turning off a stupid show? Man is a rational animal. According to the way philosophers define mankind, mankind does not watch "I Love Lucy." A woman was marveling at the blue water in another woman's toilet bowl. That blue water is good for you somehow. If I turn off the television I'll never find out. Lucy hid the shirt, and Ethel found it. She knew it was Fred's shirt, but she didn't realize the lipstick was her own. Why am I watching this? . . . and suddenly, in a piercing illumination, she understood. I am watching this for no reason. I am watching this because I am watching this. All previous philosophers were wrong. I watch "I Love Lucy"; therefore I am.

After that night, she didn't try to fight it anymore.

In the thaw of the mid-sixties, Burke had made his way back into the labor movement; he was now organizing in Connecticut for the Furniture Workers' Union, and he was away from home three or four nights a week. Hannah had become a force to be reckoned with in Teaneck's educational system; she was forever going to meetings, forever sailing into battle on behalf of open education. Daniel was usually in the library. So Sally would come home to an empty house, heat up a package of macaroni and beef for dinner, and sit in front of the TV with a baseball bat in her lap, because the vents in the house were always making spooky noises.

She had a fixed schedule of TV viewing, starting with the "Virginia Graham Show" when she got home at four. Every night had its longueurs, its periods of dead air, when she'd have to sit, say, in front of "Gilligan's Island" and do a little homework. But every night also had at least one show that was absolutely essential. And at the end of every weeknight, like a prize, like a reward, something devoutly to be waited for, the crown of the day, was the happiest hour and a half of her life.

Johnny.

For two years, Johnny Carson was her father, her friend, her guide, her guru—Johnny was her life. She loved him as one loves a lover, noticing all the little things: the way he fidgeted with his tie; the way he blinked his eyes, self-consciously, when he came out with an idea he was afraid you'd think a little strange; the way he tapped his pencil on his desk when he was in high spirits; the way he didn't smoke on his show, though she knew he was a smoker. The way he let his hair grow gray instead of dyeing it. Dick Cavett was all right too, but she disliked his intellectual pretensions—he was always proving he had a knack for palindromes. Johnny was more human. He didn't pretend to know things he didn't know; he probably pretended not to know as much as he did know— just to put his guests at ease. That's the kind of man he was, Johnny.

Not that she was a blind Johnnyphile. She saw his flaws. She saw that he didn't respect women (except for Dr. Joyce Brothers). Rooting around through her parents' bookcase she came across a book of Freud, and reading about "The Most Prevalent Form of Degradation in Erotic Life" she found a sentence that described Johnny precisely: "Where such men love they have no desire and where they desire they cannot love." Johnny respected Dr. Joyce Brothers, but he'd *never* marry her. The women who turned him on were always large-breasted starlets from south of the border, women whose English was terrible. How to explain the strange law of language acquisition whereby, when a large-breasted starlet from south of the border tries to form English sentences, every other sentence contains a sexual innuendo? The starlet would bring her pet kitten on the show and ask Johnny, "Would you like to pet my poooooosy?" Johnny, saying nothing, would look into the camera with large and startled eyes and toss his pencil over his shoulder, and the audience would go wild.

Sally's sorrow: she knew that Johnny would never want

her as a guest. She was too inarticulate—she groped for her ideas, with tortured pauses. She'd be one of the guests he'd schedule for the end of the show; if the other guests were interesting she'd get bumped. At the end of the show there was always some hapless professor, someone much too long-winded for TV. While the professor was just getting geared up to make his point the band would start blaring—the show was over; but the professor would never understand this, and Johnny would have to cut him off, thank him and the other guests for coming, and tell the audience that Shecky Greene and Phyllis Newman would be here tomorrow. As the credits rolled by you'd see the professor looking crestfallen, stunned.

The hidden brutality of "The Tonight Show."

But whatever her misgivings, Johnny remained her guide. Her dream host.

It was a pleasure, this television life. She didn't think of herself as lost. What else was there to do—study? She wasn't impressed by the people who studied hard in school. Girls who put bows on their papers and spent a lot of time getting the footnotes right. She'd read somewhere that when Franklin Roosevelt was at Harvard he got "gentleman's Cs." Sally did well in English because she liked it, and she was satisfied with gentleman's Cs in everything else. School was too stupid to get perturbed about. In social studies they read excerpts from *Walden* and *Walden Two,* and for homework they had to write a paper about their own utopias. She made an elaborate title page with bows; her paper read, in its entirety: "My idea of utopia is a society without homework, and I am actively working to bring it about." Her teacher was charmed by her sassiness, and gave her an A.

I'm just too bodacious for my own good, she thought, walking home, home to Virginia Graham.

9

When Daniel was in high school, he finally came out of his bookish reserve, but not in a way anyone would have expected. He found a girlfriend—a prematurely jaded, fingernail-painting, cigarette-smoking girl named Leslie. He stayed out a lot. He developed a loud horse-laugh. He stopped reading.

Leslie would come over and slump down on the couch and stare slack-jawed at the TV and say, "Hey, Dan, wanna pass me that ashtray?"

Sally regarded her with loathing. No one who really knew her brother would call him Dan.

After Daniel and Leslie would leave the house, Hannah would stand in the middle of the living room, fuming. "She's been through the mill a few times, I'll tell you that. I hate to think what he's gonna catch from her."

Sally was twelve, but a naive twelve. She ran her mind over the strange diseases he might catch from her. Rabies? Scurvy? Moon blindness? Malaria?

One night when Leslie and a couple of Daniel's new friends were listening to records in the basement, a strange smell began to come up through the vents. Burke was in Connecticut on an organizing campaign. Hannah paced through the kitchen in a rage.

"I know what that smell is! 'We're gonna burn some incense tonight, Ma!' Incense, hell! You and your brother might think I was born yesterday, but what you kids don't understand is that not everything was discovered when you discovered it! I used to listen to jazz in Harlem!"

Hannah secluded herself in the bedroom for the rest of the night. The next day she lectured Daniel about drugs and made him promise not to smoke anymore. He never did smoke in the house again. But three or four nights a week he'd come home with a glazed grin and an air of universal benevolence.

Sally spent a good part of that year trying to figure out why Daniel was with Leslie. It didn't make sense. Jodie came over and made her observations—"She's certainly not very literate," was her primary comment—and remarked with a knowing air that Daniel must be getting *something* out of it.

One night during a heavy snowfall Sally was sitting in her room watching "Occasional Wife" when she heard the front door slam. Daniel and Leslie had been arguing in the basement—she'd pressed her ear against the vent in her bedroom, but she couldn't make out the words.

She ran to the window and saw Leslie cautiously making her way down the iced-over front path. She put her key in her car door. Sally thought it finally might be over. And then she saw Daniel: racing out of the house without his jacket, he flew around the front of the car and caught Leslie in a tight embrace, burying his head in her hair; and they held each other for two, three, four, five minutes, the car door still open, their clothing wet with snow.

The sight of Daniel, wet and skinny in his shirtsleeves, hiding his face, haunted Sally for days. She saw it when she closed her eyes. He'd looked so . . . helpless. She couldn't understand how her brother could beg so helplessly for anything Leslie could give. What could *he* need from *her?* Jodie was wrong: it couldn't be explained by sex alone.

Daniel, as she knew him, was independent, strong. But he must have had another side that she didn't know at all. She studied him across the dinner table: he was as smart and funny as ever. But there was a part of him that no one at the dinner table could reach. And it made Sally queasy to think that Leslie, an outsider, someone who was in no way impressive or intelligent or special—that Leslie could reach a place that to Sally was forever closed.

Sally decided to make war on Leslie. She enlisted Jodie's aid.

This was the kind of thing Jodie loved. She was happy to lend her services as a last act of friendship to Sally—she was going away to boarding school in two weeks. She brought over a sheet of oak-tag to map out battle plans. "It's a two-track strategy," she said, uncapping her Magic Marker. "First, we have to make Leslie look stupid in front of Daniel. Second, we have to get Daniel interested in someone else."

The first track was simpler. Jodie came over when Leslie was around and asked Daniel literary questions. "Did Kafka mean that Gregor Samsa was no more than a bug to begin with?" Though he'd hardly read anything all year, questions like this still sent Daniel's mind racing, and he was off, talking rapidly for the next twenty minutes about symbolism in Kafka. Leslie sat with one leg over the arm of a chair, smoking a cigarette, focusing most of her attention on the TV, and occasionally glancing over at Daniel and Jodie with a bored look.

Leslie was an indoors person; she had the pale deadish skin of someone who had spent all her life in artificial light. Sally and Jodie positioned themselves in the front yard with a Frisbee and when Daniel and Leslie left the house, they'd toss it to Leslie, enjoying how idiotic she looked as she raised her hands to cover her face from harm.

But after a two-week campaign in which they systematically brought out Leslie's limitations, Sally had to admit defeat.

"He doesn't seem to care how stupid she is."

Jodie considered the problem. "It's a pity I'm not a little older. I'd be just the right mixture of brains and sex appeal that would save Daniel from people like that."

She was serious. Sally didn't say anything. But it occurred to her that sometimes she hated Jodie.

Daniel went out with Leslie for about six more months. After Sally accepted defeat, she found herself getting to like her. Once you got to know her, you discovered flashes of generosity, and a quiet, sly humor; and she seemed to like Sally, even though Sally had made her hostility so clear.

When Daniel and Leslie finally did break up—after a long arduous process during which Daniel snapped at anyone who asked him about anything, rushed upstairs to take his phone calls, and disappeared at odd hours of the night—Sally hoped that her brother would come back to her. She hoped that he'd become once again his serious, bookwormish, self-sufficient, world-ignoring self.

Hannah wished for similar things. Mostly, she wished that Daniel would stop smoking pot now that Leslie's bad influence was removed.

Both of the women in his life were disappointed. He still moved in a set they considered beneath him; he probably smoked more pot now than he ever had.

Years later, Hannah still blamed Leslie for most of what bothered her about her son.

"That damn Leslie. She was sweet, but I wish she'd stayed away from Daniel, with that fucking grass."

10

"Well?" said Mr. Manning. "Would anyone care to read a poem?" He was in his characteristic pose, half-standing, half-sitting, with his ass against the hard edge of his desk. Mr. Manning was one of the school sadists. It was obvious that he would soon be a vice-principal.

"Beth, did you complete a poem?"

Beth Black, a large, ungainly girl with long brown hair that always found its way into her mouth, nodded uncomfortably.

"Would you care to come up here and read it for us then?"

She came to the front of the room, pushed a lock of her hair behind her ear—her bright red ear—and, in a halting whisper, recited her poem:

> I am a soldier in Vietnam
> My job is to shoot, to drop the bomb.
> My general says that I must kill
> Although it is against my will.
> I quietly stalk my enemy
> A fragile, frightened man like me.
> I wish that he could be my friend

Oh when, oh when will this war end?
Please, dear God, to you I must tell
I want to come home from this earthly hell.

Without once having lifted her head from the page, lips quivering, she made her way back to her desk.

"Any comments?" asked Mr. Manning. His bald head was glinting. "Well, I have a comment. This was a poem by a thoughtful, well-meaning girl—who doesn't know what the hell she's talking about." Mr. Manning was a favorite of the school administration, and therefore he could occasionally use the word hell. "I served in Korea. The men I fought against there were the cousins of the men we're fighting in Vietnam. They weren't fragile—they were killing machines. And they don't want to be your friend. They want the destruction of the United States and everything we stand for."

He looked with self-satisfaction around the room. He had big, arrogant hands, with knuckly fingers.

Beth did not respond. She looked down at her desk, rubbing the tip of her finger against a little knothole.

Sally was trying to think of what she should say to the odious Mr. Manning.

A boy named Aaron spoke first. He was Beth's next-door neighbor. They'd grown up together; they were like brother and sister. "What about the Vietnamese Declaration of Independence?" he said.

"What's that, mister?" Mr. Manning cupped his thick hand to his ear.

"When Vietnam declared its independence from France, after World War Two. Why did they model their declaration after ours?"

Mr. Manning smiled. "Because they're Communists, and Communists are masters of deceit."

"But what about Ho Chi Minh's letters to President Truman? He wrote to Truman, asking him to help the Vietnamese work things out with the French. If he wanted to destroy the American system, why did he ask for our help?"

"You're a very well-informed young man. But you're also very naive." And Mr. Manning went on to explain to Aaron how naive he was. Before he did, Mr. Manning took Aaron in with a long measuring look, a look which seemed to promise that Aaron would be taught, sooner or later, that there's always a price to pay for being a well-informed young man.

She walked home, thinking about Beth and Aaron. She'd known them since fourth grade; she'd joked around with them for years; but she'd never really *seen* them before. It was as if they'd appeared in class just this morning, in a burst of smoke.

Jodie had been the only real friend Sally had, and Jodie was gone.

She realized she was glad Jodie was gone.

Beth walked slowly and carefully, with her eyes on the ground, as if she was in mortal fear of crushing an insect with a heedless step. In biology class, she refused to dissect her frog; instead she named him Charles, and fed him with lettuce she brought from home, and communed with him, moonily, resting her forehead against the pane of the aquarium where he sat on a rock amid plastic palm trees, his big throat bulging. Mrs. Schiller normally saw to it that not a single frog was left alive, but Beth's tender regard for Charles won her over.

"If you give him a kiss, Beth," Sally said, "he may turn out to be a prince."

"You think I should kiss the little fellow?"

"You'll get warts on your lips," Aaron observed.

Beth stared at Charles, sitting fat and contented in his ersatz jungle.

"Maybe I'll kiss him tomorrow," she said, and put her forehead back against the glass.

11

Within the family, Sally continued to play a bit part. Daniel and his troubles occupied center stage.

During his last two years in high school, he and Hannah were constantly at each other's throats. Six years earlier, when they'd moved to Teaneck, Hannah had wanted to strike a blow against the racist redlining practices of the real estate moguls, so they'd moved into the black section of town. It was a comfortable split-level on a comfortable middle-class block in the black section of town. That was in 1963—the 1963 of Martin Luther King, "I Have a Dream," and "We Shall Overcome." By the time Daniel reached high school King was dead, Malcolm was dead, the hopes of integrationists were dead. In the *Bergen Record* Hannah read of incidents of "racially motivated violence": a couple of black kids hit up some white kids for change; a greaser gang went after a black kid who'd just left the house of a white girl after a date. She grew afraid for Daniel's life. His best friends were white; they lived in the white section of town; and when he spent the evening with them he spent it on their side of town. Hannah didn't want him to walk home alone so late; she insisted that he call her for a ride home at the end of the night. Until he got his driver's license in his last year of school, this was their greatest struggle.

"Ma-ahm!" During that period he never pronounced the word with less than two syllables. "You have to let me be more independent! You're stifling me!"

"How am I stifling you? I'm stifling him by giving him a ride home!" If Burke or Sally was in the room, she addressed this remark to them; if no one but Daniel was in the room she said it anyway, a sarcastic aside to an invisible, all-wise observer who agreed with her. It was a rhetorical gesture that never failed to drive Daniel mad; with an instinctive sense of how to annoy him, she realized this.

"Your *friends* never seem to mind getting a ride home with you when I pick you up."

"But they're not getting a ride home from their mothers!"

"So what's so terrible about your mother? Am I the worst mother in the world?"

And so they would continue in an endless circle of complaint and response, Hannah with a calm and maddening illogic that could never be refuted, Daniel growing more and more hysterical as his powerlessness grew more clear.

Why didn't he just walk home, though? Why did he need her permission? Sally thought about these questions, but she never asked him.

When the time came to apply for college, Daniel's mind was on other things. He did send away for catalogs, but that was it—as far as anyone knew, he never touched them. "Things tend to work themselves out," he would say. Planning, striving were out of his realm; the future was the future. It was 1969.

Burke was the one who read the catalogs; he also read the

memos that his son brought home from school, and he marked in his datebook a seminar to be given by a recruiter from Dartmouth. The entire family trooped off to it on the appointed night. Daniel was the only one who wasn't interested, but in a spirit of large-heartedness he came along. The recruiter strode up and down the room in a manful fashion talking about how Dartmouth had imbued him with the values of competition and hard work. Daniel, his head wrapped in a bandana, his thick woolen socks for some reason pulled over the cuffs of his jeans, stretched out his legs and yawned. After the talk he and the females headed for the door; Burke shook the recruiter's hand.

They got in the car and headed for the local ice cream place. "What do you think?" Hannah said.

Daniel leaned back in the seat and smirked. "Can you see me up there, taking deep lungfuls of the crisp New Hampshire air? Later for that."

A couple of blocks later she said: "What do *you* think, Burke?"

Cleanly, decisively, succinctly: "I think he should try the early decision plan."

"And take deep lungfuls of the crisp New Hampshire air?" Daniel said. There was a slightly shaky quality to his voice. His father inspired fear.

Burke turned around in the front seat and gave Daniel a look. A look that was pure Burke. He had a way of throwing back his head and scrutinizing his own children with an air that suggested he had never seen them before.

"A couple of crisp lungfuls of air might do you good." That was his assessment. "Where *do* you intend to apply?"

"God, who knows? There's a lot of places."

"I'm aware of that. I'm simply curious as to which of them you have in mind."

"Well, actually, I was thinking it might make sense to

apply to one of the state schools, or Ramapo or something. It might not be on the same academic level as the elitist schools. But it seems to me I'd get a better human education."

There was a silence. Burke was pursing his lips.

It was Sally's considered belief that her father was the only man in the world in whom the pursing of the lips could signify an unimaginable extremity of violence held in check by an unimaginable extremity of self-control.

She decided that at the next red light she would hurl herself out of the car, hitchhike west, and establish a new identity.

But Burke did not explode at Daniel, as she had expected. Instead, shortly after they arrived at the ice cream parlor, he blew up at the waitress, who had forgotten to bring Hannah the glass of seltzer she'd asked for. In a white-faced fury, he made it clear that she was unfit for this or any other job; and though this made the rest of the family uncomfortable, it was better than having him explode at Daniel, and was a relief for all concerned. Except, of course, for the waitress; but even she was not too bothered, since, as he hotly lectured her on her dereliction, he had a spot of whipped cream on his nose, which enabled her to dismiss him as a pathetic old man.

12

Daniel continued to consider his future in his own way. His friends went on college tours, arranged for interviews, read the *Insider's Guide*. He was reading a lot of Blake and Whitman—he only read poetry these days—and he did take an occasional glance at a college catalog to see if any courses were offered on those two; but aside from that he seemed prepared to decide on the basis of vibes. All of his friends were college-obsessed that year, so as hard as he tried to rise above all that, heeding only the promptings of his own soul, he couldn't really escape from being obsessed too. He just went about it in a different way. He went around the house murmuring the names of the schools he'd applied to, eventually fracturing them all—Middlebury was Middlebunny, Harvard was Hotfoot, or, after a few weeks, Hotfood. While Sally was washing the dishes, Daniel would come up to her and whisper, "You gonna visit me at Middlebunny?"

Burke would come home from his job at about 6:30, change clothes and come downstairs every night with the same question: "Is there any mail directed to the attention of Francis Xavier Burke?" When there wasn't, he would stare at his wife in a shocked and indignant manner: "Hannah, have you been concealing my mail?" This ritual concluded, he would settle down in his chair with one of Daniel's newly arrived catalogs. He would look through them slowly, with absorption; but he probably didn't have the future of his son primarily in mind. Burke had only gone to college for one year—he'd left to support his family when his father died. And though he had read widely and seriously for the rest of his life, that he had gone no further with his schooling was something he would always regret. Not that he ever spoke of these things. "If I were you I'd apply to Edinburgh. The academic standards are first-rate, and there's always some superb grouse-shooting to be done in the autumn." After the Dartmouth fiasco, this was the extent of the advice he offered his son.

Daniel ended up applying only to Hotfoot and Middle-bunny. Middlebunny was his safety school. He had no doubt that Harvard would want him, although his class ranking was not the best and he'd distinguished himself in his final year of high school chiefly by quitting, "for reasons of principle," all the various clubs he'd been a member of. But his confidence was serene. For one thing, he had the highest SAT scores in the school; for another, "things generally have a tendency to work out."

On April fifteenth, a gray, drizzly day, Sally raced home as soon as school was over. She beat everyone else. She took the mail from the mailbox, brought it into the house, and found the two envelopes. They were thin.

One of the things that everyone knows without having been taught is that a thin envelope from a college on April fifteenth means a letter of rejection. The knowledge is innate. Sally sat on the couch with the envelopes in her lap. The shades were still drawn, but she didn't bother opening them or turning on the lights.

She considered her brother's life, with a sense of detail so close she might have been considering her own. She remembered him as a boy of nine, being lovingly reproached by their mother, every night, for coming to the dinner table with a book. She remembered how he'd seemed to know everything . . . how he'd seemed, at ten, to be a formed adult. And she remembered . . . she remembered the spelling bee. Four years ago. In her mind, her brother's life since then had been a long, uninterrupted fall.

She realized that the reason she'd hoped her brother would get into Harvard was that it would erase the record of his recent years. It would reaffirm his early promise. It would make the last four years a meaningless interlude. Rejection would mean that the last four years was the truth of his life.

There were times when Sally took her brother's life more seriously than he did.

She was still on the couch when her mother came in, carrying two big shopping bags.

"Did they come?"

Sally didn't say anything, just looked down at the letters.

Hannah put the shopping bags down. She came over and Sally gave her the letters.

She held the thin little envelopes in her hand, as if she were weighing them. As if by weighing them carefully, she could make them heavier.

"Shit," she said. "Shit on a brick."

She turned a lamp on and held the letters up to the bulb.

"Oh, Ma," Sally said disapprovingly.

"What? Don't I have the right? My own flesh and blood?"

It didn't matter: she couldn't tell what the letters said. She sat down heavily on the couch, still wearing her coat.

They sat for a few minutes, in silence. Finally Hannah sighed and said, "Well, I guess we should start dinner."

She had brought home the makings for Manhattan clam chowder, one of her specialties.

They set to work in the kitchen. Sally peeled the potatoes and the carrots and cut up the celery and the onions. Hannah started shelling the clams.

They were still at work when Burke came home.

"Hello there, ladies. How are we this evening?"

"Hi, Dad."

He came into the kitchen and gave Hannah a kiss.

"My goodness, clam chowder. What's the occasion?"

"No occasion," Hannah said.

He went back into the living room, tossed his paper on the couch, and went to the end table, where the mail was placed. "Any mail directed to the attention of Francis Xavier Burke?"

No one spoke.

"Well, well. It looks as though the day of judgment has arrived. Haven't you steamed these open yet, darling?"

He didn't understand that the judgment was already clear. Apparently this knowledge was not innate.

Hannah came out and the two of them spoke in low tones; Sally couldn't hear. Finally she heard her father say, "Well, it just proves the truth of the old maxim. If you throw enough shit at the wall, some of it'll stick. He just didn't throw enough shit at the wall."

With that he went upstairs to change.

Some time later, Daniel grooved in. He was wearing a necklace with a little peace sign.

"Hi, Ma. Dad. Salamander. What's up?"

Hannah took a breath, thought about what to say, expelled the air. Then she nodded toward the end table.

Daniel picked up the envelopes and sat down. Normally he opened his mail with casual abandon: as often as not he ripped apart the letter by mistake. Today he took his house key from his pocket and slit each envelope open carefully and slowly. When he had read the two letters he crumpled them up into little balls and tossed them, one at a time, into a wastepaper basket across the room.

Then he went up to his room and closed the door.

Hannah walked quickly to the basket and fished them out.

"Oh, Ma," Sally said. "If he doesn't want you to see them, why don't you just leave them alone?"

But she followed her mother into the living room and stood over her as she placed the letters on the coffee table and smoothed them out.

Burke was in the kitchen. He wanted to see the letters as much as anyone. But just as it was Hannah's part to rush to the basket, and just as it was Sally's part to follow—half scolding, half in league with her—so it was Burke's part to remain in the kitchen, looking through the second section of *The New York Times*.

Middlebury had turned him down succinctly. Harvard had gone into great, almost anguished length, as if to dissuade him from attempting suicide.

Hannah went upstairs to see if Daniel wanted to eat dinner. Sally and her father sat at the table, and Sally served him: thick, red, rich clam chowder, filled with vegetables.

Hannah came back to the kitchen with a tragic mien.

"How's he doing?" Burke asked quietly. Her father was so consistently a creature of an emphatic frostiness, his love expressed only in teasing, that the quiet seriousness of the question made Sally want to cry.

"Well, he's lying on the bed. He says he's okay. . . . Those fuckin' schools."

It was safe to say that Hannah, before long, would be in a rage about those fuckin' schools. It was also safe to say that Burke would soon be in a rage himself; but it wasn't so clear at whom.

"What a goddamn nerve," Hannah said. "Who the hell are they to turn him down? He has the scores. He has the recommendations. *Harvard*. They turn *him* down so they can have room for dumb jocks on football scholarships and the sons of fuckin' politicians. And that's supposed to be a great university. That's supposed to be education. I'd like to sue them. Education should be a *right*. Has anybody ever thought of suing one of these fuckin' schools?"

Burke tore off a piece of bread from the whole-wheat loaf and began to butter it. The piece of bread was microscopically small. To take a small piece of bread was good manners.

This was the first sign. When Burke got mad, his manners became more and more refined, until, at his most polite, he got up and punched you in the nose.

He put the bread in his mouth, but before he'd even begun to chew it he said, "What the hell did he expect? What the hell was his class rank?—four hundred ninety-nine out of five hundred? How much homework has he done in the last two years? How much homework has he done in his *life*? He brings his goddamn books home from school and *I* read them. He doesn't read them. You spend four goddamn years sitting on your ass smoking pot, and then you think it's an injustice when you don't get admitted to Harvard! Jesus Christ. That's the American way all right."

He paused for a moment to chew his bread.

"And what the hell are you defending him for? 'We should sue them.' Bull*shit*. If they'd *taken* him we should have sued them—we'd be crazy to let our son attend the kind of school that would accept our son."

Hannah didn't say anything. She ladled some more soup into Sally's bowl. She was an expert, after twenty years, at enduring this kind of storm. All you could do was ride it out.

"I thought he didn't want to go to an *elitist* school anyway. Whatever happened to that? Whatever happened to his theory of humanistic education? Well, he got what he asked for.

I'm sure there's still some time to apply to Bergen Community, where he can major in dope-smoking techniques."

His face was red; he got up from the table and snatched up his cigarettes, and smoked while he prepared a pot of coffee. He was still shaking his head furiously, and Sally was sure they were in for a two-hour lecture in which the themes already touched upon would be elaborated on at length.

Daniel appeared in the doorway.

"Any soup left?"

Burke looked him over sharply. Silence.

"Of course there's soup left," he finally said. "There'll be soup left for a month. Don't you know your mother always engages in culinary overkill?" And he went to the cabinet and got out another bowl and another spoon, and tossed them down with a kind of studied negligence at Daniel's place.

Daniel came to the table, raising his right leg over the back of the chair in order to sit down, as if he were mounting a horse. A recent and inexplicable affectation. Sally ladled him out some soup. He tore off a chunk of the soft wheat bread, submerged it, ate it. Then he had a few spoonfuls, blowing on the soup carefully each time.

"You make good soup, Ma," he said quietly.

13

Eventually Daniel managed to gain admission to Boston University. Burke and Hannah and Sally drove him up early in September 1971. When they got back to New Jersey, it was almost time for Sally to start school. She was entering high school that year.

It was strange, the quietness of the house without Daniel.

She arranged all her back-to-school things, her pens and pencils, her notebooks, her book covers, and laid out tomorrow's clothing neatly on a chair. She sat in her bedroom, anticipating the horrors of the next day. She planned out everything: what time she'd get up, what she'd have for breakfast, how she'd do her hair. She wished she knew what tomorrow's homework would be, so she could start off ahead of the game. She vowed that she'd change her ways this year: she'd do two hours of homework every night. Even just one hour. That was easy enough. But she made that vow every year.

There was no reason she shouldn't be able to take her studies seriously. She sat on her bed, reviewing all the objective factors. The school year hadn't started yet. She hadn't been given any homework yet. Therefore, she wasn't behind yet. If she did just a little bit of work, not even every night, but maybe just three nights a week, then she'd never fall too far behind. She tried to think of things that might prevent her from following this minimum schedule. There weren't any. But she couldn't help feeling as if she was already behind. And she knew for a certainty, without understanding why, that within a month she *would* be hopelessly behind. She'd be drawing up work schedules that would require prodigious feats of labor sustained for weeks on end, merely to catch up with the work she'd already missed. She knew that this would happen to her, just as surely as Merlin knew that it was his fate to be sealed up in a cave; and there was nothing she could do to prevent it.

To let out some of her anxiety she stood in front of the mirror popping her pimples; then she went down to dinner. Every year, on the night before school, both her parents were among the living dead. Dinner took place glumly, the serving plates passed in silence. There was no reason for it. Hannah was a teacher, but she'd already been in school a few days for orientation, and anyway she didn't hate school like Sally did. Burke had no reason at all to feel low. He probably didn't even *know* it was the day before school: he followed the events of Sally's life with a mild but distant interest, in the same way that, as a dutiful citizen of the world, he might follow political developments in Norway.

That night's dinner was made up of odds and ends: a can of chili for Hannah and Sally, a couple of fried egg sandwiches for Burke. Why was everyone so exhausted? The silence was punctuated by an occasional nicotine cough from Burke, but even his coughs lacked spirit. They went into the living room and watched a little TV, dispiritedly; there was nothing on. There was never anything on, the night before school. Burke and Hannah dragged their way up to bed, early. Sally sat alone watching a ball game, but the Mets were playing as if they too were depressed about the first day of school. At 8:30 she turned off the TV.

They had a new kitten, Napoleon. He was always tensing, readying himself, and leaping across the living room in pursuit of imaginary foes; his ambition in life was to be the cat most feared in all of New Jersey. But tonight even Napoleon seemed sad.

She sat in the living room, too fidgety and unhappy to write in her diary or read or talk on the phone. She told herself that she should appreciate these last few hours of freedom; but there was nothing to appreciate. Her freedom was gone. She sat by the window in the inadequate light of late summer.

14

Beth was sitting with Aaron in the field near the school. As Sally approached them, from fifty yards away, she was struck by how good they looked together. They were half-reclining in the grass, propped on their elbows, talking. Aaron was a conservative dresser: he was all in brown; but his socks were sky blue, and they lent a touch of color to the scene. As she walked toward them Sally felt as if the planet had shifted slightly. You practice at feelings before you actually feel them. She felt that Beth and Aaron were on the verge of something new. She admired the ease they felt in each other's presence, an ease she didn't feel with any boy; and she wondered how long it would be before Aaron, on an afternoon like this, the two of them sitting in the grass, would lean over and kiss her. She felt a spasm of jealousy, but she wasn't quite sure who she was jealous of. Of Beth, of Aaron—or of both of them, because of the stage of life they were entering, a step or two ahead of her?

15

Hannah was forever reminding her children that they had once resided in her womb. This was sufficient license for any imposition on their privacy. Sally, in fact, had spent nearly ten months in the womb. The obvious inference from this was that Sally would have liked to stay in there forever, and that if she claimed to want privacy now, such claims were spurious. So Hannah never knocked. This wasn't a problem when Sally was in the bathroom: the bathroom door had a lock. But the door of Sally's bedroom didn't. She'd be lying on her bed, reading, and her mother would charge in.

"Can't you *knock?*"

"What do you mean knock? I'm your mother."

I'm your mother was the answer to all questions.

What this meant was that Sally had to regulate her masturbating habits. Basically, she could masturbate only when her mother was asleep or out of the house.

The scheduling aspect of this wasn't hard. But what she resented, what she marveled at, was that her mother's intrusiveness had managed to extend itself even into her secret life.

Beth gave a party. At parties recently Sally had noticed a new feel. A new relationship between the boys and the girls. The days of kissing games were over: this was because they were grown up enough to kiss on their own. Now boys and girls could just be people together.

Sally was sitting in Beth's basement, being people, when Beth's mother stuck her head in the door and told her she had a phone call.

It was Hannah. "Sarah," she said.

Her mother never called her Sarah. She knew it was a hot one.

"Yes?"

"Are you a smoker?"

That was the phrase. Not have you been smoking, not do you smoke, but are you a smoker.

"Of course not."

"Then why do you have cigarettes in your desk?"

Shit, she thought. "They're Beth's," she said. Sorry, Beth.

"They're Beth's? Then what are they doing in your desk?"

"When she was over. She didn't want to bring them home."

"Well, I think her mother would be very interested to hear about this."

"Mah-ahm. I can't beleeeeve you." Five minutes ago she'd been talking with two boys; she'd felt so grown up.

"Sarah Burke, just tell me the truth. Have you or have you not been smoking?"

"I just *told* you. And what were you doing in my desk anyhow?"

She should have counterattacked earlier, but she hadn't had her wits about her.

"That's not the point. How can you be smoking? Have you gone crazy? Don't you know what smoking does to you?"

"You had no right to go through my desk." Stick to the narrow point.

"I have every right. And my going through your desk has nothing to do with your smoking. Going through a desk never hurt anybody. Smoking kills people."

It was a clash of great legal minds.

"You're not only a smoker, you're a liar too. I thought I understood you, Sally, but I guess I don't. Are you smoking tonight?"

"Of course not." But she knew her mother would be able to smell her breath across the wires.

"How do I *know* that? How can I trust you anymore? I'm coming over right now. We have to have a talk."

"You are NOT coming over."

"I most certainly am. Goodbye."

"I won't be here."

"We'll see about that."

Sally put the phone down. Tears of hatred. There was no way she could even go downstairs to say goodbye. She got her jacket from the hall closet and ran out the front door.

She ran up the hill toward Sussex Road. She hated her mother. She thought back over her whole life, and the theme of all of it was that her mother was a witch.

She was walking in the middle of the street, jumping up and down with rage. She walked for five minutes before she realized this was the street her mother would be driving on. Headlights.

She cut into somebody's yard and crashed through a tall hedge.

It was Hannah. She'd seen her. She stopped the car and scanned the yard. Sally, crouching, hidden behind a bush, didn't dare move. She watched her mother.

Hannah lowered her window. "Sally? Sally? Is that you?" She was hissing—trying both to whisper and to be heard.

Sally didn't make a sound; she didn't breathe.

"Sally. I saw you. Is that you?"

Sally could see her mother perfectly from where she hid. Hannah scanned the darkness, squinting behind her glasses. The bush was thick, the night was dark, and Sally was wearing dark clothing. But she knew her mother would see her. It was impossible to hide from Hannah. She had x-ray eyes.

The x-ray eyes passed over her, unseeing.

She had outwitted her. For the first time in her life maybe, she had outwitted her all-seeing, omniscient, ubiquitous mother. All she had to do was wait her out.

"Sally? If you're there, come out."

Nothing doing, copper.

"Sally? *Please*. You're scaring the shit out of me."

The magic words.

It was incredible. Sally was still well hidden. She could not be seen. A minute ago she'd thought that nothing could get in the way of her victory. But now she knew she was beaten. To face down her mother's wrath was one thing. To be the cause of her suffering was another.

Crouched, holding her breath, in the bushes, Sally finally understood why her brother had never just disobeyed Hannah and walked home.

But if only she could bull this through, if only she could stay hidden, she'd have a great victory. Break the grip now, and you've broken it forever.

"Sally? *Please*."

You can't win. If you win, you make her suffer. Even when you win, you lose.

"Sally?"

She emerged from the bushes, slowly, trailing her colors, while the band played "The World Turned Upside Down."

16

She moved toward regions that her brother had passed through long before. Her guidance counselor fixed her with a ghoulish stare and told her to start thinking about finding a place where she could fill her "cup of potential." College was three years away, but you had to start worrying about it now.

She wanted to do better than Daniel had. So she spent an afternoon in the library reading college catalogs, and she found out about a place in Maryland called St. John's. St. John's had only four hundred students, all of whom followed the same curriculum. The classics. In your first year you studied Greek, and read Plato and Sophocles. In your second year you studied Latin and read Caesar and Plutarch. The most modern thinker you encountered there, at the end of senior year, was Freud.

As soon as she read the catalog, she knew. St. John's. She would study the wisdom of the ages. She would go back to the origins of things, the heart of all mysteries. She would move across the courtyard with a grave, stately grace. She would converse in Latin idioms that had been moribund for two thousand years.

She was wiser than Daniel: she decided to visit the place. She spent two days there, and loved it. On Friday evening everyone in the school met in small seminars, where teachers and students practiced the Socratic method. The only thing that bothered her was that in the seminar she attended, the distinguished professor, who seemed to possess the key to all knowledge, cultivated an odd hairstyle, in which one long loop of hair, which originated somewhere below his ear, was called upon to stretch all the way to his other ear, to cover his shiny head.

She got home, after a long bus ride, on Saturday night. As soon as she opened the door she knew that her father was in the house alone. She couldn't have said exactly how she knew—when he was alone there was a sort of sizzle in the air, a hint of violence. It was like coming into a room where someone had just been using a whip.

If Hannah had been there by herself, that would have been easy: Sally and Hannah would have talked. If Hannah and Burke had been there together, that also would have been easy: Sally and Hannah would have talked. But Burke by himself: that was never easy. It hadn't been for years. Not since Sally had forsaken her interest in dinosaurs, the rivalry between Juno and Venus, and the other subjects they used to discuss with such deep mutual concern. There was still baseball, at least; but spring training was months away.

"Hello there, Sarah," he said. "The return of the wayfarer." He was in the kitchen, drinking coffee.

"Hi, Dad." She put her backpack down in the hall.

"Can I fix you something?"

"No thanks."

"You're aware that I'm a gourmet chef."

"I'm aware of that, Dad."

"I'm afraid your mother is attending an educational function, leaving her family to fend for itself. She's a very important person in Teaneck, you know. I sometimes think we won't get a solid meal around here unless we move to Leonia."

"That wouldn't help, Dad. She'll be a very important person wherever she goes."

This was their usual banter. She went to the refrigerator and poured out some cider. Beth was supposed to come over in a little while. There was just enough time for a shower.

"So how did you find St. John's?"

He wasn't supposed to ask this kind of question. This kind of question was asked by Hannah, who then conveyed the answer to him in private. This was established family procedure.

"It was great. I really liked it."

He didn't say anything. She felt as if she was supposed to say something else.

"I'm thinking of taking the early decision plan."

A clever stroke: he'd been so keen for Daniel to go to Dartmouth on the early decision plan. She congratulated herself on her ability to manipulate her parents.

She put her glass in the sink. Burke found their conversations as awkward as she did. Now that they had made their bow to the proprieties, she could go upstairs.

"Why?" he asked.

This was an unforeseen turn.

"You get a solid education there. And it seems like a real community. I really liked it."

"Yes, you mentioned that. But have you looked into any other schools?"

"Well, not really. But this one is great." She felt stupider and stupider. Her mind was locked. Whenever he asked her a serious question, she felt as if she was on the witness stand.

She was standing near the refrigerator. Burke was sitting at the kitchen table with *The New Yorker* in front of him.

"What I don't understand," he said, "is this. What if you should go to St. John's and decide after a year that you want to learn a little about *contemporary* philosophy? Or contemporary literature? Or, God forbid, that you want to take an accounting course?"

Why did he have to speak with such fury? He was trying to control himself: he was clearly trying to control himself. But his face was red, his lips were curled back from his teeth like a wolf's lips, and he was almost shouting. And he was trying to be gentle.

"It seems to me that one would want to choose a school that allows for a few choices."

The cat came into the room. Sally touched him with her foot. Everything in the room looked red and far away.

"I don't understand it," he said. "And I don't understand your brother either. Why do you both find it so painful to take a little time to think about your future?"

Burke had looked at her when he'd offered to cook something. He hadn't looked at her since. He was looking down at *The New Yorker,* and during their silences he turned the pages. If you'd seen him without hearing his words—if you'd been watching him through the window—you would have thought that he was furious about something in the magazine.

She tried to say something, but what came out of her mouth wasn't a word. It came from low in her throat—it was like the sound an animal might make if it tried to speak. Burke didn't seem to hear.

"I know it isn't easy for you kids. You have too many choices. I had it much easier. My first job was in a factory—I didn't *have* a choice. The place was like something out of Dickens—it was crying out to be organized, and we organized it, and then the union offered me a job. And I've never wanted to do anything else. So I was luckier than you kids.

But what I fail to comprehend is why both of you find your-self so *terrified* by the idea of giving your future a little bit of *thought*. Daniel seemed to think that leafing through a college catalog would be the equivalent of putting his head in a vise. And now you want to bury yourself in a place where if you change your mind, you'll have to go somewhere else. I just don't understand it. Daniel *still* hasn't changed. Now he says he wants to drop out and work in a cornfield. Your mother asks him why and he says because he's never seen a cornfield."

He'd never told her before about how he'd gotten started in union work. It had never occurred to her to ask.

He turned another page. She was leaning against the refrigerator, looking at the cat, scratching him with her foot. She was thinking that she didn't understand why she was crying. She was thinking that she'd never realized you could cry so hard and still be silent.

Burke didn't know she was crying: he hadn't looked up. He shook his head, as if she'd contradicted him.

"I'm not trying to *dic*tate to you kids. *I* happen to think that if you're not working to make things better for everyone, you aren't really alive. But I don't ask you kids to believe that. Daniel seemed to think I wanted him to follow in my footsteps. I don't want him to follow in anybody's footsteps, and I don't want you to do that either. But I do think you should give your future a little *thought*. I see these posters on the subway and they aren't wrong. A mind *is* a terrible thing to waste. You got so many people walking around not knowing what they want to do—so many people walking around the goddamn street—"

There was something new in his voice; he couldn't finish the sentence.

The doorbell rang. She ran to the door. Beth. Beth is my savior. Her savior was on the front stoop, wearing a cowboy hat.

She grabbed her coat from the hall closet, took a step or two back toward the kitchen, and, trying to sound normal, trying to sound like a model TV daughter, she said, "Goodnight, Dad." Burke nodded; he barely looked up.

At the door, a rush of guilt made her pause. Her father hadn't said anything very intimate, but she'd never heard him speak so intimately before. She came back to the kitchen and said, "I'm sorry I have to go out, Dad."

He glanced up at her, but without meeting her eyes. "That's all right, Sarah. I was just about to hit the road to dreamland anyway."

The road to dreamland. It was an expression he'd been using as long as she could remember. He used to say it when he tucked her in.

17

The great bow of the George Washington Bridge, stretching almost languorously over the river. Beth had passed her driver's test; three or four times a week they drove out to Fort Lee, to sit in the little park beneath the bridge and smoke pot.

It was early Friday evening, just after school. Beth was railing against marriage. "If you ever hear I've gotten married, that's when you'll know I've given up."

"Given up what?"

"Given up searching! If you pledge to stay with one person for the rest of your life, it's like pledging not to grow. The security of marriage is the security of death. Jot that down."

Beth was a funny mixture: she seemed all melting, blushing sensitivity, but there was something about her that was very hard. She had strong beliefs about everything, and she couldn't be moved.

"But when you say you'll never get married, isn't *that* a pledge not to grow? Maybe you'll change your mind."

"I don't think that's valid. Saying you'll never get married is like saying you'll never commit suicide."

Soon they'd start applying to colleges. And once they went to college they would begin to become different people. What they were now almost didn't count.

And so they frantically declared moral rules for themselves, to guard against the unknownness of the future.

"I wonder if we'll know each other in twenty years," Sally said. "I wonder which of us will die first."

"That'll be something. Someday one of us will be dead and the other will sit around remembering."

"Remembering this moment."

They were silent. Two philosophers at dusk.

They smoked a joint. The light began to change. The river ran slower, and the city grew soft.

You could see the whole city, softening as the light paled. The long, flowing line of it, leading the eye toward the sea.

You could see the tiny cars, you could see the movement, but you couldn't hear a thing. The city was silent.

She tried to imagine how Manhattan looked before there were any buildings. She was looking out on a green island.

She felt as though she was about to begin her life. She knew how young she was. Everything was before her. She felt as though she had the chance to live her life perfectly. No mistakes. She could be anything she wanted to be.

The sky had grown darker. The city was burning with a thousand lights. But she didn't feel awed by it. She felt something awesome within herself: something that rose out of her to touch the power of the city. She was a suburban girl, so the city was strange to her. Strange, vast, frightening. But she was even stranger, vaster. More frightening.

18

Summer. Scorching days, long mosquito nights.

She lay in bed, thinking.

You lie in bed, thinking, and after a while your thoughts turn strange . . . half thinking, half dreaming, you're nearly gone. This is how you fall asleep.

She was thinking about tomorrow evening on the tennis court . . . then she was *on* the tennis court, returning a shot from . . . who? . . . Merv Griffin. . . . A mosquito hovered around her ear and she bolted awake.

She tried to relax again, with a method she'd learned in a yoga book. You lie perfectly still . . . you concentrate, first, on your toes . . . her toes drifted off to sleep . . . she let the heaviness drift up over her ankles, up to her knees . . . she was like a submarine going under, the waters lapping. . . . Another fucking mosquito stumbled into her ear.

She stopped trying to sleep. She lay awake, waiting for the next mosquito.

July, the sluggish month. A cloud had descended on her mind. It took her a second to get people's jokes. She was having strange headaches: a burning, a pressure behind her eyes. It felt as if something was alive there, scratching.

She worked at a pointless summer job; at night she hung out at the tennis court. The court was near a swamp; the air was heavy, loaded with a yellowish thickness that seeped up into your nostrils and itched behind your eyes. She sat watching Beth and Aaron hit. She was annoyed at them: she'd been feeling weird for weeks, and they hadn't noticed. She closed her eyes. She could feel her pulse in her head. She sat with her eyes closed listening to the steady monotonous sound of the game, the sound of sneakers scraping across the clay, and behind that the sound of the traffic, and behind that a strange hum she couldn't identify.

She opened her eyes. . . . Beth and Aaron moved with intentness, returning each other's shots. They meant so little to her, really. If she had to choose whether to save their lives or save the life of a can of creamed corn, which would she choose? Beth and Aaron stepped gravely toward the executioner.

Aaron, showing off, kept one hand in his pocket as he hit the ball. What would they think if they knew the corn had been exalted, themselves put low? They didn't know her. And she didn't know them. She watched them hitting. They were unknowable. They were wrapped in flesh. Beth hit the ball off the edge of her racket and it sailed over the fence. "Little help, Mrs. Jones?" Aaron said. Sally trotted after the ball.

She didn't know what the problem was. She was having trouble waking up in the morning. Every morning, since she was little, Burke had waked her. Among his hidden talents was that he was the greatest waker-upper in the world. He would knock on her door and with a mild voice say, "Seven-thirty, Sarah—time to perform your ablutions," and instantly she'd be awake. He had a certain magic in his morning voice. Or maybe it was just that she feared him. But now he'd have to come back again, sometimes twice. She'd stopped staying up for the late movie—she'd go to bed shockingly early, and wake up exhausted, depleted, bloodshot, bleary, beat.

Something was happening, but she didn't know what it was. Last year in health class she'd read that the brain is a jellylike substance, and that if you jog your brain—for instance, if you're driving and you hit the brakes too fast—you may suffer subtle brain impairment. Maybe she had jogged her brain.

A thin film of dullness covered her mind. She started to have trouble speaking. Words turned strange. Travail. Truth will travail?

She was changing, but she didn't know what she was changing into. She'd already gone through the womanly, bodily changes, which were frightening enough, but she'd been prepared for those. She wasn't prepared for what was happening now. Things were shifting inside her. It was like the shifting of a fetus, except that she was a virgin, and except that it wasn't a feeling she could locate in any one part of her body. Why hadn't anyone told her about this?

Aaron stroked a bit of fluffy hair next to her ear. "If Sally was a boy she'd look in the mirror and tell herself her sideburns are getting good." At another time she might have smiled. Now it upset her. Maybe I *am* a boy. I'm the only girl I know who loves baseball. Maybe I'm a boy in a woman's body. Who knows? Maybe I'm in love with Beth. Maybe that's the source of all this confusion. Every year there was some guy she told herself she liked, and every year she spent hours on the phone with Beth talking about the guy. Maybe a total of three hours talking *to* him, and a hundred hours talking *about* him. With Beth. So maybe it was Beth she loved.

Anyway, love was ridiculous. At a party Beth and Aaron disappeared into a boiler room. And came out half an hour later red and smirking: a little flustered, a little smug. For about two days they went around holding hands. Sally had expected this: it was their destiny. But now that it had happened, it didn't seem right. They looked awkward. They looked as if they'd overstepped nature's bounds.

A few days later they weren't holding hands anymore. Sally, deep in her own private cavern, didn't even ask Beth what had happened. But she didn't have to: she saw. The current that was there between Beth and Aaron when they joked, when they talked, wasn't there in all realms. What she'd considered destiny wasn't destiny at all. Beth and Aaron's affection would endure, but it was something thinner than she and they had taken it for. Sally thought she'd been prepared for any grand tragedies life might have to offer. But now she saw that the tragedies life brought might be of a different kind. Tragedies of thinness.

She lay awake in the dark, waiting for the mosquito. There was a plague of them that summer. They waited until you were almost under, and then they drifted into your ear. They seemed to know. . . . She was so tense that there was no pleasure, no ease, in the mosquito's absence.

Food didn't taste the same. Her friends didn't taste the same either. Beth was boring, and Aaron was a fool. He spoke with admiration about a new guy on his block: "We took a piss on the street the other night, and he wrote his name, in script. He even dotted the i."

"Very impressive," Sally said. She thought: Someday I'll have real friends.

Her headaches persisted. In bed on a Saturday morning, she closed her eyes and felt as if she was about to burst. Lurid imaginings took hold of her, in which the throbbing of her eyes grew more severe, until finally her eyes began to bulge and crack and distend out of her head and some beast started to emerge, its beak cracking through her left eye, its claw struggling out through her right, while the body of the beast, still trapped within her, beat heavily against the inside of her head.

Her mother took her to an eye doctor, but there was nothing wrong.

There was no physical cause. Her periods were regular. Hannah was worried. She took Sally to the doctor, and the doctor called it growing pains. But Sally knew an eagle had been implanted in her skull, and was struggling to break free.

If you're depressed then you're deep. She tried to rally herself with that formula. She wrote poems about how sad she was. But they were no good. "I'm no artist," she said, throwing another poem into the trash.

That new boy, Jesse Barkin, even though Aaron had praised him for jerky reasons—he was an artist. He started to spend a lot of time with Sally and Beth and Aaron. The four of them went down to the park, and Jesse insisted on stopping at a junkyard on the way.

"This is gross," Beth said.

"Come on! You can find some great stuff!" He disappeared behind a mound of trash; the three others sat on the ground; Sally lit a cigarette. In a couple of minutes he came back carrying an armful of junk—some huge rusty wrenches and pliers and bolts.

"Great stuff," Sally said.

"Can't you see her?" He put the junk on the ground, squatted in front of it, contemplated it all for a minute, and went to work. Using two bolts for breasts and the wild bent spokes of a broken wheel for hair, he began to fashion a woman, a rusty metal nude.

"Hello, Gertrude," Sally said.

She looked at his hands. Large hands, covered with cuts, one thumb black-and-blue beneath the nail. His hands were marked by the work he was always doing, with files, saws, hammers. They were hands that knew a thing or two. Sally's hands were white, with chewed-up fingernails.

They went to the park and Jesse hoisted himself up into a tree and reclined on one of the thick lower branches. He took out a pocketknife, removed a small branch, and started whittling.

He looked good in the tree. He was built like a tree, with tangled black hair that little birds could nest in. Sparrows and starlings nested in his hair.

Sally felt reproached by his existence. He didn't have drawn-out identity crises. He was secure in the universe. He fit.

She didn't fit.

When she was little she had had a theory. The theory was that nothing bad stayed bad for more than a week. Whenever anything had bothered her, she'd thought: In a week I won't care about this. And it was almost always true.

It wasn't true anymore. Her worst problems, symptoms, whatever, went away, but she felt wrapped within a cloak of dullness. Dull August collapsed into dull September; the school year started, but nothing changed; soon dull December had come. Words were still hard to say. How do you say "Kennedy"? Do you pronounce those *n*s, or do you slide over them? She tried to avoid conversations about martyred presidents.

Between Christmas and New Year's Sally's parents went to a union convention in California. Beth's parents were also gone, so Sally spent the week at Beth's house, and the two of them got high together every night. Got high and talked. They unraveled the secrets of the universe.

Beth cared most about people: she liked to sit around analyzing everybody's motives. Sally cared most about thoughts. People were just the places where thoughts occurred.

Near the end of the fourth night of their marathon, Sally went to the bathroom, looked in the mirror, and was shocked. Her skin was so fair. Her face was so different from Beth's face.

Sitting there for four days chattering head-to-head, she'd thought that she and Beth had had the same experience. But Beth's experience must have been completely different.

Her own face seemed more exposed than Beth's. Her own face held no secrets. It just stuck out at you. "A face you could open a can of beans with," she said to herself in the mirror.

The next night, instead of staying in and getting high, they went out and got high. They went with Aaron to a park near the Hackensack River.

They sat on the swings, they smoked, they waited for the dark. Beth was off snooping around in a corner of the park; Sally was sitting next to Aaron, swaying. She was daydreaming, spacing out, feeling warm, secure, feeling better than she'd felt in months. "The Hackensack River is as beautiful as the Seine," Aaron said. "It just has the misfortune of being between Teaneck and Hackensack."

Disappointment. She'd forgotten it was Aaron sitting next to her. For a second she'd thought it was Jesse.

During her week at Beth's, as they talked, as they got high, as they cooked—destroying Beth's parents' kitchen—accompanying all this, in the background, was the rough moaning of Bob Dylan. It was as if he was taking part in the conversations. Beth had a tremendous Dylan collection; she'd stayed loyal to him through all his phases; for Sally, the week became an immersion course in Dylan Studies.

She'd always been aware of Dylan—ever since seventh grade, when Daniel used to play songs like "With God on Our Side" and Burke would chuckle approvingly at the clever way the antiwar message was expressed. But she'd never realized how many different Dylans there were. The protest singer; the psychedelic rocker, tripping out on wild imagery; the simple country crooner, rhyming "June" with "moon." All these different Dylans had one thing in common: whatever mood he was in, he didn't give a damn about anything but being true to himself. Beth told her about his appearance in the early sixties at the Newport Folk Festival: before an audience of folkie purists, he came out with an electric guitar and a howling rock band, and got booed off the stage.

By the end of the week, Sally had fallen in love with Dylan. Dylan gave her hope: he showed that you could make your life a work of art. She loved the way he remained fluid, reinventing himself endlessly, refusing to be trapped by other people's expectations. She wanted to be like that. She wanted to reinvent herself endlessly. She wanted to be fiercely, ruthlessly herself, committed to nothing except honesty. She wanted to go electric. She sat in Beth's kitchen, stoned, banging off stream-of-consciousness prose poems on Beth's little manual typewriter. "This acoustic typewriter has got to go. I've outgrown that scene. I need something with more volume."

She was coming alive. In early March, when it was still cold, she could feel the spring. She could smell the spring. The spring was nowhere in evidence. She walked to school alone on a cold crack-lipped morning with dirty old snow on the ground, the trees were bare and bony, but she was sure that the scent in the air was different, the scent in the air was new.

She still felt foggy-headed most of the time. But she wasn't sleeping so late. She would wake up and think: I'll see Jesse today.

They were new to each other. One day she thought he liked her, the next day she thought he hardly knew who she was.

That spring there was an epidemic of fire drills. It was the best thing about school. Everyone left the building in orderly formation, but once you were on the front lawn you could stand around cracking wise with your friends. She saw Jesse across the lawn, with his art pad under his arm, and she went up to speak to him. "Hello, Captain," he said.

This thrilled her. She thought about it for days. He called me Captain.

Jessie wasn't very popular in school. The girls didn't like him because he wore secondhand clothes. The boys didn't like him because he was stronger than they were, because he didn't care about sports, and because he was no good at sports. If he'd been a jock they would have admired him, but he was a bad athlete, so they treated him with the contempt appropriate for harmless giants.

He didn't seem to care. It wasn't in his nature to care. One day when Sally was in the car with her mother, she saw him with his father on the street. His father was a sculptor, with a great gray beard. He'd broken his back in the war; he walked slowly, with stiff concentration. Beside him, Jesse looked solemn. The two of them seemed to belong to another time.

Beth and Aaron and Sally stopped at his house on a Friday night. He was in the garage, which he and his parents had turned into a wood- and metal-working shop. He was building a desk for himself. He was wearing jeans, an apron, no shirt. He had beautiful muscular arms. His parrot, Hector, was perched in the corner. He'd built Hector an enormous cage, but Hector rarely used it. They smoked a joint and Sally was instantly paranoid; everything everybody said was aimed at her, a subtle put-down. Even Hector was putting her down. She sat in a corner, covering her mouth with her hand. After a little while Jesse noticed. He looked over from where he was sanding down the desktop. "You don't need to be so worried," he said quietly. "You're with your friends."

They started to have long phone conversations, late at night. He found things to admire in her—which was amazing. He admired her fund of knowledge. He said she knew everything. The truth of it was simple: a combination of her father holding forth at the dinner table every night, quoting Hazlitt, James G. Blaine, and A. J. Liebling; her utterly random reading—she read five books at a time and never finished any of them; and the fact that she was a garbagehead of useless knowledge from those years of TV. Somehow the amalgamation of all this struck Jesse as impressive.

One night they stayed on the phone past midnight, past one . . . their conversation getting further and further from the present day, their silences getting longer and more comfortable . . . Jesse was half-asleep, mumbling ever more faintly. She was under the covers. "Do you think your name is the right name for you," she said, "or is there another name that would suit you better?" He didn't say anything. He was thinking hard about this, and his answer would tell her who he really was. He didn't say anything. . . .

She listened to his breathing: slow, deep, quiet, steady, slow. She listened for a long time.

In the morning, she woke before he did. She lay beneath the covers with the sun shining in on her and the phone on the pillow next to her ear. She could still hear him. Then, a change, a syncopated rhythm of the breath. Then—cracked, uncertain, sleepy—his voice. "Sally?" "Good morning, Jess," she said.

She was happy to be alive. The songs on the radio expressed the wisdom of the ages. Everyone in the world was happy. She walked along the street and everyone smiled at her. Because she was beautiful. She knew that this exaltedness was as nuts as her depression: she passed from fever to fever. She went around town doing errands with her mother; sometimes they had to pick something up in Jesse's neighborhood, and this was thrilling. Maybe he'd be out walking his dog, maybe they'd pass his house and she'd see his light on. . . . The spring nights were keen; her life was suddenly wonderful; walking to school every morning she passed a boulder with a plaque that said that George Washington had passed this way, and she thought that it should add that Sally Burke had passed this way too, for her life seemed a thing of heroic proportions.

She wasn't so groggy anymore: in fact she needed less sleep than ever. She would wake at six in the morning and lie in bed with her windows open wide, smelling the strange things that were budding outside, plant life, idiot life bursting open in wonderful bloom. She was impatient of sleep; she woke in the morning with an inexplicable happiness, and then realized, a moment later, that she was happy because she'd see Jesse that day.

For the first time in her life she thought of herself as beautiful. She would get up in the middle of the night, get up from bed where she couldn't sleep anyway, to look at herself in the mirror. She had grown taller and firmer; she had dirty-blond hair that fell over her shoulders, and she had long muscular legs with light brown hair—she refused to shave her legs, on hippie principle. Her face, which she had never been proud of because it wasn't lovely enough, wasn't feminine enough, now struck her as honest and strong and attractive enough for any guy who had the sense to find it attractive. She stood in front of the mirror, naked, trembling with awe at how good she looked, trembling with nervousness at the thought that time could only bring changes, and how was it possible for perfection to change to something better?

She walked home from school with Jesse through the park that bordered the highway. He was carrying a large branch.

A bunch of them were supposed to go hiking at Bear Mountain the next day. But she was having second thoughts: he'd realize she'd never been hiking before; he'd think less of her.

"I don't think I can get together tomorrow," she said. "My uncle and aunt are coming over."

He glanced at her, stepped away, and with a violent slicing motion sent the branch across the highway—she heard it skimming the air above the tops of the cars. He stopped walking.

"Don't *lie* to me. I don't *care* what you're doing tomorrow. But if you lie to me—if you lie to me you're just not *in*teresting."

He was staring at her—big black eyes. She never would have thought he could be so ugly.

He was gripping her wrist, hard. She thought this was what he was doing, until she realized that he wasn't touching her at all.

"I'm not lying."

"Get *away* from me. Get away until you've learned how to tell the truth."

He cut across the highway and was gone.

She couldn't get rid of his horrible eyes, following her around for the rest of the night. For dinner Hannah made some mysterious thing that looked exactly like food, but had no taste.

She was lying in bed when she heard the tapping of the first few drops of rain against her window. It wasn't raining.

She went to the window. He was in the backyard, sitting in the fork of the elm tree. Napoleon was sitting near him, a bit higher up on the branch.

"What are you two doing out there?"

"We're talking."

She didn't smile. She was too happy to smile.

"What are you talking about?"

"He told me not to be so hard on you."

One June day, instead of having lunch on the lawn, she and Jesse walked to a park about a half-mile from school. They shared a pear and an orange and a banana, cutting them into sections with his pocketknife, and then they lay next to each other on the grass. He was lying near her, propped on one arm; she could feel his breath on her cheek.

He pulled a dandelion from the grass and put it behind her ear. A wild sweetness was traveling through the air. She took the dandelion and pressed it into his cheekbone, smeared a line of yellow stickiness below his eye. He looked like an Indian. "How," she said. He didn't smile. She thought: He's too serious for me.

His expression didn't change as calmly with neither suddenness nor hesitation he moved closer and looking straight into her eyes with an expression of absolute frankness that she would cherish for the rest of her life because it spoke of respect and feeling from an equal to an equal, he kissed her.

I couldn't have guessed how wonderful, I couldn't have guessed, I couldn't have guessed.

She had made out with other boys, in basements, in backyards, in backseats. She'd thought she'd done everything you could do with a guy, except the ultimate. But now she knew that she had never done anything at all.

They were kissing, and he was touching her face. The way he touched her was new. Maybe it was just that he was used to learning things with his hands. When he touched her face, tracing her brow, tracing her eyelids, tracing her cheekbones, she felt as if her face was being revealed to her. Now she knew what she looked like.

It was too much—it was almost too much for her, and she wanted to cry out. They were in a wooded corner of the park; the sun came down through the leaves; twenty years later Sally came back to the spot and tried to see it as the objectively shabby thing it was, but she couldn't: to her it always remained an Eden.

Finally they had to go back to school. They held hands as they walked. He had to go to class, but she had a study hall she could cut, so she sat on the lawn watching some of the boys she knew play Frisbee. All of them were graceful, all of them were beautiful, all of them were the truest of friends. Can you die of too much happiness?

She didn't understand it when she saw her mother and Daniel walking up to her. They were looking at her strangely, with kind, strange smiles. They looked like angels on a brief visit to the earth.

"Hi," she said. "What are you doing here?"

Daniel reached out and brushed a blade of grass from her hair.

19

In the best traditions of the Irish, Anne Burke was given a wake. For two days, Sally and her family sat with their relatives in one of the receiving rooms of a funeral home in Flushing, against the wall of which lay Sally's grandmother, in an open coffin.

Burke was in his over-efficient mode. He was all briskness, haleness, and cigarettes; he pumped everyone's hand too vigorously, introducing people to each other as often as he could.

For Sally, her grandmother's death was pure mystery, without grief. She hadn't gone into New York with her mother and Daniel to give Burke the news; instead she'd stayed at school so her friends could appreciate her profundity. Her grandmother's death made her profound.

She was sad that Grandma Burke had died, and the two or three things that were vivid to her about her grandmother passed repeatedly through her mind. But that this was her father's mother, that in her death he saw the death of the largest and maybe the sweetest part of his life, that in her death he saw his own—none of this registered. To Sally she was only

Grandma Burke, and somehow it seemed to her that even for her father it was only "Grandma Burke" who had died.

Grandma Burke, in her coffin, looked fed up with everything. Her lips were locked in a sneer. It was not the kind face Sally had known. Sally ascribed this to a failure of the embalmer's art. She had never seen anyone dead before.

They had dinner in a restaurant with Burke's two brothers, alcoholics who ordered food only for respectability's sake. Red-faced, red-throated, quick to anger, with the sharp suspicious vapid eyes of birds, they were like nightmare visions of what her father might have become. Uncle Jimmy put a few drinks into himself and was instantly sentimental, full of love, speaking in a poetic brogue about the importance of kin. Uncle Pat gripped his drink and didn't quite look anyone in the eye—he had the air of a man who had a contract out on everyone at the table, and was waiting impatiently for the machine-gunner to arrive.

On the second afternoon at the funeral home, Daniel and Sally and Hannah came back by themselves while the brothers remained at lunch. Hannah wandered into the wrong room. It was an honest mistake, but now she found herself in an empty room, with an open casket in the corner. Walking on tiptoe, she drew near it. "Mom," said Daniel. "I can't believe you're doing this." He hung back by the door. "I can't believe you're doing this," said Sally, as she followed her mother to the casket.

A middle-aged man was lying there in a blue suit. He needed a shave. His cheeks were heavily, ridiculously rouged.

"Somebody should teach him how to put on his makeup," Sally said.

Hannah stood near the man's midsection and peered up toward his face. "Did they clean your nose good?" she said.

It was uncanny, how little it meant when it was no one you knew.

Another long afternoon in the room where her grandmother lay. In death as in life: her grandmother had left her a legacy of interminable afternoons. As Sally became more and more tired, more and more uncomfortable, the strangeness of this vigil began to impress itself on her in new ways. All the drinking and the chattering that went on in the room couldn't rouse Anne Burke. She lay there, and lay there, as the people she'd loved stood around her.

Gradually, Sally began to find herself imagining that it was not her grandmother but Jesse who was lying there. And this frightened her. Her grandmother had never struck her as wholly alive: she was so withered, so unequipped for the modern world, so clearly a product of the past that Sally had always felt that she was, in a way, dead already.

But Jesse was different. He seemed endlessly resourceful. Sally couldn't imagine anything that could overpower him.

Except it wasn't true. Even he could be mastered. She imagined him lying in the open casket as his friends stood around him, unable to hear them, unable to move. There was a force that could defeat him; and once it had, anything, everything else could triumph over him as well . . . he wouldn't be able to brush away a fly.

She imagined him in his hospital bed, sick with some disease. She imagined death working on him: weakening him and weakening him, so that he'd finally acquiesce, he'd let go his hold on life. To die, she was convinced, is a decision: if you keep saying no to death, it won't be able to take you. She tried to imagine that last moment, when even Jesse Barkin, too weak to keep fighting, would finally say yes to death. There would be a world without him. And only now, thinking about Jesse, could Sally begin to feel something of the meaning of death.

The time to close the coffin and bury her had come. The

mourners filed past the body. The three sons were last. Sally had returned to her seat; she watched her father closely as he stepped up to the coffin. From his expression you couldn't tell a thing. He stopped at the head of the casket and looked at his mother for a long time. Then he leaned over and kissed her.

It was an excellent June day. They drove to a little cemetery in Flushing, on a hill. The noise of the traffic was faint below them. In the distance, Manhattan was gleaming. An elderly, fragile-looking priest, holding open his prayer book, read something about the victory of Christ, and then the coffin was lowered into the hole. Burke and his brothers were impassive. Next to the grave was the grave of Burke's father, dead since 1937, and of his sister, Joan. Beside these was a patch of ground that his brother Jimmy had reserved for himself. Sally couldn't understand how he could be so resigned to death. Didn't he have any hope that he might be an exception?

She couldn't banish from her mind the vision of Jesse in his coffin, without the will to brush away a fly.

Two laborers with shovels dropped earth on the box. The sun was low in the sky. Burke, white-lipped, nodded to his wife, and the four of them began their walk to the car.

Hannah was struck by her daughter's solemn face. "What are you thinking?"

Sally looked up and smiled stupidly. She didn't want to answer.

Burke put his arm around his daughter—a rare event. "She's pondering the mysteries of existence," he said.

PART TWO

20

Three years among the lockjawed scholars of Oberlin College was enough. She transferred to Sarah Lawrence, just outside New York City.

Her first few hours there were a shock. She'd known there were more women than men at Sarah Lawrence, but she hadn't thought this through: she'd contented herself with the pious expectation that the absence of men would mean one less distraction from her work. But as soon as she arrived she began to get nervous. The competition was like nothing she'd ever seen: delicate, graceful dancers; actresses with breathy voices and wide-set, little-girl eyes; European transfer students, with high cheekbones, slim brown cigarettes, and an air of incommunicable *Weltschmerz*. Galumphing around in her hiking boots, Sally began to sense that it would be a long, long year.

Because she was a senior, she was given a single room with a semiprivate bath. She was sitting on the floor putting her things away when someone slipped out from the thin space behind the half-opened bathroom door. A tall woman with purple eyeliner and anguished blond hair.

"You must be Sally. I'm your suitemate, Libby Minskin." She glanced at Sally and then checked out the room. "You're kind of a nature girl, aren't you?"

Three years at Oberlin, where the sons and daughters of Long Island dress like young lumberjacks, had left their mark on Sally. She owned three pairs of overalls.

"I'm a budding poet," Libby announced. She sat down and started to help Sally unpack her books. "What are you?"

"I don't know. That's why I transferred. I didn't really feel like majoring in anything, and I heard there aren't any majors at Sarah Lawrence. I thought I'd take a little philosophy, a little literature. . . . I like the buffet approach."

Squinting with delight through her enormous glasses, Libby pressed Sally's hand.

"So you still haven't found yourself yet. I've always wondered what that must feel like. I've known I was a poet since I was ten."

"And you haven't bud yet?"

"I've written some *won*derful poetry. But I think I'm just about to come into my own." She took a few more books from a box, pausing, with a knowing smile, over *Walden*. "We should have an interesting year together. The poet and the child of nature."

During her first month or two at Sarah Lawrence, Sally enjoyed her classes, she enjoyed the people she met, but what she enjoyed most was witnessing the tragic opera that was Libby's life. For weeks Libby told stories about her off-campus boyfriend, Ronald, a lean, lithe, passionate devil of a man. One weekend he came for a visit. Sally saw them across campus: it looked as if Libby was with a walrus on loan from the zoo. As she went to sleep that night Sally could hear them making love. "You beast," Libby called out.

In the middle of the night Sally got up to go to the bathroom. There was a light under the door. She knocked. Libby whispered for her to come in. She was sitting in her nightgown on the rim of the tub, a writing pad on her lap. "Ronald's asleep," she whispered. "I'm writing a sonnet about how the poet experiences the act of love."

In the morning, when Sally went to the bathroom, she found the door to Libby's room open, and Libby at her desk. Ronald had already left.

"You want to go down to brunch?" Sally said.

"Sure. I'll be ready in a minute. I'm writing a poem about Masada."

Large issues of Jewish identity were the dominant theme when she wrote in the morning; poems about being a poet preoccupied her at night.

One night a week, the school sponsored poetry and fiction readings in the Cellar, a dimly lit place where you could buy beer and sandwiches. Usually a Distinguished Visiting Writer would read, followed by two or three students. One night in early December, Libby read her new poems.

It had snowed all day, steadily and heavily, and it was snowing into the night. Libby was the last to read. Dressed in somber colors, she approached the microphone. She was nearly six feet tall, but behind the podium she contrived to scrunch herself up as much as she could, to become small, demure, defenseless.

"Most of the distinguished poetry we've heard tonight has been about the joyful side of life," she began. "You might say it's been daylight poetry. I want to shift the emphasis. I want to read poetry of the night."

She sipped from a glass of water. "Lately I've found myself in the grip of an obsession. I've been thinking about my ancestors, in the shtetls of Poland. I don't know why they've come to mind, these ghosts, but they've been tormenting me: when I eat, when I try to study, when I try to sleep. At first I thought they would just go away, as mysteriously as they'd come. But after two weeks, after three weeks, I realized they weren't going to go away without exacting a price. They wanted something from me. They wanted me to give their memories a voice."

And then, after a portentous silence, she began to read her new poetic sequence, *A Dance with the Rabbi of Lublin.*

Sally had spent a great deal of time with Libby in the previous weeks, and had heard nothing about these ghosts. Mostly, she'd heard Libby scheming about how to get a guy named Eric Gordon into bed. . . . But she was prepared to believe that beneath the bubbling surface tormented thoughts flowed, and she tried to listen carefully.

She found herself distracted by a guy at her table, a skinny guy who spent most of the reading shifting uncomfortably in his chair. When Libby spoke of her "obsession," he put his head in his hands. At other moments, when her poems shifted weirdly from the terrors of the pogroms to the glories of the poet herself—at moments like these he leaned forward with a strange grin.

After her last poem, Libby made a deep, deep bow. When the applause died down, she came over to Sally's table and sat next to the skinny guy, who was sipping delicately from a cup of hot chocolate.

With a long, painted fingernail she poked him in the chest. "How was I? Was I brilliant?"

"You were brilliant."

"Come on. How was I?"

"You were as extraordinary as ever."

"Sally, wasn't I terrific? Have you met this guy? Owen, this is Sally. She's my suitemate. She's studying organic farming.

Owen's a writer. But he's had writer's block as long as I've known him, and I've known him since third grade."

Owen and Sally shook hands.

"You two shouldn't even bother to have a conversation," Libby said. "You have nothing in common."

"Kindly have the good grace to let us discover that for ourselves," Owen said.

When you met a guy at Sarah Lawrence, your first responsibility was to figure out whether he was up for grabs. Sally's provisional conclusion was that Libby had no special claim on him. They seemed too relaxed. Not that she herself had any particular interest—it was just that after three months at Sarah Lawrence she performed this rapid calculation automatically.

"Since when do you smoke?" Libby said to Owen. He had a pack of Vantages in his pocket. "You pretending to be a real man?" She pulled the cigarettes out of Owen's pocket and gave one to Sally; and in the way she did this she confirmed that she waived all liens, rights, and privileges in the matter of Owen.

In three months Sally had learned that a woman at Sarah Lawrence was forever on stage. Unless you were one of the happy few who had a boyfriend, it was impossible to be alone with a guy: at lunch or dinner or sitting around in the library, it was always two or three women to every man; so you learned to make the most of whatever little exposure you could get. Although the school offered no official majors, every woman there was majoring in theater. You had to make the smallest gestures count; so as Sally lit her cigarette she knew exactly what she was doing with her mouth, with her hands, with her eyes. It was like being cast in minor parts, and becoming expert in how to steal a scene.

Very retrograde behavior, very fifties; but she fell in with it nevertheless.

Libby, obviously, had known Owen too long to waste this kind of effort on him. When she'd reached into his pocket, it was with all the grace of one of those metal claws you try to grab prizes with at the penny arcade; and now, when she flipped the cigarettes back to him, she knocked over his hot chocolate.

Owen righted the cup and sopped up the hot chocolate with a napkin. "Are you going to get me another cup?"

"Why should I? What have you ever done for me?"

"I attended your poetry reading. And wept at all the right places. Like when you described your great-great-grandfather, the rabbi of rabbis, as a fish swimming proudly toward Jerusalem."

"I'm planning to revise that line."

The distinguished visiting poet, two tables away, was momentarily unattended by admirers. Libby rose. "Well, I'd love to chat with you two all night, but I have some social climbing to do." She put a dollar on the table. "That's for the hot chocolate."

Owen watched her cross the room. "I've known Libby for fifteen years now, and I'm still trying to figure out whether one likes her in spite of her faults or because of them. Actually, I'm still trying to figure out whether one likes her."

"You do like her. I can tell you like her."

"Well, that's true. I think there's something very lovable about Libby. I just don't like to admit it."

She was talking with the visiting writer, a craggy melancholic whose main poetic theme was the temptation of suicide. He was hunched over his drink, staring at his hands, as Libby chattered on brightly about her literary influences.

"So how did you get interested in organic farming?" Owen said. "I once tried to grow a tomato plant."

"That was just Libby's little joke. I really don't know what I'm here for."

"Maybe you *should* study organic farming. It's a very fine thing. I hear they breed these fish on organic fish farms, they've got more protein than a steak, and they're also very friendly. They're kind of hippie fish."

"I don't think that's for me. I'm kind of a Burger King person, really."

"Really? I'm surprised. You look like a sixties person. There aren't enough sixties people around here."

The pleasure of being described made her ears burn.

"Well, I guess it's time for bed," he said. "Two cups of hot chocolate and I'm out like a light. Do you want these? I thought I'd try to start smoking, since it's the thing to do here, but I really can't stand the things."

She took the cigarettes. She liked him. She liked the fact that he wasn't cool. Everyone at Sarah Lawrence was studiously "intense"—smoking as many cigarettes and drinking as much as they could and constantly reminding you that they were artists. Owen seemed . . . more modest than that.

"I'm leaving too. You want to walk a little?"

They took a walk through town. It was still snowing.

"This town always makes me wish I had a house of my own," he said. "With a family. You walk around late at night, and all the lights are off except maybe one little light where somebody's watching Johnny . . . it makes you feel a little lonely."

They walked on without saying anything for a while.

"Do you really have a writing block?" Sally said.

"I don't know if it's anything so romantic. Mostly I just love to take naps. Whenever I try to do some writing I get this overpowering urge to take a nap."

"There's a lot to be said for naps," she said.

"I hope so. I read about this Indian tribe whose whole culture revolved around their dreams. They practiced dream control. When they met someone in a dream, they'd ask for a gift. And sometimes the gift would be a song or a story, and in the morning they'd teach the song to everybody else in the tribe."

"Do you practice dream control?"

"I try, but I can never control anything. The other night I tried to make a phone call, and even though I knew I was dreaming, I couldn't get through. I wonder why the telephone service is always so lousy in dreamland."

They walked on in silence, pondering this question, as the snow fell.

21

Marijuana. OPEC. Bob Dylan. These were the instruments of her downfall.

From her window she could see all the way down the hill. Brightly dressed students were heading to the cafeteria for lunch.

It was noon on a Saturday. She'd just gotten out of bed.

She'd smoked pot the night before, for the first time in months. She still felt a little high. She wondered if she should go back to sleep.

Pot. In her last year of high school she'd smoked almost every weekend; at Oberlin, almost every night. At first, pot had seemed an educational resource: when she and Beth took their endless walks, their endless drives, mapping out the universe with their conversations, marijuana had seemed an indispensable part of it all.

That didn't last. By her second year of college, when she found herself missing more classes than she was showing up for, she had come to the conclusion that the "amotivational syndrome" was not a myth. She decided to kick the habit, and she was surprised by how easy it was: she smoked every few months now, when the spirit moved her, and the rest of the time she didn't think about it much. But on days like today, as she sat in her bathrobe at noon, feeling much more tired than it was reasonable to feel, she wondered if those years had drained her of her energy.

But sometimes she thought this tiredness wasn't hers alone: the world itself seemed tired. When she was a kid, and Daniel would come home from college talking about demonstrations and teach-ins, she couldn't wait to grow up and be a rebel herself. But everything had changed. She still felt like a rebel, but she didn't know quite what to rebel against. Politics had disappeared. In the sixties, during the war, some witty senator had proposed that the United States should declare victory and come home. Instead, the peace movement had declared victory and gone home. The war had come to an end three years ago—in 1975; but the peace movement had faded away long before that. The whole "counterculture," if there ever was such a thing, had vanished. Everybody just got tired.

Life no longer seemed limitless. One night about a year ago, she and Beth, home for Christmas break, had borrowed her parents' car, intending to have one of their traditional late-night driving and talking sessions . . . and they'd run out of gas. They had to call AAA and get themselves towed. They'd fallen into a time warp—they'd thought they were back in the early days of high school, before the oil crisis, when you could put two dollars in the tank and drive all night. You couldn't do that anymore. As the newspapers were always saying, they were living in a new era of limits.

The presiding spirit over all this, somehow, was Bob Dylan. The Dylan she'd fallen in love with, in high school, was full of anger, wildness, hope. She still bought all his records; she was in love with him still. But somewhere along the line he'd been chastened. Now he wrote songs of vague renunciation, vague spiritual yearning. Even Dylan was tired.

In the spring of her junior year she'd seen Scorsese's movie *The Last Waltz,* about the final concert of the Band. At the end of the concert, all the evening's guest performers came back on stage—Dylan, Van Morrison, Joni Mitchell, Clapton, Neil Young—and joined the Band in a version of Dylan's "I Shall Be Released." It was as if they were singing an anthem.

It was one of Sally's favorite songs; sitting in the movie theater, she'd cried. Later, though, she'd wondered what it said about her time. Years before, these people might have taken "We Shall Overcome" for their anthem. Now they sang "I Shall Be Released." Released from what?

22

"When they torture you, and torture you, and torture you, with insults to the human body that I do not wish to describe, your only wish is to lose consciousness. Your only wish, and your only hope. I did not lose consciousness. What saved me was something far stranger. Suddenly my mind seemed to free itself from my body. I was suspended in the air, near the ceiling, watching the torturers do their work, and feeling nothing."

The man at the podium was a Chilean exile: soft-spoken, lean with disillusionment.

Hannah sat with a smile of contentment, knitting a hat.

Burke and Hannah were visiting on parents' day, which culminated in a teach-in against the Pinochet regime.

After the speeches were over, in the cold air, Burke nodded approvingly. "I'm glad to see that Sarah Lawrence remains firm in its opposition to Yankee imperialism."

Her parents accompanied her to the Cellar for a late snack. "Your father's famous," Hannah said.

"Famous among those who know him," Burke said.

"Did you know he was on TV last week?"

"I know, Mom, you told me."

Three years ago, Burke had become the head of District 17, a union that represented a sort of grab-bag collection of workers at nonprofit organizations, from social workers to lab technicians to home-care aides, and now he could occasionally be seen on the nightly news.

"Yes, I've become a moderately important person in New York," Burke said, "but your mother has become an extremely important person in Teaneck. I attended a Board of Education meeting with her last week. When she came to the microphone to give the board a tongue-lashing for their insufficient support of the open classroom, you should have seen them quake. She was a veritable Jeremiah."

Burke and Hannah were almost finished with their egg creams when Owen came through the door, pounding himself on the arms to shake off the cold. She felt a little jolt of tension—When Worlds Collide.

Owen had seemed very interested in her lately. When he saw the three of them he hurried over with his arm outstretched, as if he was running for mayor of Sarah Lawrence. Sally introduced everyone; he pulled up a chair from another table. He was wearing a goosedown vest, bright red. "It's not a fit night out for man nor beast," he said. "You don't have a tissue, by any chance?" He had a perpetual case of the sniffles.

"If you come down with a cold it'll serve you right," Hannah said. "You should be wearing a hat."

"Yes?" Owen perked up; it pleased him to get advice.

"Don't you know that people who wear hats retain seventy-eight percent of their body heat? You wouldn't see Sally going around in the winter without a hat."

Resting her chin in her palms, Sally smiled like an angel.

"Let me measure your head," Hannah said. "I could knit you a hat in a jiffy—I'll send it to Sally next week."

"I don't want you to put yourself out."

"She loves to knit," Sally said. "She knits everywhere. She knits at traffic lights. She doesn't look up until people start honking behind her."

"This is a great honor," Owen said, as Hannah wound a length of wool around his head.

He seemed utterly relaxed—more relaxed than he'd be if he and Sally were sitting by themselves. He had a noodly body, as if he had no bones.

"And what is it you study at dear old Sarah Lawrence?" Burke said. "Some aspect of the creative process, no doubt?"

"That's exactly correct. I came here for the fiction writing program."

"I've never quite understood the idea that fiction writing can be taught," Burke said. "Have you found that it can?"

"Actually, I wouldn't know. Maybe if I tried to write something once in a while."

"Owen has an advanced case of writer's block," Sally said.

"Writer's block," Burke said. "When some writer came up to Edmund Wilson and complained about being blocked, Wilson looked at him coldly and said, 'A writer writes.'"

There was a little silence.

"I guess so," Owen said.

Burke was dressed in his usual three-piece suit, his usual wing tips. As always, he had a curiously martial air. Even when he was dressed casually, he wasn't. Neatly pressed khakis were what he wore on weekends, and if they went out to dinner or the movies, he put on a jacket and tie. It was strange to have him in the Cellar. The room was filled with students, breathlessly exchanging intimacies; he had a look of dry amusement as he observed the human show. Somebody said "Ciao" to somebody else, and he pursed his lips, suppressing an ironic remark.

"Did you ever think about being a writer?" Owen said.

"Not very seriously. I think it's a very honorable calling, but I never thought my talents lay in that direction. I felt I could make more of a contribution somewhere else."

"That's interesting," Owen said. "I've never thought of it in terms of making a contribution. I've just thought it's what I want to do."

Burke was looking at him closely. Sally was afraid of what he'd say. To his way of thinking, she knew, the chance to make a contribution was the only reason to be alive.

She looked from one to the other. It wasn't fair to measure Owen against her father—it really wasn't fair. Burke was sixty-one years old: he'd had forty additional years in which to forge himself. But she couldn't help noticing the contrast. Burke *was* forged. She'd once heard him passionately lecturing some young union man about the organizer's role: an organizer, he said, should never consider himself a bringer of light, but merely a technician: someone who helps people learn how to organize themselves. It was a code of service, of self-abnegation; but living by that code had somehow made him the most sharply honed, the most defined of men. Even his eyebrows radiated purpose. Owen, in his puffy down vest, his hair unwashed and woolly, with a two-day growth of beard and a kind of "I'm okay, you're okay" grin on his face—it was ten o'clock at night, but Owen looked as if he'd just wobbled out of bed. It wasn't fair to compare them like this. She still didn't know Owen very well, but she knew he had virtues—of introspection, of demonstrativeness—that her father couldn't even recognize as virtues. And yet she couldn't help feeling that he seemed diminished in her father's presence.

"It's a different age, I suppose," Burke said. "One lives the life of one's time."

A conclusion everyone could live with. A few minutes later Owen said goodnight and headed for the library. "A very nice boy," Hannah said after he left.

She lay in bed, thinking about the eternal problem. The man problem. In three years at Oberlin she'd had three and a half boyfriends, and none of them had worked out.

In the darkness, near the foot of her bed, a set of golden scales was shining. On one scale sat Owen, smiling hopefully, in his goosedown vest. On the other scale were her doubts.

23

Owen had no doubts. He hung around her a lot. He'd sit down next to her in the cafeteria—always after asking permission—and he'd tell her little things he'd learned from the fillers in *The New York Times*. "Do you know how many potato chips you'd have to stack to reach the top of the Empire State Building?" She had the feeling that he made up lists of things to say, because he was too nervous for normal conversation.

He seemed to find everything about her fascinating. She told some pointless story about how, as a kid, she'd never wash her hands without washing all the way up to her elbows; Owen acted as if she'd just unfurled the Magna Carta. "Really? Up to your elbows? That's incredible." And he sat there nodding for another minute or two, trying to absorb this astonishing fact.

He was always walking into things when she was around—apologizing to tables.

"What's his problem?" Sally was sitting on the bathroom floor, talking with Libby, who was in the bath. "There are all these gorgeous women all over the place. I'm not even pretty."

"First of all, though I still don't think you and Owen are right for each other, one of his good qualities is that he likes intelligent women. For a non-poet, you're fairly intelligent. And second of all, you're prettier than you seem to think. He told me he thinks you have a beautifully frank face."

"What does that mean?" She got up and looked at herself in the mirror. She had large features, unruly hair. "A frank face."

"You know what it means. You have a natural beauty. You have an honest face."

"Is that like, plain?"

"I wouldn't say plain."

"Is that like, homely?"

"If you must know, he said he thinks you're naturally sexy."

Sally smiled at herself in the mirror.

"Personally," Libby said, "if I were a man I'd prefer the more sophisticated look."

His interest was flattering, but something held her back. She kept thinking about Jesse. It wasn't so much that she wanted to get back together with him—the past was past. But she wanted to be with someone who inspired her as much as he had. She'd had such ferocious *respect* for Jesse.

"None of them held a candle to him," she said to herself, as she sat procrastinating in the library.

Maybe it was all an illusion of high school, an illusion of first love. But no one she had met since had meant as much to her. They'd seemed less real than Jesse.

"They lacked quiddity," she said, leafing through a magazine. A word her philosophy teacher was fond of.

She and Jesse had gone off to different colleges; tried to carry on long-distance . . . it hadn't worked. There was a time when she'd thought that they could never really lose each other. . . . Now she didn't even know what state he was living in. What country.

A mostly solitary life. She spent hours in the library; she came back to her room and studied; she had dinner with Libby and a new friend, Caitlin; she took long walks. She spent most of her time studying philosophy, not because she wanted to "do" anything with it but because it roused her sense of wonder. In class Mr. Goldman lectured on Hobbes's belief that our senses are untrustworthy guides—that color, for instance, is not "out there" in objects themselves: it's something that our eye pastes onto things, that our mind invents. When she left the classroom it was a gray February day, but the ideas she'd just learned made it grayer: the color was dripping off the evergreens and the brick of the dormitory walls and the jackets of the people she passed. She walked in a world of grayness, in which the only bright and colorful presence was the mind.

This is how she got friendly with Caitlin. Caitlin wasn't a philosophy student, she was a dancer, but she had the most vivid sense of freelance wonder of anyone Sally had ever known. Caitlin was apt to say things like, "Do you ever just think, 'My God! I'm alive!'" And, of course, Sally often did. But no one else she knew had ever talked about it before.

At the beginning of the semester Caitlin bought a Bible for her religion class and after a lunch on the main lawn consisting of a Diet Pepsi and three ounces of cottage cheese, she lay in the grass reveling in her new acquisition. But if she was moved with a religious ecstasy by this book, it wasn't the glory of the Lord that moved her but the scent of fresh paper. She put her nose between two pages and said, "Only seven dollars for this smell!"

Once they had gone into New York to visit museums; Caitlin had spent the day talking about her arduous struggles to make things work with her boyfriend. They passed two older women, kissing each other goodbye outside a restaurant. "Tell me how things work out," one of them said.

"All over this city," Caitlin said to Sally, "people are working things out."

She was full of self-improvement schemes, which usually got in each other's way. She was tortured by the thought of all the things she'd never have time to do. "I figured out that if I read a book a week for the rest of my life, and if I live to be eighty, I'll have read about three thousand books." She clutched Sally's elbow. "That's not enough!"

But the main purpose of life was dancing, and the main purpose of life when she wasn't dancing was watching her weight. She had a long-legged beauty that Sally envied—she looked as if she was just about to vault onto a horse—but in her own mind she was always two pounds overweight. Sally sat next to her in the lunchroom, fascinated, as Caitlin counted out lettuce leaves for her salad and weighed a slice of cheese on a little scale that she carried in her bag.

What was beginning to disturb Sally was the fact that everyone around her knew what they wanted to do with their lives. Libby was a poet, Caitlin was a dancer, Beth was set on writing children's books. Everybody was finding their own roads. Except her. She didn't really feel like she wanted to; but she was beginning to wonder how long this could go on.

I'm roadless, she said, walking from the library to her room.

24

Burke made fried eggs, toast, coffee. As always, when he put Sally's plate in front of her, he said, "Take it away, Angelo"—no one knew why. And as always, after Hannah took her first sip of coffee, she said, "This is the best cup of coffee I've ever had."

This is why one visits one's parents.

They were having friends over for dinner that night; Hannah had shopping to do. Sally went with her.

This was one of the pleasures of being back on the East Coast: she could spend a weekend with her parents for no particular reason at all. She'd enjoyed being far away from them, in Oberlin, for three years; but now she enjoyed being back.

In the car they passed a guy on a moped. "I'm thinking of getting one of those," Hannah said.

"Why?"

"They look like fun."

She could see her mother tooling around town on a moped, pulling out her knitting at stoplights. "You might get a reputation as an eccentric."

"I already have one. That's the nice thing about getting to

be a certain age. You don't give a damn what people think anymore, so you can do whatever you want."

At the fish store they ran into one of Hannah's first-graders, with his mother. He seemed stunned to encounter "Mrs. Burke" in the outside world.

"Are we going to do a little arithmetic this week, Charlie?"

Charlie folded his arms and looked up at her sternly. "Not yet. I don't have time for arithmetic yet."

"Why not?"

"My *job* is to learn to read."

This delighted Hannah. "Every time I talk about doing some math he says, 'My job is to learn to read.' He's the stubbornest little son of a gun I've ever met."

"After I learn to read," Charlie said, "*then* I'll learn arithmetic."

"That'll be your new job?"

He nodded solemnly.

Sally went across the street to a candy store to get the *Times* for her father. Looking through the magazine racks, she noticed that there was a Dylan interview in *Playboy*. She considered *Playboy* a stupid magazine—she didn't find it offensive so much as stupid—so she wasn't happy about buying it. But Dylan was Dylan.

Finally, they drove to Hannah's brother's house. He and his wife were on vacation; Hannah came over every day to take in their mail.

Stanley and Phyllis had moved to Teaneck only recently; Sally had never been in their house before. She felt immediately comfortable there: the walls were covered with his paintings. Stanley had devoted himself to painting since his seventh birthday, when his father, the actor and painter, put a brush in his hand. In fifty-five years of single-minded work, he'd gained zero recognition. He didn't seem to give a damn: he lived to paint, and nothing else mattered.

"How's your young man?" Hannah said. She was sitting on the floor, petting the cat.

"Who are you talking about?"

"The young man we met at Sarah Lawrence."

"His name's Owen. He's all right. But he's not my young man."

Hannah was well disposed toward Owen: having had a father and a brother who'd lived for art, she took an immediate liking to anyone who declared himself an artist.

When they came back, Burke was asleep on the couch. The cat was curled up on his stomach.

"I hope he wakes up in a good mood," Hannah said.

He'd been cheerful in the morning, but that had no bearing on how he might feel when he woke. More often than not, if he lay down for a while on the weekend, some foul cloud would lower over him as he slept: he would wake up irritated, bearish, grunting rather than speaking in sentences. It was as if he woke up into the wrong life. As they unloaded the groceries in the kitchen, Sally marveled a little at the way her mother had navigated thirty years of these moods. It struck her as a kind of heroism.

The cat came into the kitchen; Burke was moving about in the living room. She heard his footsteps as he went upstairs to the bedroom. Soon they would know.

"The giant is stirring," she said.

A few minutes later he appeared in the kitchen doorway—dapper, with a fresh shirt and newly combed hair. "Is there anything I can do for the commonweal?" he said.

The three of them cleaned the house together. There was a lot to clean. Hannah was always in despair about her own messiness, but she could never bring herself to throw anything away.

Sally stalked around the house picking up old newspapers. "What should I do with these?"

"Just stack them up in the corner. I haven't read them yet."

Sally hesitated, trying to formulate some wise remark about the worthlessness of yesterday's news. Hannah pointed at her. "Don't say a word."

After fifteen minutes Burke was breathing heavily. "When are you going to give up those fucking cigarettes?" Hannah said.

He shrugged. "The day of the funeral."

At about six, the guests arrived. Two couples: the Levines and the Pollacks. The Levines were old friends—Burke and Hannah had known them since the forties. The Pollacks were a younger couple, both of whom worked for Burke's union. Mel Pollack had a beard; Debbie Pollack had a spiky, punky haircut. They looked kind of hip.

They all had drinks and appetizers in the living room, discussing the events of the day. The country was turning in a conservative direction; Jimmy Carter, halfway through his term in office, seemed to be trying to become a Republican; everyone agreed that the left in America was headed for a long bad time.

When dinner was over, Sally went up to her room and read for a while—she had to finish *The Red and the Black* by Monday. After about five minutes she started thinking about having a cigarette. But that wouldn't be smart: she didn't want Hannah to know she still smoked, and it would be hard to cover up the smell if she smoked up here. She put the thought out of her mind.

After about two more minutes she had devised a plan: she'd open the windows, then smoke one cigarette in the closet, with the door closed. Perfect. She enjoyed one delicious cigarette and went back to Stendhal.

There was a knock on the door, immediately after which Hannah opened it and put her head in.

"Dessert?"

"Thanks. I'll be down in a minute."

Hannah was about to close the door, but she stopped: holding on to the doorknob, she sniffed the air. The human smoke detector. Sally was already searching for an alibi.

"What's that smell? You haven't been smoking a *cigarette?*"

"No, Mom." She tried to assume a sheepish air. "I smoked a little pot."

Hannah shook her head. You couldn't quite say she looked pleased, but she did look relieved. "Breaking the law in your parents' house? You should be ashamed. Come soon, before the pecan pie is gone."

She couldn't quite believe it had worked. The joy of having liberal parents.

When she came downstairs, everyone had moved back into the living room; the evening was winding toward its conclusion. Her father was sitting in his easy chair, talking about the state of the labor movement. In the Burkes' circle of friends, he seemed to have an implicit authority: it always fell to him, on evenings like this, to have the last few words. For Sally, this kind of gathering could never feel complete until then—until Burke had brought together all the themes of the evening, made them cohere. She loved this, not because of any political enlightenment it conferred, but because of the way it made her feel. He always seemed at his most reflective, and somehow his gentlest, at such moments.

When he'd finished speaking she got a slice of pie and sat near the Pollacks. Mel Pollack was looking through the record collection. "I see you've got the new Dylan album. Any good?"

"Sally was taping it this afternoon," Burke said. "I came in for a few minutes, and I must say, I was gravely disappointed in my daughter's taste. I was under the impression that Dylan made at least a token effort to address social issues. But he's just singing about problems that will end up on an analyst's couch."

This was so beautifully stuffy that she had to laugh.

Hannah was coming back into the room with a pot of coffee. "She not only has the new album, she's got an interview with Dylan in *Playboy*."

Pollack looked interested. "What does he have to say?"

"You can see what he has to say." Hannah skipped over to the magazine rack. "I'm sure, of course, that that's the only reason you'd want to take a look at *Playboy*."

"Ah, *Playboy*," said the owlish Levine, relighting his pipe. "An historical journal, I believe. I consult it when I want to refresh my memory about that ancient struggle, the Pubic Wars."

Hannah stood in the middle of the living room, leafing through the magazine. "Miss February—what big eyes you have!"

Burke left the room.

The copy of *Playboy* was passed around to the obligatory naughty remarks. Hannah, however, had unaccountably lost her relish for it all. She excused herself—she said she had a backache—and went upstairs to lie down.

The guests left a few minutes later; Burke and Sally cleaned up. He rolled up his sleeves to wash the dishes, and handed her the dishtowel. "This is a two-person job," he said.

"Can't we just use the dishwasher?"

"Don't talk back to your father."

She dried while he washed. She was happy.

When they were finishing the dishes, Hannah came in. She took a bottle of aspirin from the shelf and opened the refrigerator. She hadn't looked at either of them.

"What's wrong, honey?" Burke said. "You threw your back out?"

"No."

"Well, what's wrong?"

"You."

"What do you mean?"

"I saw that look you gave me."

"What look?"

"When I took out that *Playboy*. You wanted to censor me."

Sally saw her father's face change. Instantly, the mildness was gone: his mouth grew tight with anger.

"You're goddamn right. You're goddamn right I wanted to censor you. Of course I wanted to censor you, when you talk about stupid shit like *Playboy*."

Sally wasn't very surprised by this: her father was violently puritan, violently repressed. She didn't feel it was her place to listen to her parents arguing; she went to her room.

A few minutes later Hannah came up. "You want to go back to school? Come on. I'll take you back now."

The question allowed only one answer: Hannah wanted to get out of the house. But as it happened, Sally did want to get back to school. It was 10:30: late for Teaneck, but early for Sarah Lawrence. She started collecting her things.

Hannah already had her coat on. She went out to the car.

Sally went into the kitchen. Burke was at the kitchen table, smoking a cigarette. His rage had vanished as quickly as it had come. He looked chastened, baffled.

"You're going back tonight, Sarah?"

"Yeah," was all she could think of to say.

"Well, so long. Don't take any wooden nickels."

He said this to her sometimes, instead of goodbye. It seemed to amuse him: a parody of sage fatherly counsel, from a man who didn't believe that sage fatherly counsel did any good. Tonight he said it without any playfulness, as a meaningless reflex.

"OK, Dad," she said quietly.

There was no traffic. When they drew near the George Washington Bridge, Hannah finally spoke. "Your father is a good man—he's the most moral man I've ever met—and he's a brilliant man, in many ways. But he has a basic fault. And it's held him back all his life."

Sally didn't want to hear this. It made it sound as if his life was over, as if there was no room for him to change.

"He doesn't know how to deal with people. It's hurt him at work. He can lead by example—but he can't teach."

Hannah looked as if she were wondering how much to say.

"It's not just people—it's his own emotions he can't deal with. He doesn't know how to express anger. He just bottles it up until it explodes. And he doesn't know how to show his affection either. Neither of you kids can ever understand how much he loves you. He just won't let himself show it. And it's horrible to do that to your kids."

Sally didn't think this last part was true. It was a denial of her whole experience. She understood her father loved her: you learned to understand the meaning of the hints, the jokes, the teasing. He never kissed her; he never embraced her. But when, say, he asked her to stand next to him and dry the dishes, even though there was no need for her to—this had the effect of an embrace.

But she couldn't say that now. Hannah, if only for this moment, was intent on believing that the deepest truth about Burke was his inability to express his love. At this moment, when her husband had stung her, to contradict her would be to sting her again. So Sally kept her thoughts to herself.

When they reached the campus, Hannah said, "I think you have a cold coming on. You better go right to bed."

This was irritating. Sally congratulated herself on her maturity for not saying anything.

She leaned over into the backseat and hauled up her knapsack. When she'd brought it to her lap, she sat there for a moment, feeling that the two of them, at least—the women of the family—should be able to share an expression of true feeling.

"Damn," her mother said. "I meant to give you some leftovers."

"Thanks for everything. Thanks for the ride."

"Call me on Wednesday or something," Hannah said.

She went back to her room and dropped her knapsack on the bed. It was a little after eleven. She didn't know what to do. She was filled with so many emotions—she was afraid that if she went out and socialized they'd be all wiped away. She left her dorm and walked up the hill. It was a wild, black, gusty night. She went into the Cellar, but she didn't sit down. The music was so loud she felt the bass notes jumping around in her body; people were leaning into each other's ears to make themselves heard.

She wanted to unburden herself, she wanted to talk, but she didn't want to shout. In this atmosphere, in any case, intimacy came too cheap. If you sat down with Heather she'd tell you about her alcoholic parents; if you sat down with Jill she'd tell you about her recent experiments with bondage and domination. Everyone was breathlessly ready to tell you True and Shocking Facts about their lives. Her story would be lost in the noise.

She went back out and walked farther up the hill. There

was a classroom in one of the old dorms where Owen sometimes studied after the library closed. He wasn't likely to be
there near midnight on a Saturday, but she thought she'd take
a look.

The classroom had huge windows; at night, when the
room was lit up, you could see in without being seen. Owen
was sitting at the big table, reading a book. She stood outside,
watching him, shivering, hands in her pockets. He had a thermos next to him on the table.

She went in and stood in the doorway. He looked up.
There is nothing so gratifying as surprising someone and seeing his face transformed by an immediate, unfeigned, invol-
untary expression of happiness.

"Hey there," he said.

"Hey there."

"You're back early."

"I know. Am I interrupting?"

"Not at all. I just finished my work. I was starting a spy
novel." He put the book down. "So. Let me debrief you.
How was New Jersey?"

She told him: about the pleasures of the day, about the
flare-up at the end, about her mother's speech in the car. She
felt slightly guilty telling him about her family life. But she
went on.

"My parents are a funny couple. They're complete oppo-
sites. They're like yin and yang. Sometimes I wonder *how*
they get along, and sometimes I think that's *why* they get
along."

Owen poured some tea from his thermos. "Who do you
take after more?" he said. "Your mother or your father?"

She liked this question. "Usually I think I'm more like
Hannah. I'm sentimental, I'm emotional, I'm Jewish. I think
of myself as Jewish. But sometimes I wonder. When she was
talking about how my father couldn't express his love, she

was so upset. And I wanted to say . . . you know. I wanted to say I love you. And I couldn't. I ended up just hoping she understood. And it occurred to me that I have more of my father in me than I usually think. I'm nothing *like* him, but I *am* him."

She felt embarrassed to be going on about herself like this. "What are you smiling at?"

"You're so . . . *serious,*" he said. "I was just wondering if you were always so serious. What were you like when you were a little girl?"

"Serious. I think I was exactly like I am now. Except maybe happier. More hopeful. I had more pep. Life seemed wider then."

"Don't give up on everything so soon."

She was charmed by his questions, flattered. It felt good to be here. Usually he was too anxious, too eager to please. But she appreciated him here, in this calm. She felt cared for. He took another sip of tea, and held the cup out. She took it in both hands and drew it close, so that the steam rose up over her face.

25

Libby had a get-together at her parents' house in Nyack one afternoon. After a while she and Owen got tired of ragging on each other and started ragging on Sally. "Sally's the strangest suitemate. You get up to pee at four in the morning and you notice a light on under her door. She's reading Hegel. At four in the afternoon, though, you have to tiptoe around. I'm beginning to suspect she's a vampire."

"She overslept dinner the other day," Owen said.

"Sally doesn't think about food. She has her mind on higher things."

"She just needs a watch." He took off his watch and slipped it over her wrist. "There now."

It bothered her, this. As if he thought he possessed her.

She'd had a little too much to drink; she wandered outside to clear her head. A block from the house there was a park that bordered the river. She walked to the edge of the water.

It was a bitter Sunday in the first week of March. The wind off the river was punishing. It had been threatening rain since morning; the sky was an unnatural purple; the rain when it came would be tremendous, you could feel it now.

She looked up. Owen.

He looked frail, boyishly uncombed. He blew on his hands in the cold.

"Hi," she said.

"I haven't been able to stop thinking about you," he replied.

The words you longed to hear. Though not from him. If this was a movie, she thought, those would have been the words I'd been longing to hear.

"Owen, come on," she said. She picked up a long stick and gave it to him. He dropped it on the ground.

"Look. You did this to me. Now you have to face the consequences." He was bending his head down and looking up at her from under his wispy eyebrows.

"What did *I* do?"

"I tried to write a story about you the other day. But I couldn't figure out what your name should be. So I took my usual nap, and I dreamed about you. You told me your real name was Sarah. Is that your name?"

"That's my name," she said. She felt a little weird.

"I knew it. You told me to call you Sarah. You said you don't usually like it when people call you Sarah, but it's different with people who love you."

"Owen, would you just pick up that stick and be a serious person? You can call me Sarah if you want, but I don't think you should let yourself get carried away with this dream stuff."

"I am a serious person. You said we should be together. I said this was only a dream, but you said it didn't matter. You said that what a person says in a dream is what they really feel. You said I should tell you about my dream. You said you wouldn't remember . . . but that deep inside, you *would* remember. You said it was my responsibility to help you remember."

He was staring at her. He was taking shallow little breaths.

"I think you're crazy," she said.

"I think I'm crazy too. But I think I'd be even crazier to have a dream like that and ignore it."

From where they were standing she could see the Tappan Zee Bridge, a curious bridge, low-slung above the river. The ancient river, where for countless centuries couples have stood on its shores, meaningless men confessing meaningless love to meaningless women. Jesse, she thought.

"Look. It was a very nice dream. But it wasn't me."

"But it was," he said. "We're soul mates."

Welcome to the world of emotional inequality. His feeling had such authority . . . it was so real to him. She didn't think it was properly directed at her. But maybe she was wrong. Maybe if you let yourself go you could get swept up in it, you could find out it was real.

"Let's go back to Libby's," she said. She took his watch off and gave it to him. "Take your watch."

"Souls know no time. I don't need a watch." He smiled at her, and lobbed the watch, underhand, into the river.

This touched her: it seemed a grand romantic gesture, when the age of grand romantic gestures had passed, and she only wished that there were someone more appropriate for him to bestow it on. She hardly felt she was there at all. It was the kind of day when, even when you try to feel everything as sharply as possible, try to brand the sensations into your mind, you know that you're not capturing it all fully, you're not all there. She wished she could keep this all in her mind, the battering wind, the low clouds, the harsh gray of the river, with here and there a thick white crust of ice. Yes. I wish I could keep all this in my mind, for this is the beginning of love, isn't it, the grand romantic gesture—she simply didn't have the heart to let this grand romantic gesture go to waste. She took his hand and brought it to her lips, it was cold his hand, poor cold hand, and she unbuttoned the top button of her jacket and her shirt in one movement and brought his hand to her breast, it was a curiously sexless gesture, it was just his hand on her breast, and with his hand on her breast she could feel the beating of her own heart, so strong and slow and calm that it surprised her.

26

"The pineapple is the noblest fruit," Owen said. They were at the kitchen table, eating this week's selection from the fruit club they'd joined.

She felt a kind of ease with him. He lived in an apartment in Bronxville, with a roommate who was never there. On Friday nights they would make popcorn and watch bad movies on TV, snuggling together on the couch. On Saturday night they would walk into town and buy the Sunday *Times* and come home and stay up reading it. Sally would go for the sports section, Owen for the book review; they'd make hot chocolate and sit at the kitchen table reading as Cary Grant and Irene Dunne exchanged barbs on a "movie classic" on Channel 13. And she would look up at him, reading intently, and wonder whether life had anything more to offer than this. She didn't feel as if she loved him, but she loved this life, the togetherness, the ease of it.

It was snowing; it was past midnight; he sat reading, propped up in bed. She slipped in beside him, pulled the covers up to her chin, and warmed her feet under his feet. "The purpose of life is to be cozy," she said.

27

Warm breath on the back of her neck, in the dark. On the lowest knob of her backbone, his touch.

Owen liked to wake her in the middle of the night.

It was like making love underwater. He would touch her lightly, slowly drawing her out of her dream. Half-awake, half-dreaming, she would embrace him. Sometimes, half-asleep, in the dark, she didn't quite know who he was: the lips that were kissing her were Owen's, the hands that were touching her were those of someone else. Sometimes, as she touched his face, she thought she was touching her own face.

He began a jogging regimen—getting up at six in the morning to run around the park—but he abandoned it after returning home one day with a tale of having been "glared at" by wild wolves.

"Wolves, Owen?"

"I assure you, they were most definitely wolves."

A week later he pointed out one of these wolves on the street. It was an aging husky, trotting amiably into a pizza place.

"That's your wolf?"

"That *is*, in fact, a wolf. A white-bellied Arctic snow-hound."

Whenever they went walking after that, she made sure to steer him clear of the wolves. She would point to some broken-down mutt, grab Owen by the arm, and hurry him across the street. "There be wolves in these parts! Run for your life!"

She'd never felt so childishly intimate with anyone before, so free.

Except that she always had a voice in her head, whispering: Not quite right. Not quite right. Not quite right.

28

Owen was away for the weekend. It was midnight. She realized that she hadn't checked her mailbox that day. She took the long walk to the mailroom. The campus was empty.

There was one letter in her box. Addressed in a handwriting she hadn't seen in almost two years.

She sat on a bench in the dimly lit mailroom and looked at the envelope for a long time. She still knew him so well. He'd printed her name and address in a very small, very precise hand. Even without opening the envelope, she knew his mood. This small and deliberate handwriting thrilled her. He wrote this way only when he was grave: when he was thinking of her with reverence.

Can you be in love with someone's handwriting? She was in love with Jesse's.

The letter had been forwarded from Oberlin. It had taken a while.

She opened the letter carefully and read it while she sat on the bench.

As always, it began without a salutation.

It's been two years since I've even heard news about you. I have no idea whether you'll ever read this. But I want you to know that I still think about you all the time. When something important happens in my life—or when I'm a little high—or at that very last moment before sleep . . . at times like that, I find myself astonished by the feeling of your nearness.

I'm coming to Jersey for a month or so, in March. I don't know anything about your life. But I just wanted to say that sometimes I daydream that we might get together again.

This was the last week in March. She could see him tomorrow if she wanted to.

The words on the page grew runny from the sweat of her hands.

She was stupid with joy.

Bus Riley, she thought. Bus Riley's back in town.

29

She found Owen at the Cellar, reading a book and drinking a hot chocolate. She wished he had been drinking something else.

When she sat he looked up absently, and then his eyes came alive.

"Hey," he said. "Miss Lizzie."

She put her hand on his and told him what she had to tell him. He nodded. He took out a tissue and touched it to his nose.

"I once read in a psychology book that everything depends on the role you choose. If I think of myself as Ralph Bellamy in all those movies where he ends up getting jilted, that'll be bad. But if I think of myself as Humphrey Bogart in *Casablanca*, that'll be better." He drew on an imaginary cigarette, narrowed his eyes. "We'll always have Paris."

No anger, no tears. It was a miracle.

"You're taking this awfully well," she said.

"Of course I'm taking it well. I'm a guru of seventies sensitivity. You've always been honest with me, you're being honest with me now, and I appreciate that. What can I say? I'll probably go home and shoot myself, but what can I say?"

"You won't shoot yourself. You'll probably just go home and take a little nap."

"That's true." He smiled, as if the thought of his nap had cheered him up already. "Anyway, you make him sound like a fine guy. I'd like to shake his hand some day. I'd like to engage him in a manly game of snookers some day."

In spite of herself, Sally laughed.

It surprised her, this laugh. When she'd read the letter she'd instantly rewritten her life, shunting Owen off into a footnote. She'd written him off so completely that she was surprised by the simple fact that he could make her laugh.

She decided to go to New Jersey the next day. She didn't call him—she wanted to surprise him. Maybe he wouldn't be home; maybe he'd changed his plans and hadn't come home at all. If so, she could just spend the night with her parents. The important thing was the look on his face. The important thing was to surprise him.

She slept in her own room that night.

In the morning she went to the cafeteria for breakfast. Owen was there. She sat across from him.

"Today's the big day?"

"Yeah. I'm gonna catch the train in a little while."

"Can I walk you into town? I have to buy a woofer for my stereo."

She should have said no.

"Since when do you know what a woofer is?"

"I don't have to know. I just walk into the store and ask for a damn woofer."

They had to stop at his apartment for some money. Owen went toward his desk, but when he reached the middle of the room, he stopped. "Hoo boy," he said. He stroked his chin.

On his desk, next to a few scattered bills, was a red spider.

"You think it might be possible for you to liberate that wallet for me?"

"You're not *afraid* of that thing?"

He raised one eyebrow. "Everyone has certain hidden terrors, my dear, and little beasts that creepeth happen to be mine."

"You want me to squish him?" She picked up a book.

"Don't squish him. It's not his fault I'm scared of him. As Mr. Becker used to tell us back in fourth grade, spiders are actually our friends."

There are times when you do things you know you shouldn't do. She kissed him.

"What's that for?" he said.

"For being nice to spiders."

They walked into town. She felt happy walking beside him, and once or twice she had to remind herself why she was going into town.

Two kids, about eight years old, were standing on a corner. One of them was disgruntled about his new hat. "No, it looks good," the other one said. "It makes you look like a big kid."

"You could use a hat like that," Sally said to Owen.

Near the train station they said goodbye. She watched him as he walked away. Remembering Dylan's line: "He's an artist, he don't look back." He looked back at her over his shoulder, stumbled, and then tried to recapture his dignity by jogging a step or two.

She went to the train station, bought a ticket to New York, and sat on the platform. It was another gray day. In the distance she could see the park where Owen had encountered the wild wolves.

She couldn't understand why she felt so tense. The fear that is a part of any genuine love—that must be it.

She tried to picture Jesse's face. In high school everything had been simple. Later, it had been less simple. He'd dropped out of two colleges, spent a winter living in an unheated cabin in Vermont, spent a year not reading a single printed word, in an effort to get to the marrow of himself. He'd grown more difficult after high school; being with him had often been a trial. He wasn't the kind of guy you could watch the "Late Show" with—he was all hard edges. After the shortest visit, she always felt exhausted. But it always felt worthwhile. Better to be exhausted with him than content with someone else.

While she was lost in these reflections, a train to New York stopped, discharged its passengers, and went on.

Well, the next train then.

She thought of Owen and his spider. What she felt for Owen was so different. No awe. And shouldn't you feel awe for a lover? For Owen, she felt tenderness, she felt protectiveness . . . and she felt a certain freedom. The freedom, in the morning, to be bleary-eyed and blah; the freedom to fart in his presence; the freedom to babble nonsense under the covers at night. Certainly it wasn't love; certainly it was best that it was over. She knew that if she ever had kids, she wouldn't want to have them with Owen. If she and Owen had kids, the children would be clingy, pale, afraid of life. But she didn't regret the time she'd spent with him. She would always treasure his sweetness.

The next train for New York finally came in. She stood. She felt as if she were entering a new life.

30

When the train pulled out of the station, she was still on the platform.

She sat on a bench on the platform for the next three hours, as four trains to New York passed by.

She headed back to Owen's.

31

Sally met Beth in the city on the first day of the spring break. They embraced and set off down Fifth Avenue, their eyes fixed on the ground, intently ready to discuss their latest discoveries about life.

Sally wanted to talk about her worries. "I feel like I'm being left behind. Everybody knows what they want to do. Aaron's going to be a lawyer. You're going to write children's books. Owen's going to be a writer too. I'm the only one out in the cold."

"I'm not so sure. I think I'm out in the cold too . . . in a patriarchal society." She intoned these words gravely.

"What?" Sally said.

"I've decided to become a lesbian."

"You've decided? Is that the kind of thing you *decide?*"

"It's the logical conclusion of everything I've been studying."

Beth's tale. While studying children's literature, she had been disturbed by the sex-role stereotyping she had found in it. So she took some courses in feminist theory, which had turned her in a militant direction. She proceeded to summarize the ideas of Shulamith Firestone.

They waited at a stoplight. Sally couldn't look at her. "But are you *attracted* to women?"

"I don't know. When you pass an attractive couple on the street, are you always sure you're less attracted to the woman than the man?"

"I don't know." It was a question that had bothered Sally from time to time.

32

She took a bus to Jersey, and thought about Beth.

Beth had jumped aboard the freight train of history. You gauge its speed, running alongside it for a while, hoist yourself up, and in one fluid motion you've hopped a ride . . . while Sally stood around in the train yard examining the debris by the side of the tracks. . . .

Beth had chugged out of sight. No more Beth. She'd thrown in her lot with the struggling women of the world. Sally didn't feel like one of the struggling women of the world. She just felt like struggling Sally. "That's exactly how they want you to feel," Beth had pointed out. Maybe, but it was still how she felt.

She was aware, of course, that there was a certain amount of smugness associated with not having a theory of life. She knew she had a tendency to congratulate herself on being the only person around who was unblinkered, open to the sheer mystery of the universe.

She got home and had dinner with her mother, and then they drove to the city to meet Burke.

Driving to meet her husband, with her daughter by her side, Hannah was giddy with happiness. "Horsies," she said on the highway. They were driving beside a trailer with two horses in the back.

Which promptly cut them off when the lanes merged. "What a nerve," she said. "Should I thump my nose at the horse-man?"

"Thumb your nose," Sally said.

Hannah was a master of the malaprop. At dinner she'd spoken of a friend who had "dropped me like a cold potato."

Burke was staying at the Essex House hotel on Central Park South while he negotiated a contract; Hannah came in every night after work and stayed with him. He was negotiating nonstop against a strike deadline.

"Hello there, Sarah," he said when they joined him in his room. "You've descended from the ivory tower to study the customs of the multitudes? Have a seat."

Burke had become a presence in the labor movement. He was still the head of District 17 in New York, but he'd recently been elected to the executive board of the national Public Employees' Union that District 17 was affiliated with. Once or twice a month he went to Washington, to make union policy, to visit the White House and shake Jimmy Carter's hand, etc. Hannah would come with him, thrilled to be a big shot by association. He claimed to detest it all—"I'm just an organizer!"—but it was obvious that he loved it.

But what he loved most in life, Sally often thought, were these round-the-clock negotiations. When Sally and Hannah arrived he was holding court in his hotel room during a lull in the bargaining. He looked like a leader. His people were all around him, his second in command, his third in command, about half the negotiating committee; but anyone who came in would have known instantly that Burke was the man. He stood in the center of the room, with his austere carriage; his dark blue suit was perfectly pressed; his eyes were keen with concentration, so blue they were nearly white. He was fully in command, fully alive. His people sat with their notes and their sheets of statistics; both of the phones in the room kept ringing; people kept coming in with news; but what held the scene together was Burke.

And Sally found herself experiencing a moment of sadness, somehow. Sadness at the thought that this was all he'd ever govern. She thought of the mayors, the presidents, who had served in her lifetime . . . who among them could compare with him?

The sadness quickly passed—it was trivial against her pride. After all those years in the factory, all those years working his way back after that—getting flat feet as he organized furniture workers up and down the eastern seaboard—he'd finally come into his own. You could see it at a glance. With his florid sharp-featured face and his fierce white hair and the way his bearing made him look even taller than he was, he'd become beautiful. How many people become beautiful with age? He was smoking three packs of cigarettes a day and drinking seven cups of coffee, and he looked better than ever.

Pacing across the room, Burke had another glance at his daughter. She was still standing. "Sit down before you get knocked down," he said, and her face grew hot from happiness.

This bargaining session was a small thing: it concerned only two thousand workers. But in another way it wasn't so small: these were badly exploited workers, all of them female, most of them black, most of them close to illiterate, many of them single mothers. The best contract they might get out of all this wouldn't bring them a decent wage, but as Sally understood it, the very experience of bargaining was the important thing: learning to work together, learning to stand up for their rights.

Sally and one of the home-care workers started talking. The woman was named Cecille; she had a gold tooth, a long scar across her chin, and an almost impenetrable southern accent.

Sally hated this about herself, but . . . she felt awkward. She could hardly keep her mind on the conversation because she was too busy thinking, "Here's Sally Burke talking to an underprivileged black woman. Nodding sympathetically as she tells me her troubles. She's black and it doesn't make any difference to me." Sally had all the proper leftist views, she wanted all the right things for the world, but she hadn't had any real contact with black people since high school. And so she had no experience talking with them. She knew this was ridiculous—what sort of experience do you need? But that was how she felt.

"He loved me all right, but I didn't want to marry no preacher. No preacher, no doctor neither. A preacher and a doctor's for everybody, and I wanted a man just for me." Cecille was discoursing expansively; Sally was so busy nodding that she had no idea what she was talking about. But gradually, as Cecille went on—confiding in her, woman to woman—Sally was taken with a euphoric sense of her own worldliness. She accepts me! I'm talking her language! Maybe I should be an organizer when I get out of school! Sally was still congratulating herself when Cecille got up to make a phone call. "You just stick around," she said. "When I come back I'll teach you a little more about real life."

And when she went back to Jersey that night, taking the bus alone because her parents were staying at the hotel, the memory of this began to depress her. With one look, Cecille had sized her up for what she was: a little honky who didn't know nothin' about nothin'. As a student in a small college, you're ready for anything that can happen inside that little fishbowl, and you consider yourself a very big deal. But if you travel just ten minutes into the big world, you find out you don't know a thing. She was a month and a half away from graduation. She was about to discover how little she really knew. And this evening, in which she could barely conduct a simple conversation with someone because of little differences of class and skin—this was a hint of what life had in store.

She got off the bus, walked down the quiet well-manicured street to her parents' house. She walked through the dark silent house. It was a long time since she'd been alone there. She felt ghostly: her parents were more present in the house than she was. She could feel the faint currents of their passage in the air. She went from room to room, turning on the lights.

The cat, as always, was imprisoned in the kitchen. He was sitting near the dishwasher. He'd urinated in the living room a few times, and now Hannah locked him in the kitchen when she left the house. He bore this with stoicism, like an exiled king.

Sally unlocked the little gate. He walked past her, toward the living room: huge, imperious, magisterial, slow.

She went up to her bedroom, opened the windows, and smoked a joint. There was nothing to equal the deliciousness, the security, of getting high at home when her parents were away. Once again she felt the magical expansion, time began to slow, all the impalpable essences of her life grew slower and almost touchable, what does that even mean, she put some Dylan on and he wailed away, another lost love, ah, Dylan, explaining her own life to her; and, reflecting on the thought that she was old enough to have a lover and a long-lost lover too, Sally found herself amazed by the fullness of her own life.

After the first ten minutes of bliss, as always, the doubts arrived. She caught a glimpse of herself in the mirror, and she was shocked. For most of the night she'd been among people with dark skin—she was shocked at her own pallor. She thought of Cecille. And a long-forgotten picture came into her mind: "How Ink Is Made." That poster of a black boy standing in a tub, which Grandma Burke, pathetically, had found amusing enough to put on her bathroom wall.

She should have saved "How Ink Is Made" and put it on her own wall, as a joke against herself. There wasn't much difference between her and Anne Burke. The world hadn't changed much since her grandmother's time. It had changed enough for Sally to be humiliated by the distance between herself and a black woman . . . but not enough for her to bridge it. She'd been formed by the same world that had formed her grandmother, and she was just as powerless to transcend it. She was nothing but what circumstances had deprived her from being. She was nothing.

A reversal of perspective. Sally had always assumed that she was the heroine of her own life. That if a novelist were to study her family in search of a main character, he'd choose her. The stories of her parents would be background material—their way of life, however interesting in its time, was now passé. The novelist would see that it was Sally who was on the cutting edge of existence.

But now she saw that this might not be true. What if her own story were the background? Her parents were in the thick of life: staying up all night trying to help some very poor people win a raise and a touch of dignity. While she sat in her room, dumbfounded, listening to an album she'd listened to a thousand times before. Was that heroic? Was that historic? Would that help anyone? No, no, and no. Her parents were closer to the cutting edge than she was. She was off the history train. And maybe her unwillingness to leap aboard it wasn't a sign of her individuality at all, but a sign of how her time had deformed her. If she were to be written about she'd be written about as a victim of a blank time, a time in which you couldn't fill in the blank with anything but your own bare personality. She was locked into a small story of private life.

33

"Balzac," Owen said, "was the man."

"Yes?"

"When Balzac left a party to go back to his desk he'd say, 'I must rejoin the real world!'"

Owen was at the kitchen table, reading a fat biography of Balzac. Sally was at the window, trying to do something about a dying plant.

They were living together, in Jamaica Plain, outside Boston. They'd come up the week after graduation and found an extremely cheap two-bedroom; Owen used the second bedroom as a study. He'd decided to make a real try at becoming a writer. He was working as a freelance proofreader, making his own hours, and trying to write for five hours a day.

Sally didn't quite know what she was going to do. She was just going to look for a job.

"He had all these recurring characters. You meet some angry young man in one book, and forty books later you see him as an old fart. One of these guys was a doctor, Bianchon. And when Balzac was on his deathbed, in his delirium, he called out for Bianchon—'Only Bianchon can save me!'" He shook his head, savoring this. "I think that's my goal in life. I don't even care about getting published. I just want to create a world I can get lost in."

Shopping together, cooking together, fixing the place up together: it felt strange to be living like a grown-up. As she pushed a rattling cart down the aisles of a supermarket—paying attention, for the first time in her life, to the sale announcements—she was struck by how odd it was to be doing the things her mother had always done. It seemed as if it should require a license.

"But Balzac cared about getting stuff published, didn't he?"

"That's where we differ," Owen said.

Owen's philosophy of composition was based on his philosophy of dream life. He'd wake up in the morning and put on his clothes and go directly into his study—no coffee, no shower—and start tapping away. He wanted a seamless passage from dream to page. "I don't even want to understand what I'm writing about."

Sometimes she thought writing was just something he used as a cover. Sally's idea of an artist was someone like her uncle, who painted out of a passionate need: if he were somehow prevented from painting, he'd end up in a car wreck within a week. Owen wasn't like that. If the world didn't require that you become something, if people you met at parties didn't immediately ask, "What do you do?", Owen, she suspected, would have been happy just to play.

That's what they did together: they played. They went to the movies, they went to Red Sox games, they went to bars and played Ms. Pac-Man, they made popcorn and watched the late movie on TV. They took long walks through Boston, murmuring to each other in baby talk.

With its scraggly excuse for a skyline, Boston was like a toy city. They walked through the Public Garden on a perfect day in July, watching the perfect families in their pedal boats.

Two dogs were leaping in and out of the pond; they stood facing each other on the grass, shivering wildly, throwing water off in all directions. An old man on a bench said to Sally, "They love to play all day." Owen and Sally took up this phrase: it became the motto of their life together.

This was what she loved, and this was what bothered her. Her feelings for him were strongest when he was weakest. He had a perpetual nosecold, and a perpetual hopefulness: he was always bringing home the latest cold remedy, positive that this one would finally do the trick. And she'd feel a tenderness so strong it made it difficult to breathe when, as she walked through the door after a day of job-hunting, she would find him at the kitchen table, struggling with the childproof cap of his latest miracle cure, before finally, inevitably, asking her to open it for him.

By October she gave up looking for full-time work, and put together a bunch of dumb jobs: temp jobs—typing and filing—and substitute teaching. Being a substitute teacher took only one skill. She'd come to class and get the kids to sign up for attendance, and then she'd read out the names. Inevitably half the names were things like "Dick Licker" and "Ophelia Rass," and the students' enjoyment would consist in tricking you into saying these names out loud. So Sally would peer at the list, assume a dim, befuddled expression, and say, "Dick Locker? Is there a Dick Locker in this class?" and the students would twist around in their chairs in their frustration.

Owen had pretty much stopped working. He was writing all the time now, and by an unspoken agreement she was making enough to keep them both going. It wasn't difficult—they didn't have many expenses—and as long as she didn't know what she wanted to do in life, it pleased her to be of help to someone who did.

It pleased her to be of help. She was her parents' child: she needed to feel, as her father would put it, that she was "making a contribution." She answered an ad in the *Phoenix* for someone to read aloud to elderly people. A network of old friends in their seventies, each of them crippled by age—by cancer, by heart attacks, by strokes. She ended up reading regularly to three of them, all of whom, she quickly saw, valued her mostly for the company. She would read for an hour or so—sometimes from *The Progressive* or *Jewish Week,* but more often from things like *Prevention:* magazines that taught you how to recapture your youth, the vitamin way. Soon enough she'd read something that would trigger off an old memory, and for the next hour she would be treated to long, rambling stories, sometimes stories she'd heard the week before.

She grew especially attached to one of the people she read to, a Frenchwoman named Juliette, who had terrible, incurable arthritis that made it impossible for her to undo the lid of a container of jelly. Her fingers were purple, crooked, swollen—they looked waterlogged. She took drugs for the pain, but the drugs did something to her blood, so that if she bumped her shin against a door it would open a wound, a wound that remained raw for days.

When Sally arrived, every Friday afternoon, she would find her in her reclining chair, perfectly dressed, perfectly coiffed, with a tray of cookies laid out before her and two cups sitting next to the stove in the kitchen, the tea bags already in place. One day Sally came an hour early by mistake, letting herself in with the key Juliette had given her, and found her sitting on the edge of her bed. She looked twenty years older. She looked like a puckered wax replica of herself. Sally's first thought was to call a doctor, but Juliette said she just needed a minute to make her toilette. She asked Sally to wait in the kitchen. Fifteen minutes later, Juliette emerged, looking as composed as ever. Sally hadn't realized how much her composure was a matter of fortitude.

Juliette lived in a land of ghosts. She would tell Sally stories about her husband, her friends, her family, all dead, ending them with just the barest hint of a pause before she went on to another subject. Juliette's husband, an American named Oscar, had died three years before. The only sign of her sorrow, when she talked about him, was that she would take up a napkin and fold it, and fold it, and fold it again.

Oscar, in his youth, had been a follower of Trotsky: he'd even gone down to Mexico for six months to serve as a secretary/bodyguard to the "Old Man." "He was quite a bodyguard, I'm sure. We took a vacation in Brazil one summer, and I had to look in the shower every morning, to make sure there weren't any lizards. Oscar was afraid of the lizards." She shook her head with a kind of indulgent annoyance, as if at any moment she might be called upon to go to the shower and investigate the lizard situation once again.

The role of women is to protect men from small beasts.

Oscar had broken with Trotsky in the late 1930s on some political issue of great importance at the time. Juliette referred to the issue in such a casual way that Sally, who didn't know what she was talking about, was afraid to ask.

"Trotsky attacked him in . . . what was that magazine? *The Fourth International*. He called him 'the petty-bourgeois from Brooklyn.'" Juliette related this with pride. To have been insulted by Trotsky was a high honor.

After a while Sally began to feel as if she had known him.

Sometimes Juliette would ask Sally about herself, and she soon developed a rooting interest in Sally's life. Sally would talk about Owen, her job problems, her parents. At first she thought she was telling Juliette these things just to indulge her, out of her own deep beneficence. It took her a while to realize that she had come to rely on these conversations too.

When Juliette grew comfortable with Sally, she took great

pleasure in abusing her, in a mixture of English, French, and Yiddish. It was a way of relieving some of her physical pain. "Why do you dress like a boy? Not only a boy, but a sloppy boy. You don't look . . . *appetizing*. You could look very nice if you tried."

"It's 'cause of the sixties, Juliette. I'm basically a sixties person at heart."

"Sixties, schmixties. You shouldn't go around in schmatas."

She liked the way Juliette nagged her—with expressions that sounded as if they made sense in some other language. Sally returned a book to the bookshelf; Juliette looked at her sourly. "You must keep in alphabetical order the books." She lifted herself with difficulty out of her chair, pried out the book, and put it back in its place. "You are too much in the moon," she said.

Eventually Sally began to misplace the books on purpose. She liked to give Juliette something to nag her about.

The wreckage of a life well spent. Sally made her way home from Juliette's early on a Friday night in late January, stepping around week-old crusts of snow. It was already dark. Even the life well spent ends in wreckage and widowhood.

"The great lesson of life," she said to herself. The great lesson of life was this: find a man you can be proud to be the widow of. Juliette was as happy a woman as she could be: her life consisted mostly of sorrow, but it was sorrow for a man she'd loved.

She came home with a big bag of groceries. Owen, standing in the kitchen, was preparing to electrocute himself. A piece of pita bread was stuck in the toaster; he was about to remove it with a fork.

"You'll *be* the toast." She pulled the fork from his hand. "You have to use this wooden thing here."

He kissed her. "What would I do without you?" he said.

34

She fell into conversation with the first fat man she saw.

"What do you do?" he said, fitting two potato chips into his mouth.

I go to parties and only talk to the fat guys, she thought.

Owen was home writing. She thought of it as an act of fidelity to talk only to the unattractive guys.

She started to tell him about her jobs. She was talking on automatic pilot, hardly listening to what she was saying—instead, she was listening to Dylan. Going through the host's record collection, she'd found a bootleg album that included "I'm Not There," a legendary, never-released, never-completed song from the Basement Tapes sessions—a song that she'd heard just once, the summer after high school, and that she'd been searching for ever since. It came on as she was talking; it was even more haunting than she'd remembered.

She touched the fat guy's wrist. "This," she said, "may be the greatest song ever written."

He laughed. He had nice brown eyes, when you really looked at him. Intelligent eyes.

"Anyway," she said, "I like reading to these old people—

it's more interesting than it sounds. Like, this Frenchwoman, she's a great lady. She's an old Socialist—she was in the Resistance when Hitler conquered France."

"That does sound interesting," he said. "Are you an old Socialist?"

"Me?" She took a half-step backward.

"Of course not. How foolish of me. You're a Dylanist."

"Meaning . . . ?"

"You don't believe in causes. You only believe in feelings. Am I right?"

Sally was grinning with pleasure. She didn't know quite why she was so pleased. The fat guy—she still didn't know his name—was leaning forward flirtatiously. Maybe he wasn't so unattractive after all.

"I deserve this. I come all the way up to Boston for a party when I have work to do, and I run into another Dylanist."

That sounded like he had a girlfriend. Why was she jealous? "You have a Dylanist back home?"

"About a thousand. I work for a union. I go around talking about solidarity and other corny ideas, to people who are just too hip to believe in anything but their own feelings."

A union guy.

The union guy touched her shoulder. "I'm sorry. It's just that I've got some headaches in New York. I shouldn't assume I know you. You're interested in that Socialist lady— that's unusual. How'd you get to be unusual?"

She found herself blushing. And she knew why she'd quickly felt something for this fat guy, on the basis of a two-sentence conversation. He asked questions.

In a classic episode of "Star Trek," Kirk and the crew come down to a deserted planet where they find this huge weird glowing arch, and when Kirk wonders what it's there for, the arch intones: "A question. Since before your earth was born . . . I have waited . . . for a question."

"Since before your earth was born," she said, "I have waited . . . for a question."

"I was about to ask if you needed a drink, but it doesn't appear that you do."

"But I do need a drink. I very much need a drink."

So the fat guy got her a drink. He really wasn't that fat, if looked at with a sympathetic eye. Let's think of him as husky, Sally thought.

She was about to ask him if he knew her father, but she decided not to. She preferred to remain a little anonymous. "How'd you get into union work?" she said.

"I read about the Wobblies at an impressionable age. So I thought I'd become a Wobbly myself. The only thing I didn't realize is there aren't any Wobblies anymore."

He pushed his glasses up to the top of his head and rubbed his eyes. He did have a large roll around his stomach, but he had a strong face. She guessed that he was about five or six years older than she was. He seemed . . . he seemed like a man.

"So what does a union guy do if he can't be a Wobbly?"

"He just talks union. There's probably no hope for the labor movement. People don't want to know from solidarity . . . which is just a fancy word for helping each other out. But if there's no hope for that, there's no hope for anything. So you just keep plugging away. You pretend you have a chance, even if you don't really believe it. What the hell. You might end up being surprised."

He put his glasses back down over his eyes. "It's nice of you to be interested in all this. Usually when I tell people I work for a union, they look at me like I said I was a chariot mender—like I belong in a museum." He held out his drink and examined it. "I'm talking too much. I don't know if it's you or this . . . I can't remember the last time I went off the tape."

"The tape."

"Sometimes I feel like everything I ever say is stored on tape. And if somebody asks me something I just play back the right part of the tape. But I didn't mean to tell you that stuff about pretending. That wasn't on the tape."

Sally didn't say a word, just looked at him, smiling. Thinking that maybe it would be nice to be single.

35

Owen sat at the kitchen table eating his cereal. For breakfast, every morning, he had a bowl of Spoon Size Shredded Wheat, in skim milk, with slices of banana.

"How can you eat that stuff?" Sally said.

"It helps build strong bodies twelve ways. No sugar, no salt, no nothin'. It's scrumdiddley-umptious."

He ate Shredded Wheat because it wouldn't raise his blood pressure or clog his arteries. He was a bit of a hypochondriac.

"Sure you don't want a little English muff?" she said. They were in their baby-talk mode.

"No way." Owen held the bowl away from the table, close to his chest. It was his habitual breakfast posture; he always reminded Sally of a little squirrel eating a nut in the woods, cradling it apprehensively in the fear that some larger animal might come along and take it away from him.

36

She would walk the streets, thinking: Is this really what I want? She felt trapped, and astonished that she felt trapped. Astonished to be old enough to feel this. The kind of relationship you read about in old books, books so old you got a slight headache reading them, from the strain of casting yourself into all those outmoded assumptions. "I'm trapped in a loveless marriage," she said to herself, walking down the street, and she felt like a cliché from an old movie, and she was astonished by this. There was even a measure of satisfaction in the sheer weirdness of it. She thought of the person she'd once believed herself to be, the true child of the sixties, the child of spontaneity, who followed her instincts, who couldn't promise 'bout tomorrow, man, 'cause who knows how I'll feel by then . . . how had that girl turned into this woman?

She went to the zoo. A seal looked down from his rock. She'd seen seals in the wild once, when she and Owen spent a weekend on a little island off the coast of Maine. The seals had congregated on a big flat rock, almost an island in itself. They looked lethargic, indolent, fat. But once in a while one of them would slither into the water—disappearing underwater for a minute or more, suddenly emerging far away, all leaping lightness, his back gleaming black in the sun.

This fellow here was old, discolored, dispirited. His back was mottled with brown spots. He needed the refreshment of the sea. She could disguise herself as a zookeeper, wheel him out the front gate in a wheelbarrow, and bring him back to the ocean. And what then? He'd been away from it so long that he wouldn't know what to do there. He was miserable in captivity, and he'd be miserable if he were free.

When she came home, Owen was getting up from a nap.

"I just talked to a bear," he said. He sat on the edge of the bed, reluctant to let go of the dream.

"Maybe you and I should try to coordinate our dreams," he said. "We could talk about what we want to dream, and maybe we'd both have the same dream sometimes. And eventually, if we got good at it, we could talk together in the dream, and in the morning we'd both remember the conversation. Wouldn't that be fun?"

Never to be alone, not even in her dreams: it struck her as a horrible thought. She felt like a betrayer.

37

Every Saturday they slept late and went out to their favorite diner for breakfast. It was the one day of the week Owen allowed himself to start off with anything but Shredded Wheat. They each had two fried eggs sunny-side up, plenty of toast slathered in butter, hash browns, orange juice, coffee.

She sat on the other side of the little booth, admiring him. They hadn't showered: he looked wonderfully scruffy, with his hair all wild and his collar sticking up from under his sweatshirt. He was looking through the help wanteds. Crooning softly: "Mr. President—I need a job." He didn't need a job, but he loved to look through the help wanteds; and he liked to call on the president as he did so. The sun was shining in on the table. Everything was shining. Yes. Maybe I do love him.

At home they took a shower together, and made love there, awkwardly and shyly. They'd only done this a few times before. She thought how strange it was that two people can be so intimate, still so shy.

She sat on the rim of the tub, drying her hair. Owen opened the bathroom door and put his head out. "I thought I heard the telephelone." The telephelone . . . there was something unspeakably precious about him just then.

Owen tapped at his typewriter for a while, Sally puttered happily, and it was time to leave. They were visiting some old friends of his in Worcester.

"You mind driving?" Owen said. "I don't feel so hot."

They went out to the car and she got behind the wheel. Suddenly deflated. She liked to drive, but she was annoyed that he'd asked. He didn't feel so hot. She was tired of his hypochondria. She was surprised he didn't wear a thermometer around his neck on a chain.

His Red Sox cap was on the front seat. "You should wear that," she said. "It'd make you look like a big kid."

Owen didn't say anything; he didn't even smile. As they drove on, her words lingered in the air and seemed to indict their entire relationship. They were either children pretending to be grown-ups, or grown-ups pretending to be children. She had an eggy taste in her mouth.

They drove for miles in a silence broken only by occasional stupid remarks from Sally. She tried sports, books, politics. Owen wasn't biting. He didn't say a word.

"What does that mean?" he finally said. They were stopped at a light, and he was pointing to a billboard. It said, "Check in at Barclay's Bank—Free Gift."

The master of the written word was about to inform her that the phrase "free gift" is redundant.

"I think you know what it means."

" 'Check in'? Do you check in to a bank? Don't you check in to a hotel?"

"I think they mean open a checking account."

"How are you supposed to know they mean that?"

She didn't bother answering. You know it by mystical fucking intuition. She drove on, wondering how she'd ended up with him.

"It's hard to think," Owen said.

Why couldn't people just live? Yes, it's hard to think. Everyone knows it's hard to think. Why did she have to be with a hypochondriac? Wasn't there a land somewhere where people just lived?

She drove on for another ten minutes, passing many billboards, most of which did violence to the language; but to her gratitude, the great semanticist chose not to subject them to his withering scrutiny. They were almost there.

"Do you think we could stop and buy an aspirin?" he said. "I have a horrible . . . I feel like I have an ice-cream headache."

"We'll be there in ten minutes."

"Where are we going?"

This alarmed her.

"We're going to Paul and Margaret's."

Owen nodded. Then he said: "Who?"

These were people he had known for ten years.

She pulled over to the curb.

"Owen, you're really scaring me."

"*I'm* really scared," he said. He covered his mouth with his hands.

She was a fool. Something was happening to his mind.

Owen sat staring through the windshield with a look of astonishment. He looked as if the most amazing thing in the world was drawing near.

She wanted to hold him, but whatever was happening to him couldn't be cured by her touch. It couldn't be warded off. It was inside him.

I'll never leave him. She knew this. His life was her life. I'll never leave him.

She drove back to Boston, to Mass General. Owen sat with his hands squeezed between his thighs.

She parked and led him to the emergency room. He let

himself be led, but almost reluctantly. He looked as if he thought he'd left something behind in the car.

The lamps in the parking lot were barium lamps; they gave off an orange glow. "Those lights are strange," he said.

The emergency room was huge and poorly lit, filled with row after row of people, mostly black people. They gave some information to the intake nurse, who told them to wait.

They waited for more than an hour. Owen seemed lost in concentration. He looked as if he was straining to hear a very faint sound.

Sally got up to ask the nurse if they could speed things up. But the nurse was bored with other people's tragedies; she couldn't be moved.

Half an hour later she started to get up again, but Owen asked her not to. "I think I'm feeling a little better now."

Finally they were called in to see an intern, Dr. Fish. He was young and chipper; he sat on the examining table dangling his legs; he wore a Mickey Mouse watch.

They told him what had happened—Owen talked, Sally filled in. Fish nodded eagerly—he looked as if he found it hard to keep from interrupting their story, because he had a better one himself.

He opened a drawer and took out a syringe. "This sounds like it's just a case of anemia. I've just been reading about anemia, and these are very common symptoms."

He drew blood from Owen's arm. "My mother was right—I *am* a genius. Look at that blood. It's not even red."

"It isn't?" Owen said.

"I was only kidding."

"Oh," Owen said. He seemed bewildered. He seemed stupid.

"It'll take about an hour to analyze this. Why don't you have a seat. Or better yet, get some fresh air. There's a place down the block serves authentic Chicago pizza, which, as we all know, is the greatest pizza in the world."

If your doctor recommends pizza, your problem can't be too grave. They walked through the cool spring night. Owen put his arm around Sally. They took small steps.

"Anemia," he whispered. He kissed her ear. "The most beautiful word in the language."

"It's all that health food you eat," Sally said. "You need a little raw meat in your diet."

"Tomorrow I'm having a porterhouse steak, very rare, with sausage, bacon, and kidneys. And that's just breakfast."

They went to a deli and bought some chocolate chip cookies. "We should save one for Dr. Fish," Owen said.

They went back to the hospital. It was nearly midnight. The long room was filled with families, bickering families. There were children all over the place, running around wild, screaming. The overhead TV was playing some dreary old movie—Hedy Lamarr on an elephant. The guy next to Sally wore a large button that read "Kiss My Ass." As they waited, their optimism began to drain away. They didn't make any more jokes.

Finally Fish came back out. He was grinning—he looked as if he'd just heard some excellent gossip. They got up to meet him. Owen was still holding the box of cookies.

"Well, this is fascinating. It's not anemia—your blood's just fine. But I talked to the neurologist and he's very eager to see you. He's very excited about this: he thinks you had a seizure."

"A seizure," Owen said.

"Yes. A part of your brain just—seized up." He made a clutching motion with his hands.

Sally vowed that someday she would kill this man.

Owen didn't say anything. If you didn't know him, you might not have known how frightened he was.

The neurologist shuffled out, peering at a clipboard. He looked, if this was possible, younger than the intern. When Owen saw him, he put his head on Sally's shoulder. "You expect to see the chief of medicine come toddling through in a diaper."

Whenever he joked it made her feel better; but when he picked up his head she saw that his eyes were wet. "It's like a fucking nightmare," he said.

The neurologist was a small, gentle guy named Noah Gilpin. He brought them back to the examining room, tested Owen's reflexes, shined a light in his eyes. "Did you know the pupil of your left eye is larger than the pupil of your right eye?" Owen hadn't known it; Sally hadn't known it either. "What does that mean?" Owen said. Gilpin, marking something on his clipboard, looked up absentmindedly. "It doesn't necessarily mean anything."

He told them it would be best if Owen stayed at the hospital for tests.

"Can I stay in the room with him?"

"Sure. That should be no problem. Let me just call upstairs and find a bed."

He brought them to a large empty room and told them to wait.

They waited. It must have been two in the morning. The room had the feeling of an auditorium in an elementary school. Stale, body-smelling air, drab green walls. A tired-looking nurse walked through; she was coming off duty; she slowly pulled the clip from her hair. Another followed, hands in her pockets, looking at the floor, whistling softly. If Owen had been fine tonight, and they'd spent the evening with Paul and Margaret, this world still would have been here; the nurses would still be passing wearily through this room. But how wonderful never to have seen it. Everything about the room seemed made to dampen hope. The dull green walls, the green gowns of the nurses, the rows of wheelchairs, the low ceilings that took each sound and deadened it. The morning, when Owen had sat across from her in the diner, calling softly for the president—the morning seemed a thousand years gone.

Gilpin came back with a wheelchair. Owen tried to wave it away. "I don't need that."

"It's the rule." Gilpin smiled, the picture of sympathetic helplessness.

When they reached the room, the nurse said that under no circumstances could Sally stay the night.

"This is for patients. You shouldn't be here now."

"Yeah, but I'm not leaving."

"You might not be leavin', but you ain't stayin' either." Sally pondered this. "There's a waiting room down the hall you can stay in if you want to, but you can't stay with the patients, no way."

If you argue you make her mad, and she'll take it out on Owen. If you give in you leave him in the hospital's clutches.

This was the moment for Gilpin to take charge. Boldly and decisively. He stood there, with a shit-eating grin. He was just a little boy, with a stethoscope and a smock.

"It's all right, Sal." Owen put his hand on her hand. "I'll be all right. I just want to get some sleep."

So Sally left. She kissed him goodnight, and she left.

Trying to leave the hospital, she got lost, wandering through empty ill-lit halls. It took her a long time to find her way out.

She drove home crying, with his Red Sox hat on her lap. She fell asleep on top of the covers with her clothes on.

38

Before she went to the hospital, she went to the library and looked at medical dictionaries. Stroke, seizure, tumor. Tumor, seizure, stroke. One enlarged pupil might mean nothing; it might mean brain damage.

She found him in bed. He looked as if he'd been beaten. His face was a bruised yellow, the color of a rubber glove.

"Hello, Sal." He gave her his hand, but he didn't turn his head to look at her. He lay on his back, looking at the ceiling. "After you left they did a spinal tap."

"I don't really know what a spinal tap is." She spoke softly.

"They draw out the fluid from your spine, and from around your skull, so they can analyze it. They pierce your spine with this, I don't know, this sword, and then they drain you. Except Gilpin fucked it up—he had to do it twice." He pressed his lips together to keep them from quivering. "So now there's no fluid around my brain. It takes a week or two to come back. So now, if I move, my brain hits against my skull. And it hurts. It hurts."

He cried a little. He touched his face to wipe away the tears. He touched his face softly, because even this caused him pain.

He hadn't turned to look at her because it would have hurt him too much.

She had left him alone, and this is what they'd done to him when she was gone.

"Do they have any idea what it was yet?"

"They can't analyze the spinal tap till tomorrow. Sunday nobody works."

My handsome darling. He looked horrible. They'd put him in a gown—one of those gowns that tie in back, making you feel defenseless.

There were two other patients in the room. One of them was a little fat man, shivering under a pile of blankets. He was moaning: "Laura. Lauuura."

In the other bed was an ancient man with a great deal of soft white hair and a mild, peaceful, grandmotherly face. He had his own nurse.

"Have you been feeling okay . . . mentally?"

"You mean my temporary brain deficiency? That's what they're calling it. I had a deficient brain." He closed his eyes. "I think I've been able to think all right. It's hard to tell. All I've been able to think about is how much my head hurts."

She had brought a little tote bag filled with goodies: bagels, oranges, the paper, a Walkman, a few tapes. Of course he couldn't use any of it. When she imagined him trying to put the Walkman on his head, she imagined him as a skeleton, fitting it on his bare skull.

She read the paper as Owen tried to sleep. The room was never silent. The fat man kept moaning for Laura. When the nurse changed his gown Sally had a glimpse of his bare skin: it was covered with blotchy sores, like dozens of lips— cracked red lips all over his body. The nurse quickly put his blanket back over him, but Sally couldn't get it out of her mind. In her memory his body grew more grotesque: the lips, chapped, wettish, were breathing, sucking the air.

From the other bed, the grandmotherly man asked his nurse for the time. The nurse looked as if the question enraged her. "Eleven ten." The old man thanked her, in a small, mild voice.

Sally finished the sports section and glanced at the front page. The old man asked his nurse what time it was.

"Eleven thirteen," she said.

"Thank you."

She looked at him from over her paper. His eyes were a soft and beautiful blue, as empty as the summer sky.

That "thank you" touched her. His mind had been wiped clean by Alzheimer's disease; it was doubtful that he knew his name; but the habit of courtesy lingered.

Late in the afternoon, Owen's friend Paul showed up. They'd known each other since grade school. He was as different from Owen as anyone could be: he was a carpenter—a housebuilder—with a deliberate way of considering things and the look of someone who spends most of his life in the open air. In normal life Sally had a slight crush on Paul, but she didn't like seeing him here. He had brown and muscular arms; as a gesture of kindness toward the women of the world he always wore sleeveless t-shirts; and as he leaned against the radiator, peeling one of Sally's oranges, making jokes to lighten up the gloom, he seemed too healthy, too pleased about his own good health. Owen lay under the covers, a small yellow thing.

At home, she dragged a blanket out to the living room couch. She didn't want to sleep in the bed.

The lights were off. She lay on the couch, staring at the ceiling.

She thought of Owen in his hospital bed. Staring at the ceiling. It must be terrible to lie there all night, in that strange room.

She wished she could send him strength.

She was very tired, and the room was very dark, and her rational mind began to relax its hold. She could see his face, hovering above her in the dark. She tried to make it come down, so it would fit over her face like a mask. If she knew how it felt for him to wear his face, then she could reach his mind with her thoughts. His face slowly came closer. The high forehead; the small chin; the skull, the skull in pain. It settled over hers. She breathed through his mouth.

On Monday morning a new doctor, James Freda, took charge. He didn't overdo the bedside manner: he asked his questions with a kind of self-confident brusqueness. He had a sharply cut black beard; he looked as if he drove a sports car. Sally began to feel hopeful.

They analyzed the results of the spinal tap, and they didn't find anything wrong. They took a CAT scan of Owen's brain, and they didn't find anything wrong. They examined his heart, they examined his blood, they took test after test after test . . . nothing.

"What's so strange about this," he said, "is that you start to think about the fact that your body is a *thing*. When they do all these tests, I can't quite absorb the fact that the tests have anything to do with *me*." He closed his eyes. "I guess you had to be there."

Endless hours next to his bed, ministering to his thingness. The fluid around his brain had not yet been replenished. He couldn't walk, he couldn't stand, he couldn't chew. A few more of their friends showed up, but there wasn't much they could do to cheer him. If you talked too loud you hurt his head.

She came every day, as early as she was allowed. Neither of the other men had visitors. The ancient man was named

Samuel; one day when his nurse had stepped out for a minute Sally saw him groping for his water cup, and she handed it to him. He thanked her; and after this, when she came in the morning, he seemed to recognize her. When she said hello to him he would smile and smooth his cover with his hands in an unconscious gesture of contentment.

Whatever had happened to Owen wasn't happening anymore. But something was happening to Sally. In her mind now there were two of him: Owen, and a ghostly double. Every time he had to pause to find a word, she wondered whether this was a subtle sign that his brain had been permanently impaired. Every time she looked at him she searched his eyes, she measured his pupils. She couldn't stop herself. And back at home, before bed, every night, when she brushed her teeth, she stared into the mirror at her own eyes. And reassured herself that both her pupils were the same size. And felt relieved. And then felt ashamed, terribly ashamed, of this relief.

Freda made a daily visit, Gilpin stopped in once in a while, various interns came around, and none of them would say what they were thinking. It became clear that they had no idea what had happened to him. It became clear that they might never have any idea.

Day after day after day: no change. Which was good. No tumor, no seizure, no stroke. After four days, she was able to breathe out.

But there was no release of tension. If no one could discover what had happened, they could never feel safe. What happened could happen again. One of his pupils was enlarged.

It was Friday; they had one more test to run, and if nothing showed up he could go home. They were beginning to think that it had just been an attack of migraine. Sally understood that this diagnosis meant nothing: all it meant was that they didn't know. But it seemed to make Owen happy. He was eating a little bit—Jell-O, sherbet—and dreaming of real food. "I sure could go for some Spoon Size," he said, smiling at the thought of it.

Soon the two of them would leave this place. But the prospect didn't refresh her. The man whose body was covered with lips kept moaning for Laura. Samuel kept mildly asking for the time. When you walked through the halls you caught little glimpses into every room: old people alone in bed, looking up with hostile stares as you passed. Hostile because they felt ashamed to be here. This was the side of life that was hidden away. In the outside world sickness seems an aberration, but this place showed the truth of things: here sickness ruled. Owen would get better, and they'd go back into a life in which they could be happy again, in their youth and their strength. But their happiness would be a false happiness—a turning away, a forgetting. The hospital would still be filled with sick old men and women, all of them ashamed to be dying.

When she came to the hospital on Friday, the day before he was supposed to be discharged, he was lying asleep with his mouth open. And she had the same thought that she'd had in the car: I'll never leave him. She'd moved beyond the old question of whether she loved him enough, whether she loved him in exactly the way she might have wanted. They were given to each other. They were wedded. The question of whether he was the most suitable man she might have chosen no longer had meaning. You don't choose to love your blood relations: you're born into your love for them. And Owen was the same now: he was a blood relation. There had been a slim margin of choice: the choice of the night by the river, the choice of the day she saved him from the spider. She hadn't realized, when she'd made those choices, that she was choosing a life, choosing a fate. But that was what she'd done. And now the choice was made. She'd never leave him. She knew that now, for a fact.

A nurse arrived with a wheelchair to discharge him—it was the rule. Sally walked behind them. At the door she turned to the mild old man.

"Goodbye, Samuel," she said.

He looked at her tenderly—he was sad to see her go. She knew that within ten minutes he would forget her. He raised his hand.

39

At home he lay in bed for days. He was still very weak. She cared for him tenderly. She had no needs. Her only need was to tend to him. She'd never felt so selfless, so filled with love. She sat in the kitchen in the afternoon, while Owen slept. She thought of Jesse, and she realized she'd finally left him behind. That was high school; that was girlhood. It was nothing like this—nothing like this feeling, of complete responsibility, total, unending. It stretched out before her, her feeling of responsibility for him, it unfurled through the future. She would always feel exactly like this. He would probably die before she died, because he was a man, and when he lay dead, though she would be filled with grief, she would also be filled with happiness and pride, knowing that a life spent loving him had been a life well spent.

40

Eight months later, she lay in bed, listening to the sound of Owen, in the bathroom, brushing his teeth. Slow, weak strokes. She knew that when he finished brushing his teeth, he would turn off the tap water, but he wouldn't turn it off all the way. He would come to bed, and then she'd get up and turn it off. It had always been like that, even in college.

They went out to brunch at some fresh-baked-bread place, with potted plants drooping from every wall. At the next table was a guy in a flannel shirt; he looked like the perfect mixture of macho and sensitivity. He looked like Sam Shepard. Owen was dabbing at his nose with a tissue. Why am I with *him?* she thought. How come I'm not with *him?*

They got back home, made more coffee. The phone rang. It was Owen's little sister, Michelle. Sally talked with her for a minute and passed Owen the phone.

"It's Mickey," she said.

Owen loved his sister. He took the phone with a look of shy delight. "Monkey?" he said.

In his look she could see all that was tenderest in him. She tried to recapture the feeling she'd had that night in the car, when she knew for a fact that she would never leave him. Couldn't do it.

Pressed against the coffeepot, Sally's palm was greasy with sweat. The sweat of guilt. The sweat of betrayal. If Owen were an animal, with creaturely instincts, he would know from my scent that I'm a betrayer.

That night they went to a little fair in Somerville. Owen knocked down three plastic men with a baseball and won a stuffed alligator, which he presented to Sally. Later they took a ride on the Wild Mouse; they strapped themselves in, lowered the bar into place, gripped it. Sally brought her lips to Owen's ear and whispered, "Yikes." The ride started off slowly, jerkily, picking up speed in lurches, finally accelerating to exactly the speed of terror.

"How often you think they inspect these things?" Owen shouted above the screaming of the wheels. They clutched each other's hand.

41

If she left him, it would destroy him. This was what she believed. Who else would take the childproof caps off his cold remedies? Who would make sure he ate something other than Spoon Size Shredded Wheat once in a while? How can you leave someone who needs you?

She didn't think she could leave him. She was unhappy, but she was almost resigned.

Then, one summer evening, they went to a Red Sox game.

"This is the strangest ballpark in the world," Owen said. He was admiring the Green Monster, Fenway Park's famous left-field wall. "It looks like it was designed by Timothy Leary."

They were in the bleachers—not the best place to sit if you wanted to follow the game. The view was fine, but the fans there, the bleacher bums, were mostly interested in drinking, chucking beachballs at each other, and bellowing like steers. But those were the only seats they could get.

Ron Guidry, pitching for the Yankees, had lost the fastball he was known for in his glory days, but he'd transformed himself into an artist. He was all finesse, all touch, and he was unhittable. By the sixth inning the Red Sox were down six to nothing.

In the eighth, a guy sitting just below Sally stuck a Yankees cap on his head, thrust his fist in the air, and called out, "Yankees Rule!" This was a strange thing to do in Fenway Park. He was instantly hit by a barrage of junk from the back rows—Cracker Jack boxes, scorecards, ice cubes. This provoked an odd response. He turned to face his attackers and started making monkey noises, throwing his shoulders forward and scratching his crotch. This was a language new to Sally—she couldn't figure out *what* the hell the point of this was—but it got a reaction from the back rows, who started throwing heavier things: hot dogs, chicken, anything they had.

Stuff was coming from everywhere, and it was coming *hard*. The guy next to Owen got smacked in the head with a ball, or a rock—Sally couldn't tell what it was. "Let's get out of here," Owen said. She nodded; he started to rise. She reached down for her bag; it was lost somewhere under her seat. She found it and stood up, and got slapped in the face by wet stuff—beer. Her eyes were stinging; she could hardly see. Something else hit her, on her breast. She was crying—she wasn't even sure she was crying: her face was all wet and sloppy and hot. She couldn't find Owen. She looked behind her, though there was no reason for him to be behind her. Now she was afraid for *him*. And finally she saw him. He was standing at the mouth of the exit, ten yards away, safe.

She ran to him and threw herself at him, clutching his shoulders. And was shocked to hear herself screaming: "Where the fuck *were* you?"

"I thought you were behind me. I turned around and I was amazed you were still in your seat."

They left the ballpark and walked five blocks to the car

and she didn't for a moment release her clutching grip on his arm, even though she hated him now.

In the car, she began to compose herself. Her panic center was beginning to quiet down. But she still felt shaky, humiliated, mad.

Owen's guilt center was swinging into action. All the way home, he apologized compulsively, again and again. "I thought you were right behind me. When I saw you were still in your seat, I couldn't believe it. I never would have gone ahead if I didn't think you were behind me."

She knew he was telling the truth. But the fact remained that he hadn't taken care of her.

When they got home, Owen went to bed. He didn't want to go to bed without her, but she assured him, dishonestly, that she wasn't mad at him anymore, and that she'd join him soon. She took a shower to wash the beer out of her hair, and sat in his robe in the living room, blankly watching some ancient rerun of "The Defenders." If she were happy with him, the incident probably would have meant nothing. But as it was, it depressed her terribly. She kept finding herself back in that moment of panic when she'd thought something had happened to *him*.

She sat on the couch smoking a cigarette. A question occurred to her. Which was his true self? The caring man he appeared to be in their daily life, or the man who, in a moment of pressure, had run?

Man. The word didn't quite fit.

She wished she felt tired, she wished she could crawl into bed with him and fall asleep and forget everything. But the thought of getting in bed with him repulsed her. But she didn't want to sleep on the couch either—that would be making a scene. If she slept on the couch, they'd have to have a heavy talk tomorrow, a dreary, interminable, heavy talk.

So? What was so frightening about having a heavy talk? What was the worst that could happen? That you'd leave him? Isn't that what you want? Don't you *want* to leave him?

She had been sitting. Now she stood. She walked quickly to the window, as if there were something to see from there.

You were wondering about his true self: what about yours? The person you've been for the last two years: talking baby talk, not really happy and not really unhappy . . . is that *your* true self? Haven't you known for a long time that this isn't the life you want?

She saw clearly that she wanted to leave him. She was afraid she saw it *too* clearly—nothing was ever this simple. She was in a kind of fever, in which it seemed intolerable to stay with him even one more day.

She wanted to wake him this instant and settle everything *now* . . . but that would be inhuman. Tomorrow then. But she had to work tomorrow. Should she tell him at breakfast or wait until after work?

She was pacing the living room. She stopped in front of the bookcase. She had an image of herself: tomorrow night, on her knees, packing her books in a cardboard box. Her books, which had lived with his books for so long. How could she leave him?

Her desire to leave him—wasn't it just childishness? Shouldn't she just accept this life? He was a good guy— shouldn't that be enough?

She sat back down. It was all fading. She felt her resolution fading, the black-and-whiteness of it seeping away.

She couldn't let it happen. If she let herself sink back into this half-life, she might be lost in it for years. She had to leave.

And she had to tell him now. If she went to bed without telling him, she might wake to find herself immobilized: tied down again, by threads of need, fear, habit.

She made her way slowly toward the bedroom, through the dark hall. Waking him in the middle of the night, like the secret police. It was the most horrible thing you could do to someone—wake him up so you can hurt him. But that was what she was doing. She went into the bedroom, touched him softly, whispered his name.

Owen always woke in a tender mood. "Is it time to rise and shine?"

"Time to rise and shine." She whispered it.

"But it's still dark, baby. Did you wake me up to scrumpshize me?"

This was his word for sex. From the feeling of scrumptiousness she gave him. Because it was a child's word, it had always depressed her. And because it was a child's word, it had always touched her.

"Owen. We have to have a talk."

"It's so dark, Sal." He closed his eyes and curled up, his hands between his knees. "Can't you have a talk by yourself for a while? I'll join you after I'm done with my dream."

"Owen. Please. This is important."

Owen opened his eyes and sat up in bed. What am I? How can I do this to him?

"Owen. I need to leave."

"Where are you going?"

"I've been thinking about us. I've been having problems."

"You have?"

"I'm sorry, baby, I'm sorry to tell you like this, but I'm just not happy. I think I need to live by myself."

He looked frightened, as if she'd threatened him with violence. "Why didn't you ever *tell* me?"

It was true—she had never told him she was unhappy. A few times she'd said she wished they could stop baby talking; often enough she'd picked fights with him about other things. But she had never really told him her problems. The reason was simple: she had always known, finally, that her fundamental problem was him. She'd always known that there was no way to change the fact that she didn't respect him.

"Owen, I'm not happy. I feel like we're not using all of ourselves."

"What are you doing? Sally? This is so crazy. This isn't like you."

She was sitting next to him on the bed, holding him. He freed his hand and pounded on the mattress.

"Is it because of the baseball? I'm *sorry*. I'll never do anything like that again. You have to let me tell you. It's not fair to never give a person a second chance!"

You have to let me tell you. He wasn't completely coherent. It was because he wasn't fully awake, it was because he was scared; but as always, when he said something that sounded odd, she worried for him, she worried that his illness was going to return. But she couldn't protect him. There was nothing she could do for him now.

PART THREE

42

She went to the window. The perils of living near your parents again. Burke and Hannah were coming to pick her up, and she had to intercept them before they got to her apartment. If Hannah knew Sally still smoked cigarettes, she'd faint.

For a moment she thought she saw them at the end of the block. Then the two people came a few steps closer, and she realized they were much older: a hunched little woman and a white-haired old man.

Then they came a few steps closer, and she realized they were her parents after all.

They were going to the annual luncheon in honor of the Abraham Lincoln Brigade—the American veterans of the Spanish Civil War. The handful of Americans who, when Franco launched his war against the democratic republic, had made the cause of Spain their own.

Hannah was beside herself with glee. Every year at this event she was beside herself with glee. And every year Sally wondered why she'd agreed to come along. Hannah danced around introducing Sally as "my baby daughter," fawning over her with an intensity that made Sally physically uncomfortable. When your mother introduces you as "my baby daughter," you have a choice: you can say nothing, and thereby accept the description; or you can protest, and thereby show that you deserve it.

"Look! There's Steve Nelson!" Steve Nelson meant nothing to Sally; but Hannah's voice was reverent. In the corner, surrounded by admirers, was a little man of about seventy-five, wearing a beret and smoking a pipe. He did have a certain air. . . . His beret was tilted with a jaunty combativeness; the pipe made him look the soldier-scholar; his face was ruddy—flushed with action, as if he'd returned only moments ago from a stirring military engagement, just over yonder ridge.

Hannah grabbed Sally by the wrist and bulled her way through the crowd. "Steve? Do you remember me? Hannah Burke—Hannah Salmon. I used to bring you coffee when you'd visit the *Daily Worker*. No cream, three spoons of sugar."

Nelson smiled at her warmly, without the slightest idea who she was. "How've you been?"

"And this is my darling baby daughter, Sally."

"Pleased to meet you," Nelson said. He looked a little like Bing Crosby.

"Do you know of any nice young activists for my Sally?"

It was amazing: her mother still had the power to humiliate her, with an offhand phrase.

Nelson's attention was already elsewhere: another admirer was pressing toward him through the crowd.

Hannah didn't mind; she was too intoxicated by the sheer multitude of celebrities from her youth. "That's Les Griffith. I used to have an orgasm just looking at him. He was the most gorgeous man on earth."

Most of the vets were old Communists—they were the superstars of American communism. "That's Freddy Vaughn—was he a playboy! Freddy'd make a date to meet a woman in a hotel room, and he'd proposition somebody else on the way."

As Hannah pointed out these men, she was gripping Sally's wrist. She seemed to think the appeal of these men was obvious. As if she thought Sally could look through the withered skin into their spirits, into what they'd been. Far from true. These men, who for Hannah still embodied all the possibilities of personal and moral romance, were very old. Les Griffith was cadaverous: he must have been near ninety. He passed nearby, a fragile thing, leaning on the arm of a nurse. His skull was transparent, except for a faint blush of pink.

The Lester Griffith who inspired men and women with passionate soapbox orations in the 1930s—how was he related to this man who passed in front of her today, vacantly licking his lips? It was doubtful that this man remembered that time. It hardly seemed possible to speak of that man and this as a single "he."

After the reception they made their way to their tables. The speeches were dull. A flushed, elderly historian, who was chiefly distinguished for having defended each of the Soviet Union's invasions of small neighboring countries over a thirty-year span, warned that Ronald Reagan was launching a new McCarthyism. Nelson said a few rambling things about the continuing meaning of the struggle for Spain. He called on the audience to realize that though the cause of Spain had been just, many of them, in the 1930s, had made a few mistakes. This referred to their allegiance to Stalin.

Burke chuckled as he reached for his cigarettes. "A few mistakes. Some people might say we have the blood of millions on our hands. I like that—a few mistakes."

The master of ceremonies introduced an extraordinarily

handsome young black man who had been sitting at the table of honor with Paul Robeson's granddaughter, holding her hand. He came on stage and sang a few songs—songs that Robeson had made famous during the Spanish Civil War. His voice was frighteningly like Robeson's. He looked a bit like Robeson. It must have been confusing to some of the older veterans. Drifting in and out of dream states, they must have thought that Robeson himself was before them, still alive, still young.

On the way home, in the backseat, Sally was pensive. They were so old, most of them, as to be hardly alive. But in a sense they were younger than she was. They were older than she was only through the accident of time. When they were her age, they were taking risks greater than any she could imagine. Men and women in their twenties, they had told their government to go to hell and traveled halfway around the world to fight for a cause.

Spain: when people who'd been around in the thirties spoke the word, they had a tremulous, almost a religious catch in their throats. For an entire generation, Spain had meant commitment, solidarity, the vision of a better future.

For Sally, there was no Spain.

When she got home that night, she took out her desk encyclopedia and looked at a map of the world. There was no Spain.

43

The bliss of not having a boyfriend.

She was living alone, in a tiny studio in the Cobble Hill section of Brooklyn. New York was a filthy, intimidating, brutal place; but Sally was in bliss.

The bliss of an empty bed. The bliss of speaking normally—she vowed never to talk baby talk again. The bliss of living by her own rhythms. The bliss of walking down the street desiring three out of every five men she passed, without feeling unfaithful.

Yes. Desiring all men was like possessing all men. Her life was filled with imaginary lovers: the guy on the bus every morning who looked like he played the saxophone; the Italian guy who ran the local bookshop—she'd had a dream that he was really Bruce Springsteen; the older guy who jogged near the school where she was working. In a way it was better than a relationship. If she got together with any one man, it would put all these others out of reach.

But the most blissful bliss of all was the bliss of a life without compromise. Now, if she was unhappy, it was her own unhappiness. The voice that kept saying *Not quite right*—

she'd never known if it should be respected or ignored. The voice had finally gone silent.

The night she left he'd pounded the bed like a baby. She hoped he was taking care of himself.

44

"Windblown Hector," she said absentmindedly, putting her arm around the boy's small waist. Hector was crying because he didn't know how to tie his "shoes laces."

"Come on now, my man," she said softly. "We'll teach you how to tie those shoelaces."

She was working as an assistant kindergarten teacher in a public school in Greenwich Village. She was comfortable with kids this age. Hannah had been teaching kindergarten for twenty years, and Sally had always enjoyed hanging around in her classroom.

Hannah was a tireless propagandist for the open classroom. Her main contention was that children have a natural love of learning that school too often stifles. Hannah was Rousseau.

Sally was also Rousseau. She found she was less interested in instructing children than in listening to them. Sometimes she worried that she listened too much—that she didn't give them enough guidance. Her answer to questions that began with "Why?" was usually, "Why do you think?"

The head teacher, Mrs. Keane, was a bit of a disciplinarian. This freed Sally to be friendlier with the children, goofier, than she could have been otherwise. It was a good-cop bad-cop routine.

In a few years these kids would be hardened New Yorkers, but now they were in their kindergarten freshness. At any given moment, it seemed, one of them was in tears. Hector because he couldn't tie his shoes laces. Susannah because her dog had run away. Daniel because his father had had to work last weekend and couldn't take him to the zoo. "I always get the bad luck," he said. "And I never *ever* opened an umbrella in the house!"

She wanted to protect them, she wanted to shield them from the knowledge that life is not always happy or fair. But it was already too late. What could she say to Daniel, who had never opened an umbrella in the house? What could she say to Susannah, whose dog had run away? Mrs. Keane had assured her that he'd come back; Susannah wasn't satisfied. When Sally was sitting helping some other kids with blocks, Susannah came up and said, "Do you think Milton will come back?"

Sally didn't know what to say. But she had to say something. And so she finally said, "I don't know. I hope so."

Sally didn't know if it was right to lay bleak uncertainties on such a young child. But her only strength in the classroom was that she respected children, she was herself with them.

Evidently good intentions were not enough: you had to learn how to put them into practice. And evidently Sally hadn't learned yet. Susannah avoided her for the rest of the day.

45

"My God," Hannah said. "I've never seen him so drunk."

Waveringly, perilously, Burke made his way to their table. He looked as if he was unsure about a new dance step. He kissed Hannah, and then he kissed Sally. He hadn't kissed Sally since about 1963.

"How many martinis?" Hannah said.

"Four."

"*Four?*"

"Three."

They were at Gage and Tollner's, a restaurant in Brooklyn. It was almost a hundred years old; it had the atmosphere of a dining car from the 1890s. Hannah and Sally had been waiting for him for half an hour.

"Four martinis! Why?"

"I was meeting with Edward Reilly, Esquire, to work out the final details of a contract. Edward Reilly, Esquire, is a lush."

"And you had to match him drink for drink?"

"Certainly."

"Why? Because you're macho?"

"Because," he said, "I am macho."

Sally was sitting next to him. She had never seen him drunk—never. He gave off a stale, heavy smell.

Sally hadn't wanted to come out for dinner, but Hannah had applied pressure: she'd said that if Sally were there it would cheer Burke up. He was having a tough time. These were bad days for the labor movement: Reagan, in office for a little more than a year, had dealt with an air traffic controllers' strike by firing them all, and staffed the National Labor Relations Board with a bunch of union-busting cavemen. It was hard to organize in this climate, hard to get decent contracts. And there was a much more immediate reason for Burke's gloom: two weeks ago, his union had lost an election to represent a group of five thousand social workers, an election he was sure they'd win.

He didn't seem gloomy at the moment; he seemed to be itching for a fight. He looked around the restaurant, eyebrows bristling with disapproval. "This used to be a very nice place, but now it's filled up with artists from Brooklyn Heights. Two-minute filmmakers. Look at that jerk over there—he thinks you wear a collar pin *and* a starched collar." He was a little too loud—the jerk heard him, and looked up, glaring.

"You have to be careful," Hannah said. "You're taking blood pressure pills. You have to be careful how you drink now."

Looking like a wise and patient tutor, he shook his head. "It has nothing to do with blood pressure pills. It has to do with providing a certain education for my daughter."

"Is that so?"

"Yes, it is so. It's time for this young woman to learn something about her ancestral past. If you asked her about her bloodlines, she'd only be able to tell you about this Polish rabbi stuff. Sarah, you have to get used to the fact that you have another set of forebears, who used to sit on the stoop at Tenth Avenue and Forty-third Street, drinking beer all day.

And whether you like it or not, their genes and their blood and their view of life flow through you." He turned, with difficulty, to inspect her. "And if any of them could meet you, they wouldn't know what to make of you."

A waiter took their order. Burke seemed impatient for him to be gone. He had further observations to make.

"Honey, I think it's time to admit we made a mistake with these kids. We've raised a couple of Polish rabbis. Daniel is a luftmensch, floating over the groves of academe. And Sarah, long after the two of us have shuffled off this mortal coil, will someday be residing at the Sunnyside Old Folks Home, still wondering if she's ever going to find herself."

"We have two wonderful children, and what's more, you adore them."

"These kids are not worth the powder to blow them to hell. What you don't realize, honey, is that both of them have rejected us."

"They haven't rejected us. Sally's come back to live here. It's delicious." Hannah shivered with pleasure.

"They *have* rejected us—in a very subtle way. Neither of them is planning to have children. Daniel's standards are too high for any mortal woman, and Sarah, I'm sure, feels that it would be gravely irresponsible to bring a child into a world in which so many marsupials are being mistreated in Australia. And so this great brain," he said, clutching his head, "is going to be wasted."

"I'm sure they'll both have children. They're still young."

"Well, I don't intend to wait around to find out. I've decided to take action. I'm going to have another batch of kids myself."

"Don't try to impress your daughter. She knows perfectly well that your prostate operation made you sterile."

"She knows nothing of the sort. In any case, I took the small precaution of storing some of my sperm. In the Chase Manhattan Bank. It's waiting for a receptacle."

This was too much: Burke was deeply puritanical, and this

was not the kind of joke you'd expect to hear from him, no matter how drunk he was. And in another minute, as if in payment for this, he huddled up and went silent. He was gray. Hannah asked him if he felt all right; he mumbled that he was fine. The food arrived, but he couldn't eat anything. He put his head in his hands.

Sally and Hannah tried to eat. They didn't say anything.

He mumbled something into his hands.

"Excuse me?" Hannah said.

"I said, *Too fucking old.*" He lifted his head out of his hands. "You do this job for forty-five years, you should know if you have the goddamn votes. I thought we had the goddamn votes."

"Oh, Burke, you lost one. You've lost them before. It's got nothing to do with being old. If you were in the Soviet Politburo, you'd still be one of the Young Turks. Tell him, Sally."

Sally wanted to tell him. She wanted to add a few words of encouragement. But she didn't have any. She'd never seen him like this before. She was frightened.

46

On June 12, 1982, over a million people gathered in Central Park to protest the nuclear arms race. In the early evening, they dispersed. This was the beginning of the antinuclear movement in the United States, and the end. The arms race continued.

Sally was among that million. At noon that day she went to the movies, by herself, near the park. She saw *Star Trek II*, in which Mr. Spock met his fate. Stricken with what he knew to be a fatal dose of radiation, Spock lay slumped on one side of a transparent partition as Captain Kirk knelt on the other side. The two of them pressed their fingers against the glass . . . almost touching. "I have been, and always will be, your friend," said Spock. Sitting alone in one of the back rows, Sally wept.

It was a warm, bright, beautiful day. The streets around the park were cordoned off; people were strolling toward the park, ambling down the middle of the street.

Sally walked with her hands in her pockets, marveling at the change. The city of all against all, the city of no connection—for a day, it was utterly changed. Everyone was related; everyone knew why everyone else was there; her own hopes were reflected in the faces of strangers. Everyone on these streets was against not only nuclear weapons but nuclear power as well. They all believed in solar energy. And in the glow of friendliness in every face she passed, Sally could see the beneficent effects of solar energy. For one afternoon, New York was a gentle, generous city.

In the park was the most astonishing congregation she had ever seen. A million people. No one was pushing, no one was picking anyone's pocket. She had cried a few minutes ago, because of the death of Spock; now she felt like crying again, from some mix of happiness and sadness. The city was gentle, but it would be gentle only for a day.

In a little clearing, in the midst of the million, he was standing there, talking with a woman. Like everyone else, he was idly running his eyes over the faces around him, just for the pleasure of looking. His gaze passed over Sally, passed on.

She'd recognized him instantly, though he looked a little different. Not quite so heavy; a little more tired. It had been about two years.

She walked up to him, without much regard for the fact that he was talking with someone else. He glanced at her again, without recognition. Then he smiled.

"You remember me?" she said.

"Of course. I've thought about you, from time to time."

The way he looked at her made her feel attractive.

"You have?"

"I wondered whether I'd ever see you again. It was frustrating, because I never even found out your name. I've just thought of you as the Dylanist."

47

After the demonstration, she went for a drink with him. His name was Ben.

They both ordered a beer. Sally asked him what he'd thought of the rally.

"I thought it was great. Too homogenized though. I don't suppose you went down to Washington for Solidarity Day last year?"

Solidarity Day was an anti-Reagan rally called by the AFL-CIO in 1981. She hadn't.

"That was a little more to my liking. You had New York blacks and Minnesota Swedes and Arkansas hillbillies side by side. . . . It was a good mix. Everybody today looked the same."

"Spoken like a true union guy," she said.

"Union guy." He said it with a simple pride.

He didn't remind her of her father really, but he seemed to come from the same tradition. Sally could never be a union guy, but she liked to be around them.

"Are you a red of some sort?" she said.

"A *red*? As in 'the red menace'? Is that a typical icebreaker, in your set?"

"I know some older people in the labor movement, and most of them are old Communists or old Socialists. So I was wondering if it was still true, for young lads like yourself."

"Am I a card-carrying member of the radical left? Is that what you're asking? Am I a member of the Symbionese Liberation Army?"

"That's my basic question, yes."

"I really wouldn't know how to be a red in America these days. But if the question is would I vote for Eugene Debs if he ran for president, sure."

"Dictatorship of the proletariat, man."

At the next table, a couple of guys were eating dinner and getting drunk, and they'd tuned in on the conversation. They were big beefy guys; they looked like they worked with their hands.

Ben hadn't heard them. Sally was afraid of them, and she changed the subject. "Where are you from?"

"A little town outside Pittsburgh—a steel town. That's a big part of it. Everybody in town worked for U.S. Steel, my old man included. About ten years ago, just before Christmas, the company told them it was moving south. Two months later, everybody in town was out of work. Most of them too old to find other jobs, even if there'd been other jobs, which there weren't. I was about twenty, trying to figure out what to do with myself. So that's why I decided to work for a union. And that's why I'd vote for Eugene Debs. I'd just like to see a world where the fact that you have money doesn't give you the right to push people around. Where some poor son of a bitch like my father, after he's given forty years of his life to some company, doesn't have to worry about getting tossed out of his house when the company decides it doesn't need him anymore."

"Off the pigs! Power to the people! Save the fucking whales!" The guy who was saying this was a red-faced guy with a big mustache. He was leaning over toward Sally and Ben's table, breathing on their drinks. His friend was laughing, trying not to spit out his beer.

It made Sally feel like shit. All the good feelings from the rally had vanished. You stand around among a million people who are just like you—semi-vegetarian, avid readers of the Land's End catalog, in touch with their feelings, meek as little lambs—and you think that all the problems of the world can be solved if we could all just sit barefoot in a circle and relate. Ten minutes later you go out for a drink and you realize that there are a lot of people who go through life intent on being assholes, and that they're bigger and stronger than the nice people, and that's that.

"But as for being a red, I don't know," Ben said. "A lot of the older people in my union used to be Communists—I know the type you mean. They fell in love with Russia, and they defended a lot of things they shouldn't have defended. It was stupid. 'Cause you know what's the greatest thing about America?"

"No—what's the greatest thing about America?" This was said not by Sally, but by the mustache guy, in a mincing voice.

"The greatest thing about America," Ben said, turning toward the two guys, "is that you can talk about whatever you want to talk about, and if the cops don't like it or the guys at the next table don't like it, you can look them in the eye and tell them to go fuck themselves."

Silence all around.

Very quietly: "Now, we can fucking step outside if you want to, or you can shut up and let us talk in peace. Which'll it be?"

The mustache guy didn't say anything. His friend stubbed out his cigarette. He had thick, stumpy fingers. He didn't look particularly intimidated. "Look. You don't want to fight, because we'd beat you up. And we don't want to fight, 'cause it's Saturday night and we just want to get drunk. My friend gets a little rambunctious, but he doesn't mean anything. So just cool out."

Ben looked at the guy for another second, nodded a little, and turned back to Sally. "Like I was saying . . ."

48

He'd made his point, but the mood was spoiled. They finished their drinks and left. They stood awkwardly on the sidewalk. It was still light. "If you're not doing anything, I'll make you dinner," he said.

He lived within walking distance, on West End Avenue and Seventy-ninth Street. He was tall; she had to crane her neck to talk to him. "What would you have done if they'd wanted to fight?"

"I would have gone out and gotten my nose broken, I guess."

"That didn't scare you?"

He shrugged. "What's a nose?"

"You really think that? I guess that's the difference between boys and girls." She touched her nose. She liked her nose. It was a nice nose.

"I wasn't exactly looking *forward* to getting my nose broken. But I didn't think they'd fight—nobody really wants to fight, in general. And even if they did, I wanted to make a point. When those guys think of radicals or whatever, they probably think of Castro on the one hand, or else skinny little professors with bow ties. Now, maybe they'll remember they once met a red, as you put it, who was willing to duke it out." He smiled and shook his head. "Of such great triumphs does the life of Ben McMahon consist."

He opened the door. "This is where I live."

Sometimes you like a place immediately.

"What a domestic person he is," she said. There were plants all over the living room, alert-looking and green. "How do you keep these things alive? Do you talk with them? Do you chat?"

"I don't really do too much. They seem to thrive on abuse."

His place had a nice feeling: cluttered but clean. Most of the furniture was old, a little beat-up. There were a lot of books around, mostly history books.

"I bet you have a very mature refrigerator," she said.

It was. It was filled with *things*. Milk, apple juice, beer, wine, English muffins, butter, two kinds of jam, Wisconsin cheese, coffee, an onion, two tomatoes, mushrooms, broccoli, some leftover chicken curry or something, roast beef, eggs, tomato sauce. Peanut butter. On a shelf in the kitchen there was fruit in a bowl.

"What a real person you are."

"I read this book about how to arrange your house so people think you're a grown-up."

She had a flash on Owen, a feeling of sadness about his life. She didn't know where he was living, but she knew exactly how his place must look. Neat and bare; nothing on the walls. In the refrigerator, nothing but skim milk; in the cupboard, nothing but Shredded Wheat.

She took a few steps into his bedroom. There was a pile of books on his night table. "A scholarly man. We remember him as a scholarly man."

"I haven't finished a book in five years. I skim."

A bulletin board with photographs. Family and friends. A woman—sitting in this room, on this bed, laughing.

"This is . . . ?"

Ben put his hands in his pockets, smiled, shrugged, shook his head.

"The unknown woman on the bed," Sally said.

"The unknown woman on the bed," he said.

She liked this. She liked it that he had a past.

On his desk, a pipeholder with four or five pipes. "You smoke?"

"Not a lot. Once in a while."

The place had an agreeable fullness. "This is the kind of apartment Sherlock Holmes lived in," she said. "Do you have a little Persian slipper where you keep your shag tobacco?"

"You're not from the Board of Health, by any chance? No one's ever inspected the place like this."

"It's what you've been waiting for all your life." She was a little shocked to hear herself say this.

"Yes. I guess it is."

In the kitchen, he rummaged around in the refrigerator, looking for something to cook. Sally told him about college, about her work, a little about her life in Boston. He asked her what her parents did.

"My mother teaches first grade."

"A family tradition?"

"I don't know. I like it, but I'm not sure it's me."

He seemed about to say something, but he didn't.

"And my father is . . . a union guy."

"Is that right?"

"Do you know District 17?"

"Burke. That's your old man? Old Francis X. Burke?"

"You know him?"

"I've met him. He wouldn't know me." He leaned back against the countertop, smiling. "He's the real thing, your father. He's a union man of the old school. I've heard he was quite a bomb-thrower in his younger days."

"I don't know about that," she said.

He was still smiling. "I feel pretty stupid. Here I've been giving these heartwarming speeches about trade unionism, and all the time I was talking to Joe Hill's daughter."

"I liked your heartwarming speeches."

Sally sat smoking and teasing him as he chopped broccoli, mushrooms, tomatoes. "I feel so close to the earth here." She didn't know many men who could look in their refrigerator, thaw a few things, and throw together a decent meal. "They should make a miniseries about you," she said.

They ate dinner, drank wine, talked.

"What did you want to be before you wanted to be a union guy?"

"When I was a kid I was sure I'd be a cop. I had a very sophisticated picture of what being a cop was all about. I thought I'd stand on the corner twirling my nightstick, whistling. I'd solve a domestic quarrel once in a while, and convince young hotheads not to go bad. I'd teach them all the manly art of boxing. That lasted till high school. Then I watched the Chicago convention on TV, and I thought maybe I'd do something else."

"Like what?"

He took a sip of wine, didn't say anything.

"This looks good. This looks like something embarrassing."

"You're damn right it's something embarrassing, so let's just change the subject."

"Come on."

"If you really must know, I looked into being a nurse."

She snorted.

"That's *exactly* why I didn't want to tell you."

"I was laughing because it's perfect. *Why* did Ben McMahon think about being a nurse? Because he wanted to help people. Because he'd rather be with the people who get pushed around instead of the people who do the pushing. And because he figured nurses do most of the real work anyway."

"Placed. Pinned."

"Am I right?"

"Of course you're right. You're exactly right."

She could see him as a nurse. She pictured herself as a patient, collapsing on the floor with an unnamed disease, Ben carrying her back to bed. A nurturant male.

He went to the sink, ran the cold water, passed his wrist through the stream. He was six foot something, thick-armed and square-bodied. He'd slimmed down a lot since they'd met, but he still had a considerable paunch. She was thinking that she didn't object to the paunch. She liked what it seemed to say about him. In this age of bodily perfection, Ben, maybe, had other concerns.

He put two glasses of water on the table. "Water," he said.

"Do you want children?" she said.

She'd thought of this as an innocuous question—a bit chatty, a bit disarming, a bit flirtatious. Ben was eating a piece of bread, and apparently he then and there became converted to the Fletcher doctrine of "thorough mastication," according to which each morsel of food should be chewed no less than a hundred times. When he was done with the bread he poured Sally more wine, poured himself more wine. Now he seemed ready to talk. He put his hands on his knees. Silence. He looked at her.

"Let's talk about something else. Okay?"

"Okay," Sally said.

Sitting by herself at home that night, she found herself trembling. Life. New life. She hadn't even looked for it, but here it was.

49

"Did you talk to Abrams yet, honey?"

Sally was in her parents' kitchen on a Saturday morning. Burke was making scrambled eggs. After he asked this question Sally turned and saw Hannah making a warning face at him.

"Who's Abrams?" Sally said.

"Nobody," Hannah said.

"Come on."

"Just some doctor."

"What are you seeing a doctor for?"

"Your mother's an old lady," Hannah said. "Old ladies have to go to the doctor once in a while." She squeezed Sally on the nose.

50

Bottom of the eighth. The Yankees were behind by two runs with a man on first, two out. Lou Piniella was at the plate. Dave Winfield knelt in the on-deck circle. The pitcher's job was to get Piniella out, so Winfield couldn't win the game. Piniella was a good hitter, but Winfield was the man you were afraid of.

Winfield had labored under crippling expectations all year: he was trying to make up for the loss of Reggie Jackson. He was a superb athlete, but he didn't have Jackson's drama, his power to change the flow of a game with one swing. He didn't have Jackson's godliness. George Steinbrenner had made him the scapegoat for the team's poor start, and he'd begun to get the reputation of a man who failed in the clutch. But he'd been on fire for weeks now, and the team was surging—with a win today they'd climb into a tie for first.

Piniella took the first pitch for a strike. The next pitch was inside; he held up. Then he took a big, stupid swing at a curveball in the dirt.

Another curveball flirted with the outside corner. The umpire hesitated, then called it a ball; forty thousand people, wilting with relief, gave off a long low oooooooooh.

Fastball outside; Piniella didn't swing. The count was three and two. The place was getting louder. And though everyone was watching Piniella, everyone knew that Piniella was not the most important player on the field. The most important player on the field was kneeling in the on-deck circle, watching the proceedings with a strangely disdainful smile.

Ball four. Piniella tossed his bat suavely at the batboy and jogged to first base. Winfield rose and made his way toward the plate. He was a lean, well-muscled man with tremendously long arms and legs; as he stepped into the batter's box, Sally felt afraid for the pitcher in the event of a line drive. Winfield seemed too big for this game.

It was a golden moment. This was the situation he'd been born for. Forty thousand people were standing. Each one of them knew that he would crush the first pitch into the left-field seats. Everyone in Yankee Stadium, standing, laughing, squinting in the sun, knew that Dave Winfield was about to transform himself, before their eyes, into a god.

After he struck out, somebody tossed him his glove and he walked slowly back to right field. Not a god at all, he was like the rest of us, who, just when we seem poised to surpass ourselves, always finally come up short. Forty thousand people were booing the shit out of him. Two rows behind Sally and Ben, with a high hysterical voice, a teenager was shouting "Winfield fucking sucks! Winfield sucks loose cock!"

"Loose cock?" Sally said.

"Moose cock," Ben corrected her.

"I thought he said 'loose cock.' I thought it was a form of cock you find lying around in the street."

The guy sitting next to Ben shook his head with disgust. "The money that bastard makes they should shoot him. You know what that son of a bitch makes for those three swings?"

"What the hell," Ben said. "I believe in sharing the wealth, but I'd go after Steinbrenner's money before Winfield's. Winfield, you can see it, he gives everything he's got. George just sits around talking trash."

The guy nodded; whether or not he agreed, he nodded, in a kind of ballpark, barroom, you-got-a-point-there-buddy way.

As they left the stadium Sally said, "Always on the job, eh?"

"What?"

"Union man. Union man from your bald spot to the tips of your toes." She tried to make her voice as deep as his: "Winfield, sir, despite his high wage, remains a worker. Social resentment should be more properly directed against the representative of the owning class."

"Did I sound like a dreary propagandist?"

"No. You sounded like somebody who can't go to bed at night if he hasn't done just a little something to bring about the solidarity of labor."

"Exposed," Ben said.

51

In early September, Hannah went to see a doctor at the Memorial Sloan-Kettering Cancer Center. He was a world-renowned surgeon. He looked at her x-rays, he examined the lump in her breast, and he said he would schedule her for a biopsy. Scribbling on a notepad, he informed her briskly that if the growth were found to be malignant, he would remove her breast immediately, while she was still anesthetized.

Actually, what he said was much worse. He said that by the time cancer is discovered in one breast, it has often spread, though undetectably as yet, to the other, and that his standard procedure, therefore, was to immediately remove both.

She thought she'd misunderstood him. She asked him to repeat what he'd said. He repeated it.

"It's a form of preventive medicine," he said.

Hannah left his office and walked, just walked. When she looked up, she was in midtown. She wandered over to the Museum of Modern Art. She looked at Picasso's representations of his wives. A statuette of the head of Jacqueline: her nose looked odd, until you realized that it wasn't a nose, it was a penis.

52

Sally sat in the library, reading another article about breast cancer.

Some of the articles seemed to be saying that if you have breast cancer, you can expect to live perhaps five more years. Hannah was fifty-five.

It wasn't certain that she did have cancer. She was having a biopsy the next day. They'd found another surgeon, someone who managed to restrain himself from chopping off both breasts then and there.

Sally hadn't known anything about breast cancer. She was twenty-five. She was too young to worry about such things. She'd thought that the horrible thing about breast cancer was the disfigurement. She hadn't known that it kills you.

She left the books on the table, left the library, walked home. It was early October. She cast a short shadow in the cold day. She'd always known that her father would die. With his smoker's cough, his deliberate way of moving, his stories of his youth that were stories from an unknown land, he'd been old from the day she was born. She could imagine the world without him. It was impossible to imagine the world without her mother.

The next morning she slept through the alarm. By the time she woke, her mother was already under the knife.

She dressed in a hurry. For once in her life, she put on something nice: a Laura Ashley dress she'd bought a few months before and never worn. But now, when she looked at herself in the mirror, she realized that in order to look good in a Laura Ashley you have to be a birdlike, delicate Wasp. She looked stupid.

She'd taken the day off so she could be with her mother in the hospital. She couldn't understand how she could've slept through the alarm.

Today was only the biopsy. They were just going to find out what she had. So Sally hadn't been dreading this day. But now that the day had come, she was terrified. After she brushed her teeth she still had a hard-boiled egg taste in her mouth. She brushed her teeth again but the taste remained.

On the subway up to Columbia Presbyterian it occurred to her that people sometimes die during routine exploratory surgery. Sometimes they go under and never come up again.

She sat on the subway, looking at the strange faces, overhearing bits of idiotic conversations, as her mother's flesh was being pierced with sharp instruments.

Certain things were as difficult for Sally to comprehend at twenty-five as they were for her at five. Such as: the fact that other people are living now, even when you're not there to confirm it. That Owen, for instance, was going about his business right now, somewhere in Boston. That Jesse was somewhere in the world, thinking something, doing something, right now. That Hannah was in a drugged sleep as her flesh was being seared, right now. . . .

She arrived at the hospital at eleven . . . a mere two hours after she'd said she'd be there. By now they knew what Hannah had. Sally found the building, the right elevator, the right wing, the right hall. Walking down the hall checking the numbers on each door, through each doorway a glimpse of another old person, enduring the same incommunicable sorrow. The body breaks down. That's what it's made for.

Walking down the hall. Hannah and Burke knew by now whether or not it was cancer. Less than a hundred feet away, Sally was in ignorance, but the truth was known, was waiting.

She found the room and went in.

Hannah was lying in bed. Burke was in a chair next to the bed.

Both of them were asleep.

Hannah was in a hospital gown. She had a lined, heavy face. They take you and do things that make you older than ever, and they dress you up like a little girl.

Burke, as always, was well dressed, in a brown sport coat and a burgundy tie.

Sally knew that her mother had cancer.

Burke could sleep anywhere, on any occasion. But if the news had been good, Hannah would have been awake. No matter how tired the surgery had made her, she would have been awake and babbling happily in bed.

Sally sat in the other chair and watched her parents sleep. They were before her: they were alive. She could touch them. But she couldn't protect them. Her mother's face was tired, unhappy even in sleep. Her father slept with his usual mighty breathing, each breath laboring into his lungs through the scars that fifty years of smoking had carved.

Burke woke first. He stared at her without recognition for a moment.

"Why hello there, Sarah," he finally said. "You must have come in on tippy-toe."

Hannah blinked awake. She gave Sally a smile that was barely a smile.

As a rule, when Sally visited her parents, her mother greeted her with a glee that verged on the insane. It had always annoyed her . . . and now, she discovered, it had always made her happy. She discovered this by the small shock that went through her when her mother greeted her so weakly. She felt rejected . . . she felt as if her mother wasn't glad to see her. She knew, of course, that Hannah *was* glad to see her—she just wasn't in a condition to show it. But in the core of herself, Sally still felt baffled and betrayed. Even if she's dying, your mother is supposed to care about you more than she cares about herself.

"What's the word?" Sally said.

"The word is that there is no word," Hannah said. "They can't tell yet. It's abnormal, but they're still not sure it's cancer. They're going to have to do tests on it, and they won't know till Monday."

This was Friday.

They spent the rest of the afternoon sitting around, talking, trying not to show each other how dispirited they were. Daniel was coming down the next day. Hannah would be discharged in the morning; Burke and Sally would come in and pick her up.

Sally and her father left the hospital together. They walked to Broadway, and stood awkwardly at the mouth of the subway station. Burke was going to walk up to 175th Street to catch a bus back to Jersey, Sally was going back to Brooklyn or something, she didn't know.

Being alone with her father was still difficult. When she visited her parents, even now, she found herself contriving ways to avoid being alone with him. They were afraid of each other. When he asked her questions about what she was doing and what she planned to do—the routine questions that parents always ask—she still felt a strange guilt, she still felt as if her life was a mistake. She loved him, and she loved to be around him, but not alone.

"You hungry?" Burke said. "You want to get something to eat?"

They hadn't had dinner alone together since . . . had they

ever? Maybe in the early sixties, when Hannah was at night school and Daniel was out with a friend—maybe in the early sixties he'd boiled a few hot dogs and heated up a can of corn and the two of them had sat at the table talking about Bullwinkle. The thought of Burke going home alone, fixing himself a dinner of fried eggs in the empty house, was terrible to her. But the thought of having dinner with him, trying to find things to talk about, trying to fight that feeling of inadequacy that she always had around him . . . that was terrible too.

"No, I'm not really hungry. I'm pretty tired. I should just go home."

And so they went their separate ways. They didn't touch. She started for the subway and her father headed up Broadway toward the bus station.

An observer, even an informed observer, would not have thought it an important moment. After all, they were going to see each other again the next day. And maybe it wasn't an important moment. But it was a moment Sally would regret for the rest of her life.

She looked at him, half a block away. It was a Hispanic neighborhood; the signs were in Spanish; salsa music, brassy and loud, was coming from a boom box somewhere. Burke was walking through a world that wasn't his. Or maybe it *was* his: for all she knew he went to union meetings around here all the time. She was struck by how little, really, she knew of his life. And now she was letting him walk away. She could have caught him or called out to him, but she didn't: the two of them had no emotional vocabulary for such scenes. Standing on the top step of the subway entrance, she found herself staring at him as if she had to memorize him.

Four thousand years later, long after the human race had destroyed itself, a race of aliens came to explore. They unearthed a number of remains for study, among them the remains of Sally Burke. The aliens had developed certain techniques to extract memories from the brains of the dead, to project the images on a screen. By a freak of happenstance—the vagaries of the paths of destruction, the accidents of continental drift—Sally's brain was one of the few from which anything could be extracted at all.

But not much. She'd been decomposing too long, in radioactive silt and ultraviolet light. They received only one image from her brain, and it meant nothing to them. It was the memory of Burke, walking up Broadway alone.

53

On Saturday, Hannah got out of the hospital. With Burke beside her and Sally in the backseat, she drove herself home. That afternoon Daniel arrived from Vermont.

Sally hadn't seen her brother in more than a year. Seeing each other after a long absence, they normally passed through a period of hesitance and strain, but they always finally broke through again, to that sense of mischievous conspiracy they'd shared when they were kids. There was little opportunity for that now. Daniel was solemn. He didn't express his concern, in word or gesture, but it radiated from his face; it made him grave, it made him wise, it made him beautiful. She had never seen her brother look so beautiful.

They had two days to fill before they'd find out how she was. They tried to talk about other things. Daniel was teaching at Middlebury, of all places; he told amusing stories about his students. Then he told them again.

Burke was unusually tender to Hannah. The four of them sat in front of the TV on Saturday night, watching an old movie with Jean Arthur and Cary Grant.

Brushing her teeth at the end of the night. Looking at her face in the mirror. Before she'd looked in the mirror she had expected, hoped, that her face would be like Daniel's: radiant, beautiful with grief. Instead, she looked bloodshot and peevish and pasty-skinned. She looked ugly.

She got into bed, and wondered if she'd ever felt so manless. If she had a man . . . oh, wasn't it time to admit that it didn't matter? You think that if you had a man you'd be less lonely, less afraid; but the only real relationship she'd ever had, with Owen, was just loneliness times two.

And now Ben. He'd been on vacation for three weeks, and she was beginning to forget what he looked like. She'd had hopes about Ben, daydreams; but now there didn't seem to be any point. Her relations with her family were so long, deep, thickly woven; Ben she barely knew. To think about him now seemed pointless.

When he'd left for vacation, she'd felt depressed, deprived; but now she was only half looking forward to his return. After the Owen years, it was hard for her even to imagine a good relationship. What was easy to imagine was another long emotional stalemate: months of pleasure followed by years of ambivalence.

And yet she wanted someone in her life. She'd been reading *Anna Karenina,* and falling in love—with Levin or with Tolstoy, she wasn't sure which. That night she dreamed she met Levin at a party. He was young, and strong, and warm, and he understood her.

When she woke up, for a moment, she was happy. Then she realized that Levin didn't exist. And then she remembered that her mother had cancer. She lay in bed for a long time.

54

In the kitchen, Burke stood fumbling with the can opener, trying to open a can of coffee.

"Honey, do you know what's wrong with this thing?"

Hannah came over and made the can opener work.

"There's no way I can have cancer. How could I leave a clumsy oaf like you to fend for yourself?"

There was nothing to do but wait. They sat in front of the television most of the day. In the evening they went to dinner at a restaurant in Fort Lee, where the waiter brought them the wrong food, and Burke didn't even have the spirit to get mad at the guy.

"Come on, get him, Burke," Hannah said. Burke just smiled and lit another cigarette.

Sally went to bed early. The sooner she fell asleep the sooner the phone call would come.

She woke up early. It was Black Christmas: what Christmas might be in a nightmare. You'd go downstairs to be greeted either by a wonderful present, or by the most horrible news of your life.

The call hadn't come yet. Burke had already left for work. The rest of them sat around waiting.

"Why do you two look so *glum?* Is that how I raised you, to be a couple of weepers? It'll be good news—I can feel it. And even if it isn't, I'm gonna beat this thing."

Daniel forced a smile. Sally didn't even try.

"Now, come on," Hannah said. "Who wants to play some go-fish?"

But neither of her children wanted to play go-fish. Hannah called the hospital, but they hadn't received the results yet. The three of them watched "Donahue," they watched "The Hollywood Squares," they watched the soaps. Daniel fitfully tried to read his Henry James.

"Big Hank James," Sally said. "A man for all seasons." She wanted to babble with her brother, she wanted to talk nonsense, the way they did when they were little.

In the afternoon, the phone rang. Hannah took the call. It was the doctor. She sat there nodding. Sally knew the news was bad.

Hannah hung up the phone, stood up, and sang out: "GOOD NEWS!"

In the middle of the room, they hugged one another—all three of them, in a huddle, for a long time. Finally Hannah leaned against the television, closed her eyes, and gave herself up to a long, convulsive shiver. And it was only now, only after she opened her eyes and let out her breath and smiled, that Sally realized how terrified she had been.

For the next few minutes, Hannah breathed heavily; she seemed exhausted. She plopped herself in a chair, threw her leg over the side of it, and called her friends.

Within the hour Burke came home. Hannah had been hanging by the window, waiting for him. When she saw him coming down the block she ran outside. And there, under the bare branches of Elm Street, Sally saw a sight that astonished her. Burke dropped his newspaper and took his wife's hands and kissed her, and on the lawn of one of their neighbors, he put his arms around her waist, lifted her into the air, and kissed her again.

"True love!" yelled the newspaper boy, a tough little guy of ten.

They sat in the living room, spent, as Hannah went over the conversation with the doctor. There had been some abnormality, but it wasn't cancer. She'd have to come in for checkups every three months. But it wasn't cancer.

Burke went upstairs, changed his clothes, came back down to the kitchen. He emerged growling. "What the hell! All I ask out of life is a can of Campbell's soup. But once again, the cupboard is bare! What kind of household is this!"

Hannah glowed.

Sally borrowed the car to buy some groceries. She could leave the house now. Hannah didn't need her protection.

Driving through the streets, the windows rolled up tight, she found herself yelling. Yelling at the top of her lungs. She didn't know if she was yelling for the joy of the news, or from the terror of the last few days. A long, terrible, wordless yell. She didn't try to figure it out. The yell had its own reasons.

She had to clutch the steering wheel as hard as she could. Because her mother was alive. The roadside was lined with newly planted trees: red-leafed, graceful in their slenderness. Two young girls on the sidewalk, in identical denim jackets. Sorrow: their fragility: they walked through a moment that would never come again. The world was in its nakedness. And she swore that she would hold this feeling: she'd keep faith with the knowledge that everyone dies, no matter how much you love them, and that you have to embrace life as fiercely as you can.

Yes. But at the supermarket she had to choose between skim milk and low-fat milk, and she had to choose between the cottage cheese she liked and the cheaper kind that her mother preferred to buy; she had to examine critically the various cuts of meat, numbing herself to the thought that this had been life too, this meat; and after she presented her coupons and watched the cash register girl "like a hawk" as her mother had taught her to do, and after she paid, and received her change, and lugged the two bags out to the car, and after trying for a moment to resist the temptation of turning on WNEW, Where Rock Lives—after doing all this she discovered, to her sorrow, that life was already going back to normal, and that the sense of its preciousness wasn't something she was going to be able to keep. The door to the land of insight was closing. And as she drove home through the quiet streets, the blinding sharpness of the world began to fade: the fragile young trees, the people on the sidewalks . . . their outlines blurred. They no longer astonished the eye. They weren't radiant with meaning anymore. They were just themselves.

They had dinner, and they were all happy, but it seemed an everyday happiness. Death was just a rumor again.

55

"Is this a mission of mercy?"

Ben didn't look at her: he kept his eyes on the road; which meant that he didn't like her question. "It's a mission of friendship."

They were visiting Ben's sister-in-law and his nephew.

"You like her?"

"I like her very much. But it's the kid I'm more concerned about. I've seen Priscilla throw a baseball, and frankly, she throws like a girl. Randy needs the periodic attention of Big Ben McMahon. You know what they used to call me in Little League?"

"The Ancient Mariner? 'Cause you'd stoppeth one of three?"

"They used to call me the Big Train. After Walter Johnson. They'd walk right up to the plate, and I'd blow 'em right down. 'Cause you can't hit what you can't see." He smiled with contentment.

"From now on I'll call you Big Train too."

Ben's brother Frank had flown the coop two months after Randy was born. Never been heard from since.

"Does anybody even know where he is?"

"Nope. Nobody cares."

"*You* don't care?"

"Nope."

"You? Mr. Good? I don't believe it. You raised that boy from a young pup. You whelped him."

"I whelped him. Sometimes I think the main reason I hang around with you is your vocabulary."

Priscilla lived in a garden apartment way out in Queens. Block after block of identical prefab houses, depressing to the spirit, with their carefully tended yet still undernourished-looking lawns.

"This is the kind of place a man could put down roots," Ben said.

They rang the doorbell. Sally was nervous. She didn't know why.

Priscilla in the doorway. A hug and a kiss from Ben; when Ben introduced her to Sally, she came forward and shook Sally's hand.

"Howdy," Priscilla said. "It's nice of you to come all the way to darkest Queens."

"Where's the youth?" Ben said.

"He's in the kitchen."

"What's he doing?"

"He seems to be lost in thought."

Ben disappeared in search of the youth. Sally felt left in the lurch.

Priscilla looked like a match girl. She was thin and bony and waiflike; her slip showed under her long dress. She was furnished out of secondhand stores. She looked as if this was somehow a matter of principle.

"Have you known big Ben a long time?" Priscilla said.

"A few months."

"Isn't he the kind of guy you feel like you've known him forever?"

"To me, he's the kind of guy I feel like I've known a few months."

"He's a great man. He saved my life."

"A great man," Sally said, trying not to smile.

"Gentle Ben, that's right. After Frank split I was ready to just give up. Frank was my first love. I wanted to be with him the first time I saw him. Then again, I wanted to be with *every* guy the first time I saw them. I just wanted a guy. But once I got together with Frank I thought I'd never have any problems again. And when we had Randy I thought I was the happiest person alive. Although I don't know if I was really happy, or if I just thought I was happy because we had all the things that are supposed to make you happy. Anyway. What was the point I was trying to make? You didn't happen to notice my point around here?"

She got down on her hands and knees and peered under the couch. She stood up again and brushed off her skirt. "I'll find it when I vacuum."

"Ben saved your life."

"So you really were listening." Priscilla put her hand on Sally's shoulder. "You just made a friend for life. Yeah: when Frank walked out, I just wanted to curl up with a good book and die. I didn't even care about Randy. He could've eaten catfood for all I cared. I didn't feel like a mother. *I* needed a mother. If not for Ben, I don't know what I would have done. For about six months there, Ben *was* my mother, and Randy's mother too. If I had a car I'd clean off the dashboard and put up a little plastic statuette of that man."

"You do have a car, goddammit, and you've been talking about that statuette for the last two years. Put up or shut up already." Ben came in, with a little boy in his arms. "Sally Burke, this is Randolph McMahon."

Randy, who was about two and a half, turned his head away. Ben turned around so Randy was facing Sally again; he smiled at her shyly and hid his head on Ben's shoulder.

"He's in love with you," Priscilla said. "A fool could see."

"So, Pris, what's your story these days?" Still holding Randy, Ben sat on the couch.

"I'm storyless, Ben. Sad but true."

"What did you do today, for instance?"

"I've just been trying to clean this house. It's been driving me bananas. I like to listen to music when I do the chores—I bought a tape of that Elvis Costello album, the first one, but the only song I really like is 'Alison.' So before I could finish polishing up the soup spoons I'd have to stop the tape and rewind it. So finally I just made a tape of that one song, over and over again, and now I can clean the house for an hour and just keep listening to that."

Ben nodded. He looked like he was just taking it in, but Sally could see that he was a little worried. She wasn't even sure how she knew.

"It's a fine song," he said. "I like it too. Sometimes I just lie in bed and listen to it for a month at a time."

Priscilla laughed. Sally liked the way he'd handled that.

She felt intimate with him. She curled her feet under her on the couch. It was as if he was a brother, but a brother with a sexual tinge.

They hadn't slept together yet; she wasn't sure they would. They kept not getting started. First he'd had a long vacation; now his union was sending him to Ohio, maybe for as long as three months.

But it wasn't just circumstance that held them back. For her part, she was afraid. Her years with Owen still lay heavily on her brain. She was afraid to get involved again unless she was sure, even though she knew that was probably too much to ask.

Sometimes she wished Ben would just sweep aside her doubts—just jump on her. But he wouldn't do that. Maybe he was so politically correct that he thought it was sexist to make a good honest pass at a woman. Or maybe he sensed her fear, and respected it.

So, in its slow development, it was like a nineteenth-century courtship. And she had to admit there was something she liked about this. Actually getting to know someone before you went to bed with him—it was an idea so long-forgotten it was almost revolutionary.

"So, Pris," Ben said, "you seeing any eligible bachelors these days?"

"Well, there's a few guys on the horizon . . . a few ships on the horizon, loaded with treasure. But it's kind of hard to find someone who could put up with me."

"Put up with what? You're not so bad, Pris. You got them wide hips."

"Yeah. A woman with a kid, no degree, no money, no prospects, macrobiotic, neurotic . . . everybody's dream date."

She ran her hand through her hair. Sally felt sheltered, untouched by life.

"Maybe they could get me onto the 'Dating Game,' " Priscilla said. "I sure could go for that Bachelor Number Three."

"Number Three's the man?"

"Number Three's always some foreign French guy. He could teach me a thing or two about loving, I'm sure of that."

They drove to a park nearby, in Priscilla's car. It was an old Thunderbird. "I bought this thing used and Ben fixed it up."

"You know how to fix cars?" Sally said.

"What doesn't he know?" Ben said.

"I still feel lean and mean when I drive this thing," Priscilla said. "I feel like I'm heading for a date with Elvis Presley."

In the park Ben sat Randy on a swingseat and gave him a careful push.

"I forgot the smoke," Pris said.

"You want a Lucky?" Sally said.

But Pris was already on her way to the car. "She doesn't smoke cigarettes. We're going to get high."

"Benjamin McMahon? The Big Train himself, smoking dope?"

"I smoke when I see Pris. She likes it, so what the hell."

She squeezed his arm. "You're a little more flexoid than I thought."

The three of them passed the joint back and forth, standing in the cold, as Randy wobbled off toward a little castle.

The park changed. It wasn't a hokey park anymore; nature seemed ancient again.

She walked away, sat on one of those little wooden merry-go-rounds. She propelled it with one foot, spun around slow.

Big Bad Ben. She looked over at him, in his largeness. He was standing with his hands in the pockets of his suede jacket; the tip of his nose was red from the cold. Pris had her hands in her pockets too; the wind put some of her hair in her mouth as she spoke. They were talking quietly; Sally couldn't hear what they were saying. Ben had a smile of interest on his face. Randy was crawling around through the wooden castle, through an ascending passageway that led to a slide. Priscilla and Ben never entirely took their eyes off him as they talked . . . and she marveled that she was old enough to be part of this. You never quite shake off your past. She was sitting in a park, high on marijuana, just as she'd been a hundred times in high school, with Beth or Jesse. But now she was sitting in a park high on marijuana while her friends kept an eye on a child. She'd thought that adulthood, having a kid, meant graduating into the past—the past that existed when you were growing up, the Ozzie and Harriet past. But that isn't what happens. Everything you ever were, you remain.

Priscilla. Old and young. The way she'd blurted out half the secrets of her life seemed like something only a young person would do. But then again, she had a child; she had responsibilities more grave than Sally could imagine.

A single mother. How *would* Priscilla find a decent man? There was a big man shortage out there.

Priscilla was talking; Ben was biting his lower lip; he looked as if he was about to tease her. Sally felt she should join them, but she wanted to hang back for another minute and watch, just look, be apart. Big Ben. He seemed the paragon of virtue, going around helping in people's lives. A Johnny Appleseed of moral acts. She still didn't have a clear sense of where he was in all this—Ben himself, the inner man. He seemed a creature of pure aid, a kind of overweight, masculine Florence Nightingale. She could have this man if she wanted him. He had beautiful generous lips, a nice enough face. She could probably come to love him, maybe.

Pris had a birdlike body, an arched back; she walked with delicate steps. Ben said something that made her laugh, and she skipped a little—she skipped back two steps and skipped forward again, with girlish grace. For a moment she sloughed off her worries, she was young. And Sally smiled at Ben's goodness, his purity. He was like a greathearted oafish giant in a fairy tale. Oafish, because he didn't even realize that Pris was in love with him.

56

Hannah Burke had gone mad. This was Sally's conclusion.

After their kids leave home, many couples move to someplace smaller. Hannah had her heart set on a twelve-room house.

"What on earth do you want to move for?" It seemed to Sally that she was forever trying to dampen her mother's youthful enthusiasms.

"I'm telling you, Sally, you have to see this place."

So Sally saw this place.

Hannah had a friend who was in real estate—she was a "real estate mongol," as Hannah put it. Sometimes Hannah went around with her on weekends, looking at houses, just for fun. And two weeks ago, as she'd told Sally, "I saw my dream house."

The house was huge and ancient—built in 1760. They went there with Hannah's real estate friend, who was also named Sally, and trooped from room to room to room, twelve grim rooms in all, grim because she didn't understand what had come over her mother, each grim room with its grim little fireplace and its grim little smell of the past. For all she knew it was a magnificent house. It was hard to see it. All she knew was that her folks had lived in the same place for almost twenty years now and she didn't understand the point of this.

They were accompanied on their tour by the owner's little gray terrier, Bob. Sally concentrated most of her attention on him. Bob, a refined dog, a dog with manners, stayed slightly ahead of the group, ushering them from room to room. They'd seen every room in the house and started for the basement, Bob still in the lead. But when the other Sally opened the door, he drew back, whining.

"What's the matter, fuzzy?" Sally said, kneeling and scratching his head.

"It's strange," said the other Sally. "Every time I show this place, he hangs back at the basement. But the basement is perfectly fine. Totally dry. Come on."

They went down to the basement, and it was perfectly fine, to their human eyes.

When Sally and Hannah got out of the place and walked toward Hannah's car, Hannah was staggering slightly, drunk with joy. It was embarrassing—Sally felt as if she'd just met her mother's lover. "What do you think?" Hannah said.

When they were in the house, Sally hadn't spoken to anyone but the dog. She turned to her mother. "I think you're out of your fucking skull."

Hannah looked stunned. "How could you not love it? It's so gracious! It's so spacious!"

"So what it's spacious! You need to move to a fucking castle? What do you *need* all that room for? You need room for a torture chamber? You need a hall for fucking jousting tournaments?"

"But, Sally! It's a landmark! It's been declared a landmark by the federal landmarks commission! It's in the Library of

Congress! It was built in 1760—before even your father was born! George Washington may have slept there, Sally! Think of it!"

Hannah was besotted.

"Does Dad want to move?"

"Dad won't even notice. He just has to get off at a different bus stop."

"So he doesn't want to move."

"I don't think he cares one way or another. But he'll love the house after a while. He's kind of an amateur historian. It was made for him. Sally, we'll be as happy as kings!"

When they got back home, Burke was sitting in his easy chair, doing the crossword puzzle. He lifted up his glasses. "So, Sarah, you took the grand tour?"

"Yep."

"What did you think?"

"Well, it's certainly large. Have you seen it?"

"I've seen it in my mind's eye, through the lyrical descriptions provided by your mother."

The old cat cruised slowly into the room. Slowly, majestically, he crouched at the foot of the couch on which Sally sat, measuring the distance, and he jumped onto the pad beside her.

Sally picked up the cat's brush from the coffee table and brushed him. He purred, arching his back with pleasure. He had become loving, almost docile, in his old age. Though not completely. After she brushed him for a while he bit her, which signified that he wanted her to stop. Then he curled up, resting against her hip, and went to sleep.

He was twelve years old. He walked stiff-legged, slowly; he rarely went out. Mostly he sat around, sleeping and eating.

"He's lost all interest in life," Sally said.

"That's the problem with early retirement," Burke said.

Sally spent most of the afternoon giving her tenderest attentions to the cat. She was mad at her mother, and she didn't understand why.

Everything that Hannah did annoyed her. She never seemed to be in control of her life. Her eternal vows to clean the house. But how could she clean the house if she couldn't throw anything away? If you went down to the basement you could find everything Hannah had ever owned—spurs from an ill-fated horseback riding lesson at Camp Kinderland in 1936; sandals she'd worn when she worked on a kibbutz for a few months in 1949, and couldn't bring herself to part with.

Her eternal dieting. She announced proudly that she had lost five pounds, through a new method. During the day she observed the Dick Gregory diet—nothing but fruit juice; "and after five o'clock, I eat anything I want." She said this as she sat down on the couch with a spoon in one hand and a pint of Häagen-Dazs in the other.

"Mom."

"It doesn't matter how you get the calories, it's the amount. And even with the ice cream I'm burning enough calories to lose ten pounds in the next month. That's my goal. I'll have you know I lost three pounds this week."

"You know, Mom, in the last ten years you've lost five thousand pounds."

She didn't understand why her mother was so hot to buy the house. She didn't understand why she was so upset by her mother's desire to buy the house. She didn't understand anything.

It was a gray day. Sally sat by the window. All the lights were on. She was trying to read *The Rainbow*. She loved the book, but today she was bored by the incantatory rhythms. And she beat him off, she beat him off. Where could he turn, like a swimmer in a dark sea, beaten off from his hold, whither could he turn? He wanted to leave her, he wanted to be able to leave her. For his soul's sake, for his manhood's sake, he must be able to leave her. The monotony of it seeped down the wrong tube of her brain and made her feel as if the grayness of the day would be eternal. It was the same feeling she used to have on certain rainy Sunday afternoons of her childhood, when there was nothing on TV, nothing to do, nothing to think. You'd be desperate for something to take you out of your mood, so you'd finally turn on the TV and endure whatever was on. Usually it was something about giant radioactive crabs chasing people around the desert, cornering them in a cave, to the accompaniment of incongruously sluggish music.

Hannah was making phone calls, crowing to her friends about the house.

"It has the original beams. They say George Washington slept there. There's a mysterious passageway in the basement that leads to nowhere. I think it was probably used to hide runaway slaves during the Underground Railroad."

"Your mother has become a history buff," Burke observed.

It started to rain. Burke lapsed back into his puzzle. A spectral presence. His quietness frightened her: when she'd visited lately, he'd seemed too subdued. He seemed resigned to dwindling into mineral form. He did the crossword; occasionally he looked over his glasses at some instant replay on the tube; but there seemed to be no spark there, no sign of life. It scared her. She wanted to say: "Do not go gentle into the night, Dad."

Say it—say *something*. Why not say something? She couldn't. That's why not.

The weather. A variety of weather doom. The weather made her feel as if there was no point to life: whether you worked hard didn't matter, whether you found someone to love didn't matter, because even if you worked hard and found someone to love, a day like this would come, when a strange damp coolness seeped in through the windowpanes and seeped in through you, making you see that everything was meaningless.

And the mood of the day finally made itself so baleful that even Hannah was subdued. She grew quiet, she grew pensive, and instead of making a real dinner she asked if anyone minded if she ordered pizza, and the three of them ate in a silence that Sally thought of as desultory, even though she knew it wasn't the right word.

So they ate in a desultory silence. The TV was still on in the living room, but Burke switched on the one in the kitchen. Leonid Brezhnev had died that day, at the age of around six hundred; Sally didn't care about this, but she was surprised that her parents didn't seem to care about it either. She would have expected them to show at least a bit of interest. After the news there was a special about a woman who had chosen her own death: she was terminally ill, so she chose to take an overdose of morphine. She discussed it with her family and friends, she set a date, she made her loving farewells, and she died as she wanted to die.

It didn't interest Sally much, but her parents watched it in silence, with absorption.

After dinner Sally hunted around in the bookcases, looking at Hannah's books on education. There was nothing recent—it was all stuff Sally had already read. *Teaching as a Subversive Activity; The Way It Spozed to Be; How Children Fail.* The faded classics of sixties idealism.

For the rest of the night they watched television. This was what her parents did with their lives. Cultivated people, dedicated to overarching social ideals, able conversationalists . . . they had somehow been reduced to spending most nights in front of the tube.

After her parents went to sleep, she stole some cigarettes from the pack Burke had left in the kitchen. She had been filching her father's cigarettes for almost ten years. She tried to do it discreetly, but she couldn't always control herself: sometimes he left a pack with five cigarettes in it when he went to bed, and she couldn't stop herself from smoking four. He never said a word. And she never knew whether it was just his famous obliviousness—whether he really didn't notice—or whether he did notice, and saw it the way she saw it: as a small communion, a secret sharing.

She stole a few cigarettes and went outside. The night was misty. Without knowing where she wanted to go, she got into her parents' car and drove slowly through town. She didn't even realize where she was going until she was there . . . outside the other house.

The house had an enormous yard, and it was across the street from a park, so it was all alone. She sat in the car with the window open, smoking cigarettes and staring at the house. Trying to understand why it disturbed her.

Sally flicked her cigarette into the street, put her head back against the headrest, and closed her eyes. It was cool here, and it was silent. The only sound was the wind. With her eyes closed she tried to concentrate her mind; when she opened them she looked again at the house, its wide, quiet, dark lawn. The sight made her shiver. She understood.

The house was death, yes?

That made it a little clearer. The house was death.

A picture of the cat came into her head, the gentlemanly cat. The cat was old: to get to your lap from where he stood beside you on the couch required a complex strategy, a tricky climb. To get used to a new home, to face down the dangers of a new neighborhood—that would be altogether beyond him. In one stroke, the cat, old enough as he was, would turn ancient.

But you don't put off plans you've set your heart on just because they might discomfit the cat. And the fate of the cat, she understood, was not what disturbed her. What disturbed her was that the house would bring the death of her father.

This realization was no realization at all: all it meant was that her father was old. What did it matter where they were living? It's not as if the house would make him any older.

It was just that the house her parents lived in now had been the site of so much of their lives. He had been young when they moved there, still in his forties. In that house he'd still dressed up as Santa Claus, for a year or two; in that house he'd received the offer to become the head of his union; in that house he and Hannah had made love.

If he died in that house he'd be dying in a place that had seen him through much of his life: that had been fit for growth, fit for the increase in strength and mastery. The house she looked out on now had seen nothing of this: all it would ever see of him was his old age—his weakness and his weariness and his sleepiness, the slackening of his will.

So now she knew. She lit another cigarette and looked out at the old stone house. She'd thought that if she reached the source of what bothered her about the house, then the house would cease to bother her. But it bothered her just as much now. She knew that her disquiet was irrational; she knew that her real fears had nothing to do with the house. But the realization of what her real fears were hadn't made the place any less dreadful.

The clock on the dashboard made it half past two. Why was she always awake when the rest of the world was asleep? She always seemed to be the last person on earth.

There was nothing mystical or mysterious about the house. It was nothing but wood and stone. But to her, it was the future. And though the future would come no matter where her parents lived, that house, blank of any relations with her father, seemed to embody that future starkly.

At a quarter to three, Sally sat in the car, smoking, staring with dread at a house that was really nothing more than a house. While her father, the man who held the world together, turned in his sleep.

57

Three months later, the move was history. The cat hadn't batted an eye. The move had made him young again: he made his way over every inch of the house, sniffing intently, pausing to impress certain key scents on his memory. Hannah as usual tried to keep him locked up in the kitchen, but now his wish to escape was born not merely from his pride but from his thirst for knowledge, and so he grew adept again at the old forgotten art of leaping barricades.

There were other cats in the neighborhood, glimpsed by Sally briefly and from far away; Napoleon quickly established himself as the ruler of the land. During their first few weeks there he would wait at the door to be let out, trot out gracefully, and disappear into a bush; within minutes hissing and snarling would come. Finally all pretenders had been cleared away, and Napoleon could be found every afternoon sitting at a little distance from the swimming pool, blinking with a pleasurable somnolence in the sun.

Burke hadn't helped out with the move: he didn't even see the new house until the week before they moved there. "Very nice," was his comment. But once they were there, he seemed to flourish. The house had three fireplaces, and he became the keeper of the fire. Carrying the logs in from the porch on a frosty day, he moved with the caution of a fragile old man, but still with a certain grace. Stepping pigeon-toed over the crusty ground, he had the grace of the former athlete who knows his limitations and moves smoothly within them. With his habit of devotion to the smallest details, he was a pleasure to watch as he made the fire, peering cautiously into the fireplace as the fire caught on, fanning the embers with the bellows Sally had bought him as his housewarming present, and then, when he was satisfied that the fire would last, removing neatly his blackened pigskin gloves. Once the fire was made, reading or doing the crossword or watching TV, he would stay near it for the rest of the evening.

When the summer came, he took a few Fridays off, and sat by the pool for most of the long weekend, reading and smoking and enjoying the quiet. He and Hannah had breakfast and supper outdoors most weekends when the weather was fine; when Sally visited, which she did more often now, she marveled at the change in him. Early one evening they sat at the picnic table near the pool, finishing dinner—Hannah had picked up coleslaw and potato salad at the deli and grilled some hamburgers and hot dogs. Burke poured his daughter some ginger ale—she never drank soda but she made an exception now, for the sheer foolish pleasure of having her father pour it for her. She had never seen him so relaxed. In his old age, he had sailed into an extraordinary mildness. She knew that her father had accomplished a great deal in his life: as an organizer he'd walked into many hopeless situations and turned them into victories, into little monuments to what the power of solidarity can do. But now he'd accomplished a transformation beyond all the others, a transformation she would never have dreamed possible. He had turned himself into a man who could enjoy old age.

Most of the credit for the transformation, of course, went to Burke himself, and Hannah. But surely some little part of it—the stage on which the transformation could show itself, complete itself—was this large, long, ancient, dreamy, many-windowed house. Sally held her cup forward as her father poured her some more ginger ale. You never know about things. You never do know. . . .

58

They lay together in a field in Central Park.

They still had not yet made love.

The park in the middle of the city: structured greenness, structured nature. And Sally and Ben structured as well.

Their lying together in the field was one event in a structured sequence of events whose meaning and end were known. They would be sleeping together soon.

Neither of them could turn to the other and say, "Both of us know we'll be sleeping together soon, right?" But though it was impossible to comment on the existence of the preordained sequence, both of them knew that it existed.

They were in Sheep Meadow, a beautiful wide green field. Signs around the field informed you that it was only for quiet activities. Picnickers, Frisbee throwers, couples on blankets.

"We're having quiet fun," Sally said.

The summer air was hot, wet, shaggy. They lay about ten inches apart. Between their bodies was a slight field of friction. At any moment, in the middle of a sentence, he might stop talking and bring his lips to her lips. But the moment had not yet come, and until it came it would seem impossible: a violation, almost, of the laws of nature.

They were talking, about nothing: talking just to talk, savoring the deliciousness of anticipation. Ben was telling her an anecdote from his childhood, but she wasn't really listening: she was watching the way his lips moved as he spoke.

She smiled up at him, shielding her eyes with her hand. There was a silence. Stretched out on the soft grass, her lips a little parted, she felt eminently kissable. She felt young, she felt alive.

Ben's face was inches from hers. She was no longer a human being: she was a quality: she was readiness personified. She had no idea how he kissed . . . he might have any kiss in the world. Soon she would know.

"Big Train?" she said. "What's your biggest wish?" Just to talk.

"My biggest wish?" He pulled a spear of grass from the earth. "My biggest wish . . . is a world where people could work together, with nobody pushing anyone else around."

Strike up the band. McMAHON DECLARES HOPES FOR LABOR HARMONY.

She felt suddenly deflated.

"What's your biggest wish?"

She tried to think, but she couldn't. All she could think about was the question of why his biggest wish struck her as so lame.

It was so *public*. No intimacy. If he kissed you, you'd feel like you were being kissed by the entire political action committee of Local 259 of the Amalgamated Clothing and Textile Workers Union.

She was sure that at another time she'd be able to think of her biggest wish. But now she was feeling deflated. "Oh . . . I don't know."

And now she knew that they weren't going to kiss each other, not today, maybe not ever.

He seemed to know it too. He sat up and reached over to his backpack.

She wondered what he thought had happened. She knew what had happened on her end: what had happened on his?

He zipped open his pack and brought out a plastic bag filled with large purple grapes.

"You don't know how I suffered during the boycott," he said.

She sat up and brushed the grass from her jeans. She was smiling. "Union man," she said. "From the shine of his bald spot to the tip of his toes."

This is what happens when you get to know someone. What used to be said in admiration is said with a trace of a sneer.

Doom.

She wrapped her arms around her knees. "Have you thought about the fact that you'll die on one particular date? That you have a deathday, just like a birthday, only you don't know it yet?"

"It's nice to have you around to remind me of Last Things," Ben said. He snapped off some grapes and put them in her hand. Her reflection seemed not to have wowed him. Maybe he was as tired of her shtick as she was of his.

"Maybe every year you get a premonition on that day, but it's so subtle you don't know what it is. A little dizzy spell."

"Could be," Ben said. "Could very well be."

59

Beth came closer in slow motion, like someone in a commercial.

Sally saw that she shouldn't have come.

Beth's hair was short and bobbed; she was wearing a skirt-suit and running shoes; she was a businessman.

Then they embraced. Beth's embrace was as strong as ever, and Sally was glad she was here.

The summer was almost over. Sally was taking a trip, a whirlwind tour of some of her female friends. Beth in Chicago; then Caitlin, her dancer friend from Sarah Lawrence, in Pennsylvania.

Sally was cramped and sore from the train ride, so she wanted to walk for a while. Beth took her bag. She was bigger than Sally, but not as strong; as she set off with it, she tilted. They walked toward Beth's apartment, along the park, near Lake Shore Drive.

Beth was speaking excitedly about law school. Sally still trying to absorb the fact that she was in Chicago, city of big shoulders—she'd never been there before; but Beth gave no quarter: she was off on a tale about how brilliantly she had performed in moot court.

The sun was coming down over Lake Whachamacallit. Sally had momentarily spaced out on its name, and Beth hadn't paused for breath.

Sally was thinking that their friendship was over. This was the sure sign of its death. After Beth stopped speaking about her life, Sally would speak of *her* life, and Beth would listen, saying little, as Sally was saying little now. When conversation collapses into two monologues, you can be sure friendship is dead.

"The judge said he'd never seen such an uppity woman," Beth said. "If he could've made it stick he would have held me in contempt."

"What happens then? They throw you in moot jail?"

They walked two by two by two by two, at the head of a procession of ghosts. The ghosts of who they'd been.

Beth stopped to tie her shoe, and Sally stopped, and all the ghosts behind them stopped as well. Sally took the opportunity to turn and look at the long line of them, and she noticed a curious thing. All of her own ghosts were basically the same as she was now. All of them were unhappy, because they didn't know what they wanted.

All of Beth's ghosts were sure of what they wanted: and that was the only thing they had in common. The earliest of the ghosts was swearing she'd never get married. The next ghost, the college ghost, was saying that the key to life was living on a lesbian separatist commune in Northampton. And today's Beth, bouncing exuberantly in her Adidas, was talking about the University of Chicago Law School as if it were wider and more populous with luminaries than the Milky Way.

All the ghosts of Sally, meanwhile, were girding themselves

to ask the big question. This was her role. The big question was always different; but there was always a big question. Why are you so sure you won't change your mind about marriage? Or: Why are you so sure that all men are oppressors? Or: today: What the hell are you doing with your life? Why law school?

"Steve saved my life this year," Beth said. She was talking about her boyfriend. "Saved, my, life. He's very real-world-oriented, and when I start to flip out about school he's like, 'Will you cut it out? Don't you know how meaningless it is?'"

"If it's so meaningless . . . ," weighty pause, ". . . why are you doing it?"

They walked on without saying anything. Beth watched the ground, with that old expression Sally loved, that "to think is to be full of sorrow" look. As if she were taking care not to step on any defenseless insects.

Sally's question had disturbed her. Beth had lost her bounce. But that was good. Sally's job was to rid the world of false bounce.

"I'm just trying to survive, Sally."

She looked anguished, as if law school had been the only alternative to certain death.

"Did the SS give you a cruel choice? Attend the University of Chicago Law School or lose your son?"

"What *should* I be doing? What do *you* advise?" She considered Sally with a rude smile, as if she might as well ask career advice from a baboon.

"I don't advise anything, but I think there must be something you want to do more than be a lawyer. You used to be such an idealist. I'm sure the law pays well, but so what? It just seems so *boring*. It's like moving to Florida."

"Just because I'm not committed to living on bread crumbs doesn't mean I'm not still an idealist. I'm just as much of a feminist as I was in college. Did you know that less than half of one percent of all corporate law partners are women? If I become a partner, I'll be a role model. And feminism is about role models. Feminism is about women and power."

"You know, when Maggie Thatcher conquered the Falklands, that just made my day. That was the greatest thing for the women's movement since *The Second Sex*. And wasn't it glorious when Indira Gandhi showed you didn't have to be a man to put an entire country under martial law? If only there could be a woman Hitler . . ."

"Oh, Sally, you're really such an asshole sometimes. Are you aware of that?"

"I'm aware of that," Sally said. "I'm perfectly aware."

They could still enjoy their arguments: that was something. But she wondered whether they were friends only because they had been friends.

Beth's apartment was on the fifteenth floor, with an astonishing view of the lake. In the black of the evening, the lake was filled with tiny moving lights.

"Do you ever just unplug the phone and sit here and watch the boats?"

"I'd love to, but I never have the time."

It was painful to turn away from the view. A huge color TV, two VCRs, a souped-up state-of-the-art stereo/cassette deck, track lighting with dimmers, an extensive bar.

As Sally stood there scowling in judgment on all this, she was vaguely aware that she'd become the kind of person you don't want to invite to your house.

Beth worked out at a health club; in the summer she went to the islands and in the winter she skied; she was as scrupulous as ever about her eight hours' sleep; she looked great. Sally looked all right, but she didn't look great. She didn't like to exercise and she was one of the last people on earth who smoked—cigarettes, marijuana, whatever you got. If I'm still so morally questing and she's not, shouldn't I look better? Shouldn't it show?

They walked around, they ate out, they called out for Chinese food, they watched romantic comedies on the VCR, they gossiped about old friends, they lay on Beth's bed and looked at catalogs. They avoided the difficult subjects.

In the background, looming balefully, was the shadowy figure of Beth's boyfriend. His name was Steve; Beth called him "Stee." Which irritated Sally, for some reason.

Steve was a corporate lawyer. He was older. He was in SDS in the sixties; he was teargassed at the Chicago convention; he'd gone to law school so he could fight for poor people's rights; and then, one summer vacation, as he was traveling on the road to Damascus, an angel appeared before him, holding up a big dollar sign.

Beth wasn't normally easy to influence. So Sally wondered if she was just looking for someone to blame. But she couldn't help feeling that she wouldn't have taken the corporate road if not for "Stee." He was in California, sewing up a big deal. But he'd be coming back the day before Sally left. So they'd spend one evening together. Just to think of it made her stomach secrete sour juices.

The bout was held on a drizzly evening in late August. The usual crowd of celebs was at ringside: Norman Mailer; Joyce Carol Oates; Jack Nicholson—badly in need of a shave.

Sally came into the ring first, shadowboxing, while Angelo Dundee went over the strategy. Stick and run; stick and run. Don't go toe-to-toe too soon.

A roar went up through the crowd. Stee swept down the aisle, surrounded by toadies and photographers. Red-white-and-blue trunks. He danced into the ring, waving, clowning, confident. His hair was perfect.

The three of them were in a dark little Thai restaurant that Stee had "discovered" during his law school days. Stee was already there when Sally and Beth arrived. He quickly made Sally ill at ease by mentioning scornfully that the people at the next table had asked for chopsticks. "*Chop*sticks in a Thai restaurant."

And Sally, despite all her resolve to take him on, found herself joining in an initiate's smile of disdain, as if she too could think of nothing so vulgar as asking for chopsticks in a Thai restaurant.

Stee was handsome: tall, racquetballishly athletic. During the meal it was established that he'd received his BA at Harvard, that he was fluent in French, that he preferred Bach to Mozart and *L'Education Sentimentale* to *Madame Bovary*. He didn't actually *say* any of this; but he somehow let it be known.

Sally felt outclassed, and it made her afraid to cross him. She had this discreditable thought: I wish Ben was here. He'd put this faker in his place.

"Where do your journeys take you next?" Stee said. "Now that you've done Chicago."

"I'm visiting a friend, a Sarah Lawrence type, in Pennsylvania, then back to New York."

"And when you get there?"

"Back to the old grindstone. I'm teaching first grade this year."

"And you're going to stay with that job indefinitely?"

"Until I think of something better to do."

"I should think you'd be able to think of a thousand better things."

"Such as?"

"Anything more in keeping with your natural inclinations."

This rudeness was so sudden and so unexpected that she forgot she was afraid of him. "Why do you think you know what my natural inclinations *are*?"

"Well, I don't know anything about *you*. But everyone

seeks to maximize their own existence, and by working for coolie wages you're not maximizing anything. You're going against nature."

Beth looked as if she wanted to be far away. There was a candle burning at their table; she ran her finger up the side of it, gathering the hot soft wax on her nail.

"Against nature?" Sally said. "I didn't realize that chipmunks and beavers could be observed competing for those hefty paychecks in the wild."

She was sweating wildly. She wasn't very good at arguing. She wasn't very good at arguing against men.

"Actually they can. They forage in the places that have the greatest yield. You won't find a chipmunk making a martyr of itself and going hungry out of altruism. But I'm talking about human nature. The essence of which is to pursue one's self-interest."

She looked at Beth. "Survival of the fittest," Beth muttered with a tight smile. This meant nothing. It was Beth's way of distancing herself slightly from Stee without saying anything to challenge him. What would she say if Sally asked her opinion flat-out? She was afraid to ask.

"Maybe you're right about a certain kind of person. But some people value other things above self-interest. I've got a friend, a union organizer, I think he's sincere, who'd probably say he values the common good. I can't hold myself up as an example, because I can't really say I know what I'm doing with my life. But I do know I'd rather be teaching some kid to read than helping some company devour another company. Can you really go home at the end of the day and feel *proud* of what you do?"

He'd attacked her first, so she had a right to attack him back. But as soon as she'd spoken she felt the tears come to her eyes.

Stee was smiling at her: lazy-lidded, calm, condescending. "Even if the common good *is* your goal, I'm not sure you're in a position to lecture me. I'm about to become a partner, in a fairly well-regarded law firm. In a few years, without false modesty, I should be rather powerful. A powerful person can *do* . . . a martyr can only whine. Andrew Carnegie was a businessman and a capitalist and a robber baron and any number of other dreadful things, but precisely because he had power, he could build libraries and universities—and thereby do more for education than all the martyrs of his time, who undoubtedly despised him, and whose names have been mercifully forgotten."

Beth didn't say anything: she just sat there looking uncomfortable, pushing a piece of rice around with her fork.

If his point was that he planned to become a philanthropist, Sally didn't believe him. But she couldn't really argue with him either. She could have worked up some rap about the sanctity of the teacher's calling, but it wouldn't have been an honest representation of who she was. She wasn't that committed to teaching: it was a job she felt good about, but it was a job.

Stee reached for the wine and refilled everyone's glass. He had an excruciatingly self-satisfied look on his face. The conqueror. The new Andrew Carnegie. Sally cast about for a devastating rejoinder, but she couldn't find one. She was tongue-tied. She felt tears coming on again, tears of frustration—but she was damned if she'd let him see her cry. As he leaned toward her, pouring out the wine, she smacked him in the face.

After this, her mind went blurry; the table, the dishes, the glasses seemed to be sliding away. Someone called for the check. Her first sensation, after her head cleared, was a desire to abase herself, beg his forgiveness, crawl. She managed to repress it.

Stee insisted on paying; casually flipping his credit card

onto the table, he wore a calm, sardonic smile, as if he were holding a few withering remarks in reserve.

Beth was staying at his place; Sally was spending the night, her last in Chicago, alone at Beth's. When they said goodbye, Sally and Beth shared a long embrace. What it meant, whether it meant anything, she didn't know.

At the end of the night she sat on Beth's couch, alone, with the lights out, watching the boats on the lake. She wasn't pleased with herself. If she could have defeated him with words, she would have. The slap was an admission of ignorance. An admission that she didn't know what she was living for.

60

Caitlin was living with her husband and daughter in Valley Forge, Pennsylvania.

Howard was away for the weekend, which was just as well. Sally liked him a lot; but with the mood she was in, if they'd gotten into a serious discussion, she might have slapped him too. Howard was in advertising, and he liked to corner you and tell you that all the true artists today are making commercials. He used to particularly enjoy telling this to Owen.

Andrea, fourteen months old, was fanatically attached to her mother. If Caitlin looked away, Andrea cried out. Whenever Caitlin had to leave the room for a minute, she surrounded Andrea with a fortress of toys. Andrea examined each toy and tossed it aside with disgust. It took her about thirty seconds to go through ten toys; then she screamed for her mother.

"She's been like this from the beginning," Caitlin said. "It's interesting. Maybe I've played into it, but I really don't think I made her this way. You really are born with certain qualities."

Sally and Caitlin were in the living room, stretched out on separate couches, with tea and cookies on the table between them. Sally admired Caitlin's long legs, her long, capable hands. Caitlin was the only woman whom Sally sometimes felt faint stirrings for.

Andrea, sitting on the rug, performing obscure procedures on the disembodied head of Yogi Bear, looked like the most serious person on earth.

"Life is strange," Caitlin was saying. "Who would ever have thought I'd end up a housewife? Sometimes I walk along the street thinking, 'Life is amazing! I'm a housewife!'"

She wasn't complaining—it was just her freelance wonder. This was what Sally loved about her.

When she laughed, or when she spoke about something that evoked her sense of awe, she looked as beautiful as ever; but when she fell silent she looked as if life was grinding her down. She'd finally given up on her ambition of being a dancer. She'd been injured too many times.

"You haven't ended up as anything," Sally said. "You're twenty-six years old."

"I know—I'm a fairly youthful human being. But when I try to think of what I want to do with my life . . . I can't think of anything. I feel like all the creativity has been drained out of me. Not that I was so creative in the first place. But I used to have this tremendous *desire* to be creative. Now it's like I don't really want to do anything."

Sally sipped her tea. It was hard to hear this. It was painful to think of Caitlin not wanting anything. For as long as Sally had known her, with her perpetual self-improvement projects giving her perpetual headaches because of how little she'd accomplished so far, she'd always seemed the personification of the desire to become. What she wanted to become might have changed from week to week, but finally that didn't matter: it was the sheer joy of becoming that had thrilled her.

Well, now she was a mother. That was that.

Caitlin looked beautiful, but tired, tired. It was hard for

Sally to imagine her life. Never having a moment for your-self . . . not having a self anymore, in the old sense.

"Have you thought about the fact that she'll have to take care of your funeral arrangements someday?"

"Not really, but thank you for mentioning it. I do like to think about all the traumas I'm giving her, even now. She'll spend years on a psychiatrist's couch because of me. Because I'm the most important person in the world." She picked Andrea up and lay back on the couch and held her up at arm's length. "Am I the most important person in the world? More important than Albert Einstein? More important than Martin Luther King?" Andrea, in the air, was in raptures.

They drove to a park. In the car Sally brought Caitlin up to date on things with Ben.

"You know, when you talk about this guy, I can never fig-ure out what I think. Sometimes I think you're too good for him. But sometimes I think he's too good for you."

On the radio, John Fogerty sang, "Sometimes I think . . . life is just a rodeo."

"You know," Caitlin said, "that's what *I* think sometimes. That's what I think exactly."

In the park they walked toward a gazebo, crossing a long field. Caitlin was exulting in her ability to move—she'd just recovered from an ankle sprain. When she was a dancer she used to blame herself for all her injuries: she thought she didn't practice enough; but this time she'd simply slipped on an ice cube. "The beauty of pure accident," she said.

When they reached the gazebo, Caitlin immediately noticed the echo under the dome. "An echo! Hear the echo, Andie?" Excited, tense with attention, Andrea looked for the sound.

Sally was impressed with the way Caitlin was thinking for two.

Caitlin walked to the top of the hill, Andrea riding on her hip. She had that same long athletic stride she'd always had.

Caitlin would never be a dancer: her fifteen years of work had come to nothing. Years ago, when Sally admired Caitlin's walk, she'd thought it was obviously the walk of a future dancer. But Caitlin would never be a dancer. So the walk, as graceful and as full of freedom as ever, was now just the way she happened to walk. It said nothing about her future, her career, her fate. It was disheartening: her lovely loping long-legged walk, shorn like this of all significance. Caitlin would have to find something else to do. And she'd have to invent a new justifying mythology for it, a new understanding of her life, according to which everything she'd ever done had been done in secret unknown preparation for this calling.

The next day Caitlin drove Sally to the bus station.

"Well, you're off to further adventures," Caitlin said. "And I'm off to feed Andrea her snack."

She looked defeated, and Sally hated to see it. She wanted to say: "Don't you see that your adventures are more astonishing than mine? By the end of the day you'll have seen her learn to do something she's never done before. You'll have touched the central mystery of life."

She didn't say it, though. For she knew that in the course of a day, a mother doesn't feel close to the central mystery of life. All you know is that now you have to feed your child, now you have to change her, now you have to keep her occupied for a minute while you make a phone call, now you have to try and get her into bed.

So she didn't say anything. She just kissed Caitlin and said goodbye.

Later, after the bus started to move, it occurred to her that what she didn't say was exactly what Caitlin would have loved to hear. She felt inept, incompetent at friendship. She closed her eyes.

61

She was sitting near the bathroom of the crowded bus. After a few minutes, the funk of the bus got into her mind—the mixed smell of piss and disinfectant and bodies and gasoline exhaust. Her head felt large and oblong: the first faint traces of a fever.

Across the aisle was a woman in her late thirties with her son, a kid of about four or five. The woman's hair was long and unwashed; she wore a peasant blouse and a long print skirt. A superannuated flower child.

The son was a whiner. Mile after mile after mile after mile, he whined.

At issue was a pack of Strawberry Twinkies. He alleged that his mother had promised that he could eat them before Philadelphia. His mother, hereafter "the Defendant," held that the promise had been of Twinkies *in* Philadelphia. Plaintiff argued that he wanted a Twinkie. He wanted it, he wanted it, he wanna wanna wanna wanna, real bad. Plaintiff in addition climbed on Defendant's lap threatening to "Fart in your big fat face" if said Twinkie continued to be withheld.

"Ethan, you're hurting Mommy." Ethan was pinching her,

digging his nails with an evil precision into her arm. "Ethan, when you do that, you're hurting Mommy's arm." I think he gets the picture, Sally thought.

Ethan finally prevailed. The Twinkies were produced, he enjoyed them. "Can Mommy have a bite?" "No."

For two minutes, all was quiet. A middle-aged woman emerged from the bathroom and hurried up to the driver, gesticulating tragically; the driver nodded, unclipped his microphone from the dash, and told everyone that the toilet wasn't working, but that they'd have a chance to leave the bus if they needed to in Philadelphia.

"That means you can't make pee-pee until Philadelphia. You don't have to make pee-pee, do you?" said Mommy, running her fingers through Ethan's hair. He snapped his head back with annoyance.

Within minutes, Ethan was announcing his agonizing need to make pee-pee.

Sally got out her Walkman, put in *Planet Waves,* and fast-forwarded to "Hazel."

Dylan made her invisible. She watched. The more she watched the woman, the more she understood her. She'd come of age when the sixties got locked in that long bad skid . . . the acid years. A desiccated flower child, a detoxed hippie. She was thin, she was maybe even pretty; but with a haunted, ravaged edge. The bags under her eyes were permanent: she looked as if she needed ten years' sleep. But even if she got that ten years' sleep, she would wake from it groggy and unrefreshed.

She and Ethan were locked in mortal combat over a peanut butter and jelly sandwich. He clutched it; peanut butter oozed between his knuckles; she gripped his hands, exerting no force, but attempting through moral suasion to induce him to relinquish his claims.

Ethan, at the age of five, was doomed: he was an annoying

little bastard, and he'd be an annoying little bastard for the rest of his life.

This woman was a casualty. Sally, omniscient, knew this. A casualty of the sixties. She'd been young in a time in which everything was taken on trust: in which it was believed that if your heart was pure, no harm could find you. In which it was believed that if you lived fully in the moment, tomorrow would take care of itself.

She was the wreckage of that dream. Still wearing period clothing—a walking antique. Her face was gaunt: beaten down to the skull by acid, by pot, by angel dust, by a vast array of prescription drugs cunningly procured . . . you cunningly procure the substances that will retard you. She had placed her trust in experience for its own sake. She had placed her trust in some guy, who had spermed her and then walked out. And she was left with the refuse of the relationship, the refuse of her all-embracing trust, in the form of this bratty kid, the mirror and victim and punishment of his mother's innocence. Ethan was a casualty of the sixties too.

Sally believed that this woman's life was over. Her life had been shaped by certain premises; and the rest of her life was the unfolding of the logic of those premises. Even if she lived to be ninety, her life would be nothing more than the further monotonous unfolding of that logic. Thus spake Sally.

And yourself? What about you?

Except for a weak reading light here and there, the bus was dark. She looked at her face in the window. It had no lines.

She was twenty-six. No lines. Untouched by experience. Unformed.

The evil blossoming of her fever. She wondered if her own life was over as well. She had been formed by different currents than the ones that had formed Ethan's mother; but they were just as debilitating, and she'd bear the mark of them as long as she lived. Apocalyptic longings for what life might be, and utter cynicism about what it was. Scalding idealism, chill disenchantment, had mixed in her to make a tepid stream. If you refuse to commit yourself—to love, to work, to any cause, to anything or anyone but your own freedom—then you wind up a blank.

She hadn't even traveled in her life: she'd never been past St. Louis. Travel would have been defining. Her freedom consisted of the refusal of any commitment, the refusal to give herself.

She was another casualty. At the age of twenty-six, she'd reached the end of the line. Maybe this was her sole contribution: that she'd lived out a certain set of premises, and discovered that they led nowhere.

On her headphones, Dylan was hoping that she'd "stay forever young." He seemed to mean it as a benediction; it sounded more like a curse.

She got back to her apartment and dumped her things on the floor. She went through the mail: junk mail, bills. She sat on her couch and felt cold. It was August, but she felt cold.

That late-August loneliness was in the air. After two months of blistering heat, the weather had broken; suddenly the nights were chilly, that late-August chill that makes you feel hollow in the bones.

She went back out and took a subway to his place. Rang on his doorbell and found him there. He had his glasses up on the top of his head; he was holding a copy of *The Other America*.

"How were your journeys?" He looked happy to see her.

"I made a buffoon of myself in two different time zones."

"Well, I'm glad you've decided to come back and make a buffoon of yourself here."

She started to tell him about her trip, about her multiple

bemusements. But that wasn't why she'd come. She'd come to define herself. He made some tea, placed the cups on the coffee table, sat next to her on the couch and said, "Go on." Instead, she pulled the rubber band from her ponytail and shook out her hair so it fell loose around her shoulders, and she smiled at him. Whatever this meant, he understood it. He kissed her.

62

Dripping, wrapped in a towel, she walked toward the bed. Watching her come near, he drew a long breath. "Did anyone ever tell you," he said, "that you're the most beautiful woman in the Western world?"

She wasn't the most beautiful woman in the Western world, but she flourished under his gaze. She felt like some nineteenth-century city, just after the birth of electric light. On a cool Friday evening in late September, she came to his place after work. His apartment was cheerful, filled with light. From his window, over West End Avenue, you could see cars and people rushing along Broadway—you could take in all the dazzle of the city. They made dinner together, drinking wine and listening to music and talking. It felt utterly intimate; but at the same time she felt as if this apartment, this room, was at the heart of the city.

He saw her as unusual, he saw her as interesting. He thought about the things she said. Two days later he would say, "But on the other hand—"

It was astonishing, it was instructive, to see how things could change. Lying in bed with him on a Saturday morning, with no obligations and the weekend stretching endlessly ahead, she experienced a revelation that made her feel the equal of Einstein. She finally understood why people get together in couples. It's because it makes them happy.

Late on a Saturday night, for no reason, they decided to take a ride. They crossed the bridge and went north, alongside the wide dark river, and then turned off onto roads they didn't know. They'd been talking all night, and now there was a new kind of pleasure in silence. There are too many words in the world. Love is finding someone you can shut up with.

They found themselves near Bear Mountain; he parked the car and they walked until they came upon a small black lake. She took off her shoes and walked barefoot along a ledge of rocks over the water. She felt graceful. He walked a step or two behind her, awkwardly. Everything was quiet. The moon was on the water; they hadn't said a word for an hour; she felt as if the two of them were outside of time. He wasn't a man born on a certain day of a certain year: he was something more than that. She was more than her biography. She felt as if they were on the verge of great discoveries.

Walking with him through the city, her arm through his, she felt like a fortunate woman.

She worried that it couldn't last.

63

All the little boys this year had ancient names. In her mind, some of these six-year-olds were bearded scholars of the Talmud; others, majestic African kings. "Hannibal," she said, grabbing the roughest kid in class and hauling him in. "Stop smiting Noah."

She sat at home reading her students' diaries—they were learning to read and write at the same time. Each of them kept a diary, for Sally's eyes only. They were excited by the secrecy, the gravity of this; it helped them think of writing as something mysterious and thrilling. After reading each entry she would write a short question or comment on the bottom of the page. Below that, she would correct their spelling. She never circled their mistakes; she'd just write the words correctly at the bottom of the page. She wanted them to feel free when they wrote, reckless, not worried about mistakes.

All this—the diaries, the manner of correcting them—she'd picked up from her mother.

When Ben was in the neighborhood, he'd sometimes drop in on the classroom. The children were wild about him, mostly because he was so large. If he made the mistake of sitting down they'd swarm all over him, hoisting themselves up onto his lap.

One girl walked up to him and stood there scowling, with her hands on her hips: she looked as if she was about to ask him for two forms of identification. Ben said, "Hello, Winnie."

Winnie was amazed. "Howjou know my name?"

"You look like a Winnie," Ben said.

The truth was that he'd recognized her from Sally's description.

The idea of a romance between Ben and Sally was thrilling to the children—scandalous. "Ben likes Miss Burke! He likes Miss Burke!"

With this man, with these children around her, she was almost beginning to feel as if she had a life.

64

"I've had it."

On a Saturday morning in September, Burke was complaining.

"I think it's just about time to pack it all in. It's time to move to Surrey and keep bees. Are you ready to live in Surrey, honey?"

"Uh-huh," said Hannah, who was poring through the lifestyle section of the *Bergen Record*.

Burke was stalking around the living room, picking things up. "I don't think you're aware of the gravity of this question, honey. I'm not talking about living on Belgrave Square and holding Tuesday afternoons at home. I'm through with the life of the literary lion. I'm talking about a lonely existence in Surrey, with only the craggy majesty of the moors to divert us. And the murmuring of innumerable bees."

"Bees," Hannah said. She was reading about the sorbet diet.

Burke shook his head. "Your mother thinks I'm joking, Sarah."

Burke had started to make little jokes about retirement. He'd done nothing more than joke about it; but even this was new.

"I don't like it," Sally said to Ben.

"Don't be so hard on the man," Ben said. "He's sixty-six years old. And through no fault of his own, his union is coming apart. It's amazing he's been able to hold it together this long."

"I know that. But I always thought he'd die in harness. When William O. Douglas was practically senile, I remember my mother said he should resign, and he got furious. He gave a ten-minute speech about how a man has the right to die on the job."

"You were so happy about the way he's learned to relax. Give the man the privilege of changing."

65

They went to a party given by a guy Ben knew. They were introduced to a friend of the host, a young woman visiting from France. She was a philosophy student; blue-eyed, with thick, blond, wild, pleasure-loving hair, she held a drink in one hand and a Gauloise in the other. When Sally asked her a question, she addressed her answer to Ben. After a minute or two of this, Sally turned her attention to a nearby television, where a Mets game was on. Mookie Wilson fouled off a curveball.

"Why did you decide to study philosophy?" Ben said.

"When I was . . . yoong," she said slowly, "they told me that the *philosophe* . . . understands the world."

Ben was obviously tickled by this. Sally didn't like the look on his face. "And do you understand the world?" he said.

The young philosopher smiled mournfully, lowered her eyes. *"Je ne comprends rien."*

Sally felt like slugging her in the jaw. I'll give you something to comprend.

Stretching a line drive single into a double, Mookie slid headfirst into the bag. The crowd was yelling, "Moooo!" Ben snuck a look at the screen.

The philosopher turned to see what he was looking at. She waved her cigarette, with an air of distress. "The baseball—in America, everywhere the baseball. I do not understand the baseball."

"Sorry," Ben said, looking away from the screen. "I love baseball. I probably couldn't explain why. I guess it just comes with being an American."

She smiled knowingly. "I think you love the baseball, not because you are an American, but because you are a man. And for this, you must not tell me you are sorry."

Sally walked away. She went to the bathroom and looked at herself in the mirror. "I do not understand ze baseball," she said softly.

She looked in the medicine cabinet. She felt so unhappy she might have taken something if there was something to take. But there was only Pepto-Bismol.

On the way home she didn't feel like talking, but she talked just enough to prevent him from asking her what was wrong. Why do couples stay together? Inertia. In an honest world, Ben would be going home with the philosopher tonight.

In bed he turned to her. He was hard.

She touched his penis, lightly, just enough to tease him. Then she turned away.

He put his hands on her shoulders and pressed himself gently against her.

"Better put that thing away, Mookie. You're in the wrong ballpark."

"What's that supposed to mean?" He let her go.

"You know damn well what it means." She put on a soft breathy voice: "I do not understand ze baseball. Put away zat bat."

"Oh, Sally." He put his hands over his eyes. "Are you bent out of shape about *that*?"

"Yes, I'm bent out of shape about that. If I wasn't there you would have ended up sleeping with her."

"That's ridiculous."

She was at a loss for a moment, because she knew it *was* ridiculous.

"Well, you would've liked to sleep with her. Wouldn't you? Wouldn't you?"

"Oh, Sally. Stop it."

"Can you tell me you didn't think about what it would be like to sleep with her?"

Ben was silent.

"You shit."

He sat up and slung his legs over the side of the bed.

"Did the thought cross my mind? What can I say? Am I the only man in the world *you* ever think about sleeping with?"

She didn't say anything; she hardly heard the question. She was trembling. Broken glass, slamming doors—she wanted violence.

"I'm gonna take a shower." He left the room.

She lay in the dark. She tried to understand exactly what was bothering her. It was an article of faith with her that, on some level, everybody wants to sleep with everybody else. So why was she so tortured by this?

What *is* jealousy? What is it? She heard the water in the shower hitting the floor, hitting Ben.

He came out of the bathroom with a towel wrapped around his waist. She liked his body. She liked his casual strength—she liked the fact that his strength wasn't something he cultivated or even thought about. And she liked the slight friction, the slight tension between them now. She wanted him to come over to the bed and pin her down.

He didn't do that. He was standing in front of her, holding the towel around his waist like a skirt, pressing his other hand against his chest in a gesture that would have been theatrical if it weren't so obviously deeply felt. "Sally, you can be jealous if you want to be jealous. It's true that I thought about what it would be like to sleep with that person. If I never thought about that kind of thing, I wouldn't be human. But the fact is that I'm your man. I'm just not thinking about anyone else. It amazes me that you don't see that."

He was near-naked, he was painfully sincere. He had his hand on his chest, his white chest. No escape from love: this phrase went through her head.

66

It was soon after this that she started to resemble the Wolfman.

They wanted to spend a long weekend somewhere; friends recommended Sag Harbor. At their motel-room door they encountered the couple staying in the next room, a man and woman in their sixties. The man was huge—he seemed to have about six shoulders—with an oversized head. The woman, full of vim, looked like a former cocaptain of the cheerleading squad.

It was a drizzly afternoon. Ben went out to buy a snack. "Get something sort of Chinese," Sally told him.

She sat on the bed reading a detective novel. Trying to get comfortable. The feeling of the thousand other people who had passed through this room.

In the next room, the man called out, "Bun?" His voice came clearly through the wall.

"Be out in a minute, Norm."

"Don't hog the john, now."

Sally turned the page.

She heard the man moving around, the closet door sliding

open, the little squeal of hangers on the rod. Softly, he began to speak. "Bunny hog the john," he said. "Bunny hogga john."

All across America, people were speaking gibberish. People who had been with each other so long it was almost like being alone.

Was that good or bad?

Her essential morbidity. To her it was bad. Sometimes she thought you can chart the history of a relationship by its failures of attention. The first time you touched your lover with a negligent touch: a playful push, a pat on the ass. The first time you spaced out while your lover talked—nodding at the proper cues without hearing the words. The first time you found yourself saying stupid things just because there was nothing else to say.

"Bunny hogga," the man said.

Ben came back with a bulging plastic bag. He'd found a takeout place where you could get dim sum lunches; he had shrimp rolls, chicken dumplings, baby spareribs, pork buns. They spread it all out on the little table near the window, and they ate until she felt slightly stupid. Since they'd become lovers she'd gained four pounds. She knew she shouldn't worry about four pounds, but she worried. She saw herself turning into a pork bun.

When the rain cleared they left the motel and took a walk on the gray beach. She didn't know why, but she didn't feel close to him. They were silent, but it wasn't like the intimate silences they sometimes had. She didn't know what was missing.

Maybe it was the world that was making her edgy. It was late October; in the last week more than two hundred Marines had died in a bombing in Lebanon, and Reagan, in one of his masterstrokes of distraction, had invaded Grenada, apparently because the government there was building a new airport. She had a feeling of imminent doom. She felt as if, at any moment, things were going to start falling out of the sky—rocks, bottles, missiles.

Later they drove around, went to a bookstore, went to an antique show in a big barn.

At the antique show, Ben got into a conversation with a watchmaker. He was a young, bony, dippy-looking guy with a huge Adam's apple—he looked a little like Prince Charles. Once Ben expressed an interest in watch repair, the guy was uncontainable, hustling back and forth behind his little table, holding up his products for Ben to get a better look. Ben didn't give a damn about watches, but he was nodding and asking penetrating questions—you'd think he'd been searching all his life for someone to enlighten him about the mysteries of the timepiece. Ben had this knack: he drew people out. He seemed to be interested in everyone. He *was* interested. It was one of the things she liked about him—but somehow, standing a few feet off, she resented it. He makes you feel as if you're the most interesting person in the world; but is it worth much if he does it to everybody?

"Of course the man who really knows this stuff is James Browning, over in Greenpoint. He's a real traditionalist. You could give him a call."

Ben nodded, as if he just might do that. "Jim Browning," he said. Sally, standing with a thin smile, found herself annoyed by that "Jim." You haven't met the guy—you have no *intention* of meeting the guy—but somehow you're ready to put him in your will.

They had dinner in a restaurant; they didn't say much. Later they came back to the room and read. She expected that they would make love soon. She looked forward to it—she thought it would heal this apartness. She lay on the bed reading one of Robert B. Parker's Spenser novels, he lay beside her reading a book on Reconstruction, and she looked forward to the moment when he would put down the book and touch her.

They heard the couple in the next room coming back, opening and closing their door.

"Did you like the whole atmosphere?" the woman said.

The man said, "It was . . ."

One of them turned on the television.

"Hi, I'm Chuck Scarborough," the man said.

"I wasn't overjoyed," the woman said. "I liked those little hot dogs."

Ben looked at Sally with a small, regretful smile.

She woke in the dark, startled by an unfamiliar sound. The snoring of the man in the next room.

It was only after she'd been listening for a while that she could make out the woman's sound, a thin whistle.

Ben slept. His broad body. His calm.

She lay awake, contemplating the history of her betrayals. She didn't understand herself.

It made sense that she had left Owen. Something important was missing with him. But with this man it was different. What was missing with Ben was probably not worth having. What was missing with him was what would be missing with anyone.

She put her arms around him; he remained asleep, but with his natural friendliness he returned her embrace. She wanted to make herself small in his arms, she wanted him to protect her. But what she wanted him to protect her from was herself. She was certain that she was going to leave him. She didn't *want* to leave him, but she was certain that she would.

Can't you fight it?

This man wants you. This man may be the best person

you've ever known. Can't you fight whatever it is that makes you want to flee him?

She didn't know if she could fight it.

By day, according to legend, the Wolfman was a normal man, even a good man. He had no desire to kill, no control over what he became during the full moon.

Help me.

She wanted to whisper, "Help me." Softly . . . not loud enough to wake him . . . just loud enough for the words to enter his thoughts in his sleep. But she didn't. She was afraid that the woman in the next room was awake. If she was awake, she might hear.

Her arm began to ache under the weight of his body. With difficulty she tugged it free.

Ben stirred, and the man in the next room stirred in response. His snoring died down.

She felt wired, wide awake.

She lay on her side, with her eyes wide open, staring at nothing. She listened to the breathing: the three sleepers, and herself. In the darkness, it was as if they were all in one room.

Slowly, their breathing fell into place. They breathed together, in and out, as one.

67

It turned out that Burke was serious. Not about England, but about retirement. He'd reached the point where he couldn't do the job as well as he expected himself to. DiMaggio.

When she called her mother to chat one night in March, Sally learned that he'd handed in his resignation. He wasn't leaving until the end of the year, but he was leaving.

"What the hell *is* this, Dad? Man is the animal who labors!"

Burke looked up from *A Journal of a Tour to the Hebrides*. She had come out for the weekend; she was pacing back and forth in front of his chair.

"What are you going to do with yourself if you retire?"

"Why does one have to *do* anything?" he said mildly. "Why can't one just be?"

"Who the hell *are* you, Buddha? I thought doing *is* being, in your book."

"When you reach a certain age, Sarah, you attain a new perspective. Your mother and I are moving to England. I've picked out a little cottage in Surrey. I'm going to keep bees, and once a week your mother will drive to the farmer's market in London and sell the honey."

"He's talking about the bees again?" Hannah came into the room with cheese and crackers on a tray.

"Sarah thinks it's a superb idea. Don't you, Sarah?"

Sally didn't say anything.

"Your mother isn't so sure she wants to move to Surrey and keep bees. Your mother enjoys being an important person in Teaneck."

"I'm sure she'll be an important person wherever she goes."

"Very well put, Sarah. Honey—did you hear that?"

She hadn't meant to say anything that would blunt her attack on his decision to retire. But it was what she had to say: it was the line she was obliged to speak; it was a family tradition.

Sally and Hannah went out to buy things for dinner. First they went to the fish store.

"What's your pleasure? You're the guest."

"How about some bluefish?"

"We'll have to get some shrimp for the old curmudgeon. That's all he ever eats anymore."

They went to the fruit store and stood squeezing melons side by side. Mother and daughter. Hannah squeezed Sally's head. "Not quite ripe."

On the street Hannah drew Sally's attention to the window of a knickknack shop, full of the kind of kitsch that Hannah loved. A statuette of two old people on a couch, the man in a cardigan, bifocals, reading a paper, the woman knitting, white hair, bun.

"That's what I'm going to get him for his birthday. The two oldsters."

"It's hard to believe he's really going to retire."

"I know. It's funny to think of what it'll be like with him underfoot. This new phase."

Sally thought, but didn't say: The last phase.

"There's a new store that sells gelata." Sally silently corrected her mother: gelato. "Wanna buy a pint and demolish it on the way home?"

She simply couldn't imagine what he would do once he retired. Maybe he couldn't either. During dinner he kept babbling on about England. "I don't know if your mother is quite prepared for the lonely solitude of the Shropshire valleys."

68

When she was in Manhattan, the city seemed strange. The only thing that had changed about it was that in a few months Burke wouldn't be working there anymore. It would no longer be his city.

Burke was a lover of the city, an intimate of every street. He told its stories. Walking down the street he'd point to a hotel and say, "Eugene O'Neill died there, Sarah. His last words were, 'Born in a hotel, dead in a hotel—goddammit!'"

She hadn't been aware of it before, but she realized now that she had always held her father and the city in the same thought.

She sat in a bus on Broadway. Through the smoked glass of the window, the buildings were a flatter brown. It would be strange to walk through the city, a few months from now, knowing he wasn't there. It needed him, to tell its stories.

69

His last bow. Burke and Hannah were going to the Soviet Union as part of an AFL-CIO contingent. Ben and Sally took them to the airport.

Hannah was wobbly with glee. "I just can't wait. I'm so excited I'm not even scared to fly. All my life I've been thinking about this country, dreaming about it. When Hitler invaded and the Soviet people defended Stalingrad house-to-house, I read so much about it, I saw so many newsreels, that sometimes I would wake up surprised to be in New York. I just can't believe I'm finally going to be there. Burke!" She pinched his arm. "We're going to stand under the Russian night!"

Burke wasn't going on about it, but he was excited too. He kept stubbing out his cigarettes as soon as he'd lit them.

When they got to the airport Hannah and Ben went to look for the departure information. Sally and Burke were left to deal with the suitcases.

Hannah had fitted the suitcases with wheels. But neither Sally nor Burke had the mechanical aptitude to understand that you have to grab the strap of the suitcase and pull it along behind you. Instead, Sally stood behind the suitcase and pushed it, and Burke cautiously followed her example. The problem with this method was that when you pushed it, the suitcase tended to go its own way, veering off crazily in all directions. Sally and her father made their way slowly through the airport, hunched over their suitcases, pushing them with one hand and trying to steady them with the other, taking little crisscross steps to try to follow their zigzag paths.

Ben and Hannah were standing at the end of the corridor. Hannah watched them with a look of astonished amusement. "You dopes," was all she said when they got there.

After her parents had boarded the plane, Ben and Sally had french fries in the snack bar.

"I love airports," he said. "I love to see people coming in from England and Senegal and Thailand. What a world."

The cool spring air. The sound of planes rushing overhead. They were in the parking lot. The plane overhead might be her parents', taking them to the motherland.

Sally didn't share her parents' feeling for the Soviet Union; but it was good to know that they would finally see the place that, for so many years, had been their spiritual home. Russian soil.

70

He was sleeping.
She was sinking.
They had just made love.

Ever since that night in Sag Harbor, she felt as if a gypsy had put her under a curse.

There are an infinite number of ways to touch: every man she'd been with had touched her differently. But it's an infinity like the infinity of fingerprints. Each man's way of touching was as invariable as his fingerprints; and no matter how much she'd cared for him, each man's touch had finally— maybe not completely, maybe only a little bit—bored her.

She loved the way Ben touched her—with a great gentleness. But tonight, as they made love, it had occurred to her that if she stayed with him long enough to grow bored by his touch, she already knew the form her boredom would take. She would grow tired of too much gentleness.

She turned in bed to test him: to see if the movement broke the rhythm of his slumber. It did not. Slowly, she passed her hand through the air above his face. He slept on. She lowered her hand to his chest, letting it rest there on the long slow rise and fall. After a time she ran her hand along his chest, the hairy chest of the man, the hairy chest of the Other, until she found the secret passage, the spot through which she could plunge her hand. She laid her hand directly on his heart and felt the push and pull. His heart was slick and bloody. She touched other organs, identifying, through their shape and feel, their functions. Finally she reached the valve through which his kindness flowed. Slightly, ever so slightly, she adjusted this valve. So that the milk of human kindness in his veins was just a little thinner. With a twist of another valve, she mixed the milk of kindness with the grit of resentment, the bile of bitterness. That was better. That was much better.

She searched, beneath the warm organs of his love of life and the pulsing thing she couldn't identify, for the tiny knobs in the lowest reaches of his abdomen. Finally she found the knob of sexual affection, and turned it from where it was set—on an embracing, full-hearted, self-abnegating love—until there was something mixed with that compassion, a touch of toxin, a tincture of hate: something that might lead him, if only so rarely, to bite her too hard, to clutch her too roughly for a moment, to pull her hair. This is what I want sometimes.

In the morning he kissed her awake, kisses wet with goodness. The knobs had slipped back to their old settings. The adjustments hadn't stuck.

71

Hand in hand through the island of lost souls. They were in the lower East Village. People were living on the streets, in wretchedness.

Some of the people were begging; Ben gave them change until he didn't have any left. Some of the people just stared at them. Sally was afraid.

About ten feet in front of them, an old black man, leaning against a wall, silently, gracefully keeled over.

Somehow she'd known he was going to fall. It was as if she'd lived through this before. Something bad was about to happen.

She grabbed Ben's arm and tried to steer him across the street. He resisted.

She should have left well enough alone. But she tightened her hold and said, "Let's get out of here."

She was afraid, but he was too preoccupied to understand this. He looked over at her—quickly, coldly, as if he didn't know her—and then he forgot her. She let go. He knelt beside the man and put his hand on his chest.

Sally drew near. The stench was overpowering: piss and

vomit and booze, and the horrible reek of the unwashed, ill-used human body.

Ben had his ear to the guy's chest. Then he had his ear to the guy's mouth.

He looked up at Sally with a kind of surgical coldness. "Do me a favor and get to a phone booth and call 911. Tell them to get an ambulance, heart attack—Third Street and Avenue A. Wait—say it's a cop with a heart attack."

This impressed her: he knew what would make them come.

But something else had struck her more than this. He'd told her what street they were on. He'd assumed that, in her usual fog, she hadn't noticed where they were. She was shocked that he'd sized her up that way. It was as if he had a core of contempt for her under his show of gentleness and respect.

Of course it was true: she hadn't known where they were.

Stop thinking about yourself.

She went to look for a phone. But not before she had watched, horrified, as Ben lowered his mouth to the other man's mouth, breathed into him, and the other man's chest and stomach heaved out in response.

She found a phone a block away. As she was telling them to get an ambulance, she was thinking: I'll never let him kiss me. I'll never let him kiss me again.

When she'd finished talking she stood there, pressing the receiver against her ear, because she didn't want to take that first step back. She didn't want to think about what she had just been thinking. Ben was trying to save this man's life. Risking the smell of him, risking germs, risking AIDS, who knows? And her first reaction was to be revolted. And her second reaction, and her third reaction, and her fourth. She knew there was goodness in what he had done. She knew that if she were a better person she would have loved the goodness, would have loved the man. She tried to find the core of goodness in herself, to answer his. Couldn't find it.

An ambulance and two police cars came quickly. The cops had a few words with Ben and then two of them got back in their car and disappeared. The other two hung around. The ambulance guys put what looked like little suction cups on the man's chest; the suction cups were wired to some machine. They talked to themselves in a language Sally didn't understand.

Ben leaned against a wall with his hands in his pockets, terribly white. He watched, bleak, drained, dispirited, as the technicians did their work.

Sally came over to him and they exchanged a look almost without affection. "You got one of them firebreathers?" he said. She gave him a cigarette. He tried to light a match but he couldn't. Sally lit his cigarette. She was careful not to touch him. She wanted to touch him—her repulsion had passed—but she knew he didn't want her to.

The ambulance guys got the man into the ambulance and disappeared. The cops hung around, writing in their mysterious leather notebooks.

The cops were younger than Ben. One of them, with a mustache, boyishly pink flesh, came over to him. He pressed his knuckle to the side of his nose and hawked out a gob of junk from the other nostril. It was a practiced move.

"Good Samaritan?" he said to Ben.

Ben grunted, barely looked up.

"Ass breath," the cop said.

That apparently completed police business.

Ben had a twisted, ironical smile. She couldn't understand why he was smiling. "Is that what they do instead of give you the key to the city these days?"

"He was right," Ben said.

"Why?"

"Because maybe that guy will live, thanks to me, and stay in a coma. On the other hand, maybe he'll be lucky ... maybe he'll just have massive brain damage. Or, if he's really lucky, he'll recover completely, and he'll soon be able to resume his place as a valued member of society." He looked at Sally coldly. He seemed to be as disenchanted with her as he was with himself.

72

She lay on the floor.

She wasn't sure why she had chosen that position. Probably it had something to do with making herself seem vulnerable: it was a way of declaring that she wasn't the bad guy; that she too was a victim.

It didn't work. Ben knew. He knew who the victim was.

He stood at the window looking out on the traffic on Broadway. He had his hands in his pockets. He wouldn't look at her.

After the ambulance and the police had gone away, they'd taken the subway to Ben's place. They didn't speak.

She knew he had performed an act of goodness. She didn't understand why she was so disturbed. But she took it for a sign, a revelation about the two of them. She felt as if she was carrying a heavy stone inside her body.

When they got back to his place, he tossed his jacket on a chair and said, "Well, should we have a talk?"

"What do you mean?" she said. Even though she knew what he meant.

"We went through something strange tonight, didn't we? I don't mean with the guy. I mean you and me."

She nodded yes.

"I'll tell you what was strange to me if you tell me what was strange to you."

He was smiling as he said this. He looked relieved. Clearly, whatever was bothering him wasn't big enough to drive them apart. He was picturing a rosy future. They would share their thoughts, they would solve their problems, and they'd reach a new level of togetherness—with new problems, deeper problems, the problems of people who are more deeply in love.

"I think I have to go first," she said. She sat on the floor, resting against a bookcase. "I think we need some time apart."

He looked as if he wasn't sure he'd heard her correctly. "Why?" he said.

She didn't know what to say. Because there really was no why. There was no sequence of reasoned observations leading to the conclusion that they should be apart. There was only the truth of her feelings: that he had performed an act of goodness that had left her cold; that one night when he slept she had tried to rearrange the elements of his nature; that when the couple in the motel had acted out the emptiness of marriage, his warmth had not been enough to warm her. That after two lost years with Owen, she was terrified of domestic life. That she had a stone inside her. If she tried to explain all this, Ben, being Ben, would sympathize with her, put her feelings in context, show her that her drastic conclusions weren't warranted. He'd wrap her in a warm web of understanding, and make it impossible for her to move.

She couldn't let him do that. She resolved to make nothing but me-statements: to say nothing he could contradict, nothing he could muffle with his understanding. On the night they met, when, with an inspired guess, he had called her a

Dylanist, he'd said that this meant she only believed in her feelings. So he'd known from the first what he was getting into with her. She brought this to mind now, trying to make herself feel less guilty about abandoning him.

"Ben," she said, "this just isn't working for me."

"What's not working?"

"This relationship."

He was looking at her blankly. "Why?"

"I don't *know* why. That's the problem."

"Well . . . what *about* it isn't working?"

"I don't know. It's so confusing."

He spoke in a soft voice: "How can we get unconfused? How can I help?"

"Ben. I don't know if you *can* help."

They could have gone on like this, easily, for hours. She had to bring it to an end.

"I think we just need some time apart."

Ben seemed to consider this. "But . . . why?"

"To figure things out."

He smiled: a tight, unhappy smile. "I feel like we're playing twenty questions. I'm not trying to persecute you, Sally— I'm just trying to understand you. What are the things we need to figure out?"

This was when she lay down. As if to persuade him that she was helpless, that she shouldn't be blamed. "I need," she said, "to figure out if I want you in this way. I need some space. I know I love you but I'm not sure that I don't just love you as a friend."

I need some space. I know I love you but I'm not sure that I don't just love you as a friend. She felt ashamed of herself for speaking this way. You think you have an original relationship with someone, something that's his and yours alone; but at difficult moments you can find no language for your emotions other than the language of self-help books.

Ben was staring at her, with his mouth open. He looked as

if he wanted to break something. He looked stupid. "What the hell did I *do?* I just don't get it. I committed the unpardonable sin of giving some guy CPR? I wasn't aware that that was grounds for fucking *divorce*."

He went to the window. For a moment she thought he was about to punch through the glass. "I just don't understand how this happened. I felt you drifting away lately, but I thought it was just a passing thing. I thought I should give you *space,* as you put it, to go through whatever you were going through. But before that, we were getting along great. I thought we were getting along great."

She had to stop herself from saying: We *were* getting along great. Maybe he was right; maybe she should stick it out, work it out with him. But she couldn't. After sticking it out for years in a relationship that was a mistake from the first, she was terrified of another mistake.

"Ben, I need room to figure things out."

And so Ben was defeated. He didn't look at her as he spoke. "I don't understand you. But I can't, you know, I can't twist your arm."

He stood at the window looking out on who knows what. From where she was lying, she could see, over his shoulder, the moon.

At a lecture she'd attended in college, a Chilean exile had spoken of how his mind had left his body during torture. Her mind seemed to leave her body now. She felt as if she were watching the scene from somewhere overhead: she felt as if she had died, as if she was looking back into the past, on a scene from her life. She saw herself lying on the floor, with her head resting in her palms; she saw the man staring glumly out the window; and what struck her most about the scene was the enormous waste. After she died, what she would most regret would be the waste. Two people, mortal, flawed, well-intentioned, fearful: they couldn't help each other. Ben with his massive goodness, his goodness so good that it was almost too good, as if he was afraid of the regions of himself that were darker, more ambiguous. . . . And herself. It was probably an illusion, brought on by the pressure of the moment, but from her vantage point outside her body she felt she had her first full clear view of who she really was. She was still a girl, a fearful girl. The stone inside her was made of fear. It was fear that had made her so revolted when he put his lips to the lips of the homeless man. It was fear that had kept her so long with Owen; it was fear, now, that was causing her to leave. Fear was what kept her from moving, and fear was what moved her.

Later that night he went outside with her and hailed her a cab. They had several tortured phone conversations during the next few weeks, and then they stopped talking. She thought about him all the time, but she didn't see him again until after Burke died.

PART FOUR

73

It took her about five seconds to get on the phone. In those five seconds, she was able to look at the clock and see that it was 7:15; to wonder why anyone would call so early; to be afraid that something had happened to her father; and to look forward to the mixed relief and irritation that would come when she'd find that it was just a wrong number, just a rude friend. "Hello?"

"Sally?"

All Hannah needed to say was her name. Her voice was low and wild: Sally knew something horrible had happened.

"Mom?"

"I can tell I don't have to tell you. I can tell from your voice that you already know."

Sally had known that something horrible had happened. But until Hannah said this, she hadn't been sure of what it was. Until that moment she had hoped that the news was merely horrible: a heart attack, a stroke, a coma, but still life, still hope. Now she knew there was no hope.

She had sometimes wondered, through the years, how the news would come. Wondered who would tell her, what words would be used. She'd imagined many possibilities. The only possibility she had never imagined was that she herself would be the one to say the words: that she would tell herself.

She said: "Daddy died?"

Hannah told her to take a cab. "There's money in the house," she said.

Her parents had never been rich; but there'd always been money. It was taken for granted: it never needed to be said. So that Hannah had to say this now meant that it was no longer taken for granted. It was a glimpse of the changes, the small changes, that would take place within the large change.

After Sally hung up, she realized that she didn't know how it had happened, or when, or where.

She had to dress. She had to move quickly. This is it, this is it, this is it, kept repeating in her mind. A moment that she'd been afraid of all her life, woken up worried from dreams about . . . it had come.

This was the way it had come. This room, this phone call, this moment. This was the way the moment was to be, forever. She went to her dresser. She had done her laundry the night before, so all her clothes were clean. She looked through her dresser for one of her newer pair of underpants, not the old ratty ones—this was what she always did when she dressed, you wear the ratty ones last. As she was looking through the pile she realized that this was madness—to be sifting through her underwear now, in the same old way— and she reached into the drawer and grabbed up everything in it and threw it all over the room, bras and underpants everywhere, and she pounded the dresser and screamed.

All her life she had wished that she could live in the moment. It was an ideology of the age: the belief that few of us are ever fully awake. Be here now.

Now she was living in the moment, as she never had before. The past did not exist. The future was unfathomable: she had no idea even of what the next hour would bring. She was fully awake now.

She got the phone book and called a cab company. When she got off the phone she noticed that she had lost all feeling in one of her hands. She wondered if she were having a stroke.

When she told the cabbie that she was going to New Jersey, he clenched his fist. "New Jersey, the Garden State—awright." He unclipped his mike from the dashboard and talked to his dispatcher. "Teaneck, New Jersey, big man—what's the damage?"

On the highway he pulled up sharp—there was a briefcase lying on the shoulder. He opened his door, leaned out, and snagged it. "This could have fell out of Donald Trump's limo. There could be ten thousand dollars in here." He put it next to him on the seat without looking inside. Apparently he was afraid that Sally might lay claim to a share of the fortune.

Sally was glad that he was like this—a bumbling hustler— it did away with the temptation to confide in him. She didn't want to seek wisdom and comfort from the cabbie who was driving her home.

She sat in the backseat, not speaking. All she was thinking was: This is it, this is it, this is it.

She was encased in a shell. She felt a sticky substance being secreted from her pores, covering her face, covering her eyes. A shell. A thin but indestructible shell of permafrost.

"You goin' to work?" said the driver. He was in the mood to chat.

"No."

She didn't want to be rude, but that was all she could say.

She had him drop her a few blocks from home, on the other side of the park. It was a beautiful day. It was the first of November, but the temperature was in the middle sixties, the sky was clear. She walked in the bright ten o'clock sun on the rim of the brown park. Five or ten sparrows were in the outfield, hopping in mysterious formation. On the tennis court, at the far side of the park, a man was practicing his serve.

When she drew near the huge secluded house, she saw her uncle Stanley's car. Hannah's brother. Foolishly, she was shocked. She'd thought she'd be alone with her mother.

She went in, as always, through the back door. There was no one in the den. With cups and newspapers all about, the room was in its usual cheerful disorder.

A woman was at the kitchen sink, washing dishes. Aunt Phyllis. Sally wanted to find Hannah, but Phyllis rushed toward her with her arms outstretched. She rushed up on twinkle toes—that was the phrase that passed through Sally's mind. They embraced. Sally felt nothing. She didn't want to be embracing Phyllis; she wanted to find her mother. But there was a mysterious hidden television camera in the room, recording everything she did, and Sally therefore had to obey the proprieties, and so she put her arms around her aunt.

And immediately felt horrible for that moment's delay, because now she heard her mother saying, "Sally? Is Sally here?"

Hannah lurched into the room. She was still in her nightgown, a mini-nightgown that didn't even cover her knees. She looked both heavy and insubstantial. She embraced her daughter, clutching her, for a long time.

Sally still didn't know what had happened.

They didn't have a chance to talk. The doorbell rang and five or six people from Hannah's school came in. They sat down in the living room. Hannah didn't want to let go of Sally. She stood holding her hand.

The phone rang; Sally answered. She had a brief conversation with someone; when she hung up, she couldn't remember who it was. Phyllis approached her shyly. "Is there anything else I can do? I washed the dishes and cleaned out the refrigerator. It's funny—I'm normally at work this time of day, and I've got such a strong work ethic I feel like I have to keep working. Maybe I could tidy up in the basement?"

The basement? You want to clean the basement? You want to clean the basement? Sally was astonished, but she didn't let it show. Phyllis was a warm, sweet-natured woman who sometimes, when she was flustered, said silly things; it would serve no purpose for Sally to betray her astonishment. She felt in no danger of betraying anything, because she was encased in permafrost.

The phone kept ringing. People kept giving her their coats. The house was strange to Sally. If she had been there the day before, she would have seen her father. But she would never see him again. She tried to let this thought enter her mind. It was a simple thought; it was a thought she should have been able to grasp. But it wouldn't go into her mind.

The phone kept ringing; Hannah kept running to the foyer to answer it. People offered to get it for her, but she wanted to talk. Sally, sitting in the living room, expertly making small talk—expertly, because of the permafrost—heard her mother say to someone: "The dominant figure of my life is gone." Hannah hung up the phone and pressed herself against the bare white wall.

Sally went over to Hannah. "Is Daniel on the way?"

"I haven't been able to reach him. Let me try again."

Daniel was still teaching at Middlebury. She called his office. "Jill? This is Hannah Burke, Daniel's mother. Yes. Yes. Could you have him call me? His father died."

He was going to hear it from someone at work.

People were still coming in. Hannah was talking.

"He wakes up around six. He'd get himself ready and bring me my coffee around 6:30. I woke up at seven and he was still in bed. I thought he overslept. I reached over, I said, 'We're late!' But as soon as I touched him I knew.

"I went crazy. I was screaming like a banshee. I ran downstairs—I don't even know why. And then I thought I hadn't really seen it. I thought it was a dream. I don't know what I thought. I went back upstairs and he was still there. And I started screaming and ran downstairs again.

"Finally I called 911. The ambulance came so fast I hardly had time to hang up the phone. They tried to revive him but they couldn't. Maybe if I'd called them sooner he'd still be alive."

Hannah had one foot up on the couch; her nightgown was barely longer than a shirt; she was almost nude. Sally wished her mother had her clothes on.

"They couldn't take him away until his doctor came to sign something. And that bastard came an hour late. The bastard gave him a clean bill of health a month ago. So he just stayed there for an hour, and then they took him away. I don't even know if he had his teeth in."

Two women whom Sally didn't even know were sitting in the corner; one of them leaned toward the other with a look of puzzlement and interest. "Burke had false teeth?"

The phone rang. Someone answered and called Hannah over. "Daniel? Yes. It's your dad. He died."

Somehow the house had filled up with food. There were twenty or thirty people there. Sally was suave, she was humorous, she was the good hostess. She had retreated miles and miles and miles below the frost.

None of her friends knew. It was odd to think of this. The world had changed for her as much as if an atom bomb had fallen, and yet none of the people who loved her had any idea.

The house was filled with chattering people holding paper plates, gabbing nose to nose in little groups. Sally kept expecting Burke to walk in and exclaim, "What the hell is this, Grand Central Station?!" But he didn't.

She went to the kitchen to make coffee. The ancient coffeepot sat on the stove. She started measuring out the scoops. One, two, three, four, five, someone asked her where the bathroom was, five, six, or was that seven? She dumped the coffee back into the can and started over. One, two, three, four, who was that, five, five? She dumped it out and started over. Two more times she tried to measure out seven scoops. She couldn't do it. She gave up.

She cleaned up in the kitchen. She wiped off the kitchen table with a sponge. On the table was a long tube of ash that had fallen from one of her father's cigarettes the morning before. She stood over it for a long time. Finally she closed her eyes for a moment, took strength, and wiped away the ash.

She cleaned the den, she cleaned the downstairs bathroom. Finally there was a chance to slip away. She went upstairs, into her parents' bedroom. Everything was as it had always been. His scent filled the room, as always: that heavy but somehow delicate smell, tobacco mingled with a sort of bakery sweetness. Slowly, she approached the bed. The bed he had slept in, night after night. The bed he had closed his eyes in, the night before. Voices came up faintly from downstairs. Slowly, slowly, she let herself down. Facedown, she stretched across his side of the bed. It was quivering with his nearness, with his presence. So close, my father, so close.

Daniel arrived that evening. When she embraced him, Sally saw into his soul. They shared a long embrace, their bodies pressed together as if they were lovers; and in this embrace he communicated everything that he was. She felt his unhappiness, she felt his loneliness, and she felt his longing, for something that life had never yet given him. She understood something she had never guessed before: that he conceived of himself as radically incomplete. She didn't understand why he believed this, but she understood that this was what he believed. They broke the embrace and, after looking her for one second in the eye, he turned away, as if he were embarrassed—as if he knew that she knew about him now.

At about eight she started to call her friends. No one was home. She hung up on a lot of answering machines.

She didn't try to call Ben. She kept dialing the first few numbers and hanging up. They hadn't spoken in months.

She dreaded the moment when the last guest would leave. As each one left, she felt diminished; she felt as if a subtraction was made from her being. She didn't want the noise to go away. She dreaded being alone with Hannah and Daniel.

But the moment finally came. Sally saw out the last guests, the Levines, then leaned heavily against the door. Daniel was sitting, exhausted, in Burke's chair. Hannah was lying on the couch, wearing one of Burke's sweaters. The television was on, and she was looking blankly at the news.

Sally was cold; she put her denim jacket on. She sat on the loveseat, next to the cat. Old and smelly, he was huddled lumpishly, unknowing.

On the news, they were going on about a stabbing, they were going on about a fire in the barrio, they were going on about the presidential campaign. Reagan was poised for a sweeping victory; Mondale didn't have a chance. How insane that they could report on this trivia and not mention the death of Burke.

Hannah kept going over the details of the night before. "He looked so gorgeous. He had a meeting, and he came home late. As he walked in the door I remember thinking how proud I was . . . how beautiful he looked. I was watching the news, and usually he'd stay up with me. But he said he was exhausted—he said he'd go upstairs and read a little S. J. Perelman and hit the road to dreamland. And when I came up he was asleep."

She'd given that same account about twenty times already that day.

Sally was bottomlessly tired, and bottomlessly confused. A year earlier, an old friend of her parents had died, someone she had known all her life. Her emotions then had been so simple. They'd had precise location in her body: in her abdomen, in her chest, behind her eyes. Her emotions now had no location: she wasn't even sure that the feelings were inside of her. They seemed to be present in the objects in the room.

"He must have known," Hannah said. "He really must've. He called me in class yesterday—he called twice." She had a phone in her classroom, so the kids could talk with their parents and learn telephone skills. "He never calls twice in one day. And both times he stayed on for a long time. The first time he was surprised I could stay on: he said, 'Hey, don't you have some children to look after?' But they were out of the room, for art." She was silent for a moment. "He really must have known."

The processes of consolation were starting to take effect. Sally wanted to resist the processes of consolation. But she'd been thinking all day about the fact that, on an impulse, she'd taken her shower the night before. She never took a shower at night. It was as if she'd wanted to be ready.

Hannah went rummaging in her bedroom and came down

with a photograph album. The three of them settled on the couch and looked at the pictures. Burke in his late twenties, just before he met Hannah. The four of them on a summer vacation, 1965. Burke and Hannah in Moscow six months ago.

If she had looked at them one night ago, these pictures would have been pictures of an accessible world. Even the pictures from the sixties. Burke and Hannah hadn't changed—Burke still "performed his ablutions" in the morning, still "hit the road to dreamland" at night; Hannah was still prepared to "eat my hat" if she didn't lose five pounds by next Friday. Sally and Daniel, for their part, though they found it difficult to talk as two adults, still found it easy, frighteningly easy, to slip back into the babble of their childhood. When the four of them were together, the past had not been past.

Now that was changed. The bridge to the past had been cut away—like some rickety swaying footbridge from an old movie, stretching from cliff to cliff. The bridge was gone; the past was inaccessible. She stood on one cliff, and her entire life up till this morning was on the other. The life she knew when she was ten years old and the life she knew yesterday—these seemed closer to each other than yesterday and today.

Daniel went to bed. Hannah went to bed. Sally, as always, stayed awake.

When Burke and Hannah had moved into this house, they were confronted by the problem of what to do with all these rooms. They made use of them as best they could. One small room had nothing in it but wool for Hannah's knitting. She called it the wool room. Another small room was a sort of dressing room for Burke.

Sally made her way up to that room. It was quiet. She opened the door of the closet—it was a huge closet—and went in. A long row of beautiful suits. The smell of him. How can the smell of the man be so vivid when the man is gone?

In the quietness, the long row of suits seemed to be at attention.

She leaned against the wall of the closet and let herself slide weakly to the floor.

She sat on the floor, tired, tired beyond thought, so tired and numb that his death seemed a purely intellectual experience. Where had he gone? She knew that he hadn't been translated into any higher realm. Burke was a confirmed atheist: if his soul had risen up after death and he had been offered an afterlife, he would have refused it.

There was a desk in the room; she went through the drawers looking for traces of him. But there was nothing there. With the exception of his clothes and his books, Burke's possessions could have fit into a file folder. He'd accumulated nothing.

Finally she came upon a little picture of him, taken when he was nine or ten years old. A handsome, earnest-looking boy, wearing a tie. He looked open to life. Looking at the photo closely, she could see the later evolution of his face: the places where the lines of strain and strength and care would grow.

He was looking directly into the camera; he was looking directly into her eyes. In her exhaustion, her mind blurred, and she was filled with a feeling of helplessness at the thought that this little boy had died. This little boy who looked so frankly and calmly into the camera . . . this little boy would someday die. This little boy had died, and there was nothing she could do to protect him.

After the picture was taken, the little boy had turned back toward a world of which she knew nothing. The little boy had become her father, and she'd thought she knew him; but she knew nothing about this world of his childhood. Burke's extraordinary rages, the extraordinary blackness of his moods, the foul cloud that lowered over him when he woke up from his afternoon naps . . . she'd always taken it for granted that this foulness, this blackness, was the heritage of his youth. The dark, ceremonial, guilt-haunted, Catholic world that the little boy had turned back to after the picture was flashed. The mix of historical and familial currents that had come together to create Burke—to create his extraordinary acuteness and his extraordinary blockages—currents that had gathered like a tide from history, cresting at the moment of his creation: these forces from the nineteen-teens and nineteen-twenties had been active in him until yesterday. The early years of the century had still been alive, in him. Now that he had died, this tide fell back into the past. No one else would ever be formed by these currents; they fell back into their proper place in the early twentieth-century world.

She slipped the little photograph into the breast pocket of her jacket. She covered her pocket with her hand, and pressed it against her breast.

She went to what was called her room. She didn't think she'd be able to sleep, but she slept.

She had imagined that waking would be like this: you wake up happy, as you usually woke, and then you smash against the knowledge. But that wasn't the way it happened. She felt as if she hadn't slept at all: as if she'd spent the night thinking about him. When she woke the knowledge was with her, as if the interval of sleep had been no longer than the closing of her eyes.

She went downstairs. Hannah was sitting in front of the television watching "Good Morning America."

Daniel came down as the coffee was perking. He sat down heavily at the table, casting a disapproving look at the TV. He was showered and dressed but still groggy; he sat for a minute rubbing his eyes.

"I had a dream that Dad would have appreciated. I dreamed I lost my wallet."

They drove to New York to make arrangements for the funeral. They went over the George Washington Bridge—a route they had taken a thousand times with Burke in the front seat. To the south, the city was sparkling. The river was calm.

At the Riverside Memorial funeral parlor they were introduced to a young woman who was to handle the arrangements. Daniel did most of the talking. He seemed to have grown a little stronger than Sally remembered him: he sat up straighter, he spoke with a new authority. The father dies, the son becomes a man—is that it? She felt a moment of sharp contempt for him, for playing out this tired scenario.

The woman, Andrea Ollman, spoke with a lugubrious slowness; her deliberateness, her studied, stupefying calm, testified to her knowledge that she was dealing with people who were insane with grief. Her every gesture was rounded and slow; nothing sudden, nothing sharp. It turned you into a patient. Sally felt like giving her a fat Bronx cheer—anything to break through that wall of concern.

They went over the details. Cremation. A secular ceremony. The urn not to be present. Obituary notices in the *Times* and the *Bergen Record*. They worked out the language of the notices. Hannah kept pumping for flowery phrases about his love of his family and his years of service to the labor movement. Sally would have preferred something drier and more factual, but she had enough sense to be quiet about it.

Andrea Ollman punched the keys of her calculator and made out a bill. She passed it across the desk to Hannah.

Hannah raised her eyebrows. "Isn't this a little steep?"

Here Andrea Ollman was magnificent. She spoke calmly: "We put in a good day's work here, and we belong to a strong union, which has done its best to win us good wages and benefits."

Hannah smiled. "I don't see how I can argue with that."

Before Burke could be cremated, his body had to be identified. Andrea Ollman led the three of them into an elevator. A strange taste rose in Sally's throat. The elevator went down, and the doors opened. Andrea Ollman slipped off into a little room to the left. They didn't notice. Directly in front of them, just outside the elevator, on a wheeled table, covered to his shoulders with a sheet, was Burke.

For the second time in her life, Sally saw that death does not bring peace. There was no expression of peace on Burke. His mouth was rigid, locked. He seemed to be under a great strain. It was as if death was not something that does its work and departs, but a force that comes and stays: that continues to restrain you, to violently hold you down. It was as if death was holding him down.

His teeth had not, in fact, been in his mouth when he died. This was only the second or third time that Sally had seen her father without his teeth. It made his head look smaller. With his shrunken, shriveled jaw, he looked much older than he'd looked when he was alive. And for the first time, Sally saw a resemblance between Burke and his own mother.

His hair was combed straight back. This was not the way he combed it. Someone else combed my father's hair this morning.

Sally, Daniel, and Hannah were howling. They were making terrible animal sounds.

She had thought that when the moment came she would kiss him. She remembered how moved she had been when she saw him kiss his mother in her coffin.

But perhaps the embalming job had been imperfect; perhaps it was the delay in his doctor's arrival that had caused it; or perhaps when one is to be cremated one is not embalmed at all. Whatever the reason, something had gone wrong with his ear. His right ear had begun to shrivel and turn purple at the lobe. Her father had had lovely, delicate ears. He was not himself anymore. He was turning into inorganic matter. For sixty-seven years the mysterious processes of life had guarded the integrity of his skin. One day of death had undone it. He was turning into something else. And she found that she couldn't kiss him. She wanted to kiss him, she wanted for all her life to kiss him, but she couldn't do it.

The three of them had been howling since the elevator doors had opened. Now Daniel turned and made a fist and, with all his strength, pounded again and again on the wall. It was like a signal: Andrea Ollman emerged from the room where she'd been waiting, and ushered the three of them back into the elevator.

They went back to her office to sign the death certificate. Daniel picked up the pen, then hesitated. "That wasn't him," he said. "Never saw that guy before in our lives."

Hannah's house was filled with people. They kept coming, and Sally found herself a kitchen slave, serving coffee and cake to people who took the cup and the plate without thanking her or glancing her way. People streamed in bearing cake, and she cut it for them. She made coffee, cut the cake, washed the dishes, picked up what people dropped, and her grief was overswept by her resentment. So perhaps there was some healing purpose to all this.

She still hadn't heard from any of her friends. She resented them for not helping her when she was so clearly in need. It's true that she hadn't told them; but it seemed obvious that if they cared about her, they'd know.

Daniel's woman came down to join him from Vermont. She was a tiny dark shy woman named Penelope. She had a way of standing at an angle to the room so that she seemed to be sinking back into the shadows. Ever since Sally had known her, she and Daniel were forever slinking off into another room to be alone, and even when they didn't slink off they seemed to exist in a closed, impenetrable circle. When she wanted to address the room she'd whisper into his ear, and then he would speak. This might have only been shyness, but Sally saw it as a novel way of dominating Daniel—through reticence, through retirement, through an affectation of weakness.

Then again, she'd always had trouble with Daniel's girlfriends.

Sally was standing by herself in the kitchen, drinking coffee, confused, tired, numb; wishing that these people would go away at the same time as she was thankful for all the noise. Ben came into the room.

He reached out and took a strand of her hair away from her mouth. Quietly: "How're you feeling?"

They were silent for a minute. He'd put on weight again. He didn't look good.

"I've been better."

"Nobody did any work at my office today," he said. "We sat around trading Burke stories. We've got a guy who used to work for your father's union. His first day on the job they sent him out to observe a bargaining session—this was before he'd met your old man. He showed up early; Burke was the only one there; and when he got a look at the collar pin, and the fountain pen, and those menacing white eyebrows, he took it for granted Burke was management. And he thought, 'Christ, we're never gonna get a penny out of this guy. This is the toughest-looking boss I've ever seen.'"

They looked at each other for a long time. They didn't touch.

After a little while he said, "Let me say hello to Hannah."

He was there for the rest of the day. Without being asked, without making a point of it, he began to take over the responsibility of keeping things together. Sally was preoccupied with the onrush of people, but she saw him washing dishes, making coffee, greeting people and channeling them in the right direction, performing all the duties of a member of the family.

There was something frighteningly natural about his being there. And frighteningly reassuring. In the calm way he took care of things without being asked, he seemed to embody some masculine principle. . . . Don't sleep with him. It would be a bad idea to sleep with him now.

She watched him as he went to the door and paid off the newspaper boy. And didn't wonder why he was doing this. And didn't wonder what it meant about the future. The future, in any case, was something she couldn't imagine.

That evening a few of them sat in front of the television. The presidential election was a few days away. Hannah, Sally, Ben, Daniel, Penelope, Stanley, and Phyllis sat listening to a preelection report.

"That fuckass Reagan is going to be president again," Hannah said.

"The people want him," Stanley said. "I thought you believed in the people." This was a continuation of a political argument they'd been carrying on since 1939.

"How could they want him? Don't they see he isn't even real? He's run by computer. That wasn't a new hearing aid they put in his ear—it's a microphone. His aides tell him what to say."

"I don't think people respect Mondale," Phyllis said. "People respect Reagan. He's a thinker."

"A thinker! How can you call that idiot a thinker!"

"I think he ponders things very deeply. He has a philosophy. Anyway, that's my opinion."

"A thinker. I've got news for you. Reagan hasn't had a thought in his life. He's not a thinker, he's an idiot. And anybody who thinks he's a thinker must be an idiot too."

Hannah buried her head in Sally's lap. She'd never really accepted Phyllis; it occurred to Sally that her own difficulty with Daniel's girlfriends was just a family trait. Phyllis didn't say anything; she just sighed.

After a while Phyllis and Stanley left. Nobody talked much; they watched the TV.

"Do you think I offended her?"

Daniel laughed and closed his eyes. "Why on earth would you think that?"

"I'd think she'd be downright pleased to be called an idiot," Sally said.

"I didn't really call *her* an idiot."

"What's the term, Ben, syllogism?" Daniel said. "People who consider Reagan a thinker are idiots. Phyllis considers Reagan a thinker. Therefore . . ."

"Don't worry," Penelope said. "I don't think she'll know she was insulted. She's too much of an idiot."

None of this had much to do with Phyllis—Penelope didn't even know her. It was just that a little spasm of pointless nastiness made everyone feel better.

"Maybe I should call them and tell them you didn't really mean it," Sally said. "You're not yourself."

"Yeah," Daniel said. "Tell her not to take Mom seriously. Tell her she's too tired to be dishonest right now."

"I'm not sure Sally's the best diplomat," Hannah said. "You should have seen her yesterday. Phyllis volunteered to clean the basement—I thought Sally was about to take her head off."

Sally was amazed to hear this. Apparently the permafrost didn't conceal her emotions quite as effectively as she'd thought.

She went into another room and called. Stanley answered.

"I just wanted to apologize for my mother. She's not herself right now."

"She's herself all right. She's her true self. This is the way she really feels."

Sally hadn't anticipated an argument. She couldn't think of anything to say.

"Phyllis said to me on the way home, 'This is the way she's always felt. Burke kept her in check, but now that she's free this is how she'll be from now on.'"

Sally closed her eyes. "Okay," she said. "Well, apologize to Phyllis for me, okay?"

When she came back into the living room Hannah said, "Whad she say?"

"I talked to your brother. He said not to worry about it."

Penelope and Daniel went to bed. Ben stood up. "I'll see you tomorrow." Sally saw him to the door. They didn't kiss.

"He's such a nice guy," Hannah said, drowsily, from the couch.

Sally and Hannah stayed in the living room, watching television. Hannah lay on the couch, Sally lay on the rug. Before too long Hannah fell asleep, and soon she began to moan, softly. Sally got pillows and blankets, covered her mother up, and went to sleep on the rug.

The memorial service was held the next day. First you stand in a little receiving room and people come in and annoy you. A third cousin forty thousand times removed on Hannah's side, a little scrunched woman, came up to Sally and said, "Remember me?" Sally drew a blank. "You don't remember me?" The woman was outraged. Sally turned away and greeted someone else.

Stanley and Phyllis came in. Sally apologized to Phyllis, who threw up her hands as if she was warding off a spell. "That's the way she feels. I'm glad the truth came out."

The hall filled with people—people of all ages and colors and backgrounds. The death of a union man.

The service began. People trooped up to the stage and spoke about Burke. Half of them ended their speeches with the phrase "Don't mourn, organize." Fuck you, Sally thought. The other half ended their speeches with embarrassed little pauses—they'd planned to say, "Don't mourn, organize," but had decided not to, in view of the fact that everyone else had said it already.

Daniel, displaying his new sonly characteristics, made the last speech. It was just right: lightly, humorously loving at the beginning; sadly, movingly loving at the end. Fuck you, Sally thought.

She hated to hear all these people talking about him in the past tense.

It ended. She was standing near Daniel. Someone stuck his face near Daniel's face and mugged toward heaven. "He heard you. He heard you loud and clear."

They drove back home. Hannah drove, as always; with her free hand she clutched the urn.

The ashes were in a plastic bag inside the urn. When they got home she put them in a samovar she and Burke had brought back from the Soviet Union.

"Mom . . ." Sally said.

"What?" Hannah turned on her with an ugly, defiant face. "Does that offend your sensibilities?"

Sally didn't say anything.

Hannah was sitting in a pile of condolence cards. Everyone outside the inner circle had left. "The fourth day is the hardest," she said.

"Look at this fuck." Hannah tossed a card over to Sally. It was from a journalist Burke had known.

Burke was a remarkable man, it read. *I guess you don't need me to tell you that. I'll always remember him.*

"I thought he was supposed to be a writer," Hannah said. "Is that the best he can do?"

Her mother's anger disturbed her, but she was the same way: her anger sometimes choked her grief. She knew she wasn't really surrounded by fools and boors; it only felt that way. Was this normal—a normal way to manage grief? Or was it a sign of some flaw in their family? Caller after caller told them how lucky Burke had been to have died in his sleep. When the tenth person, filled with goodwill, told her this, Sally said, "He didn't exactly win the fuckin' Irish Sweepstakes."

People kept coming and coming, for days. Sally was a slave, Daniel was a slave, Hannah was a slave, Penelope was a slave, Ben was a slave. But it was good to be a slave—it was worst at night, after the guests had left. The five of them would sit around for a while and amuse themselves by cutting apart the people who'd been there, but after that was over they had nothing to cushion them. And even the cutting up of the visitors lacked that edge of fine wit it would have had if Burke was there.

Daniel and Penelope went to sleep; Ben left immediately afterward. Hannah fell asleep on the couch, with the television on.

Sally stayed up. She went to the room that Hannah called the library. She could be alone with her father there. She ran her hand over the spines of his books. Somber-colored hardcovers that had been the backdrop of her life for as long as she could remember. There were photos of her as a baby playing with dolls in front of these books. *The Mind of the South. And Quiet Flows the Don. This Was Normalcy.*

Till four in the morning she went from bookcase to bookcase, looking intently through books that had been around her all her life. But she was thwarted: she couldn't find him. Not even in the books he'd loved. Last summer he had spent two weeks helpless with laughter over one of S. J. Perelman's posthumous collections. Sally sat for an hour with the book on her lap, trying to find what he'd loved in it. But the book was filled with false elegance, overwritten phrases trying to do the work of wit. She couldn't find what her father had liked about it. She couldn't find him.

His books had no meaning without him. Most of them were history books. She didn't know much history; but she knew enough to know that if she ever decided to study the subject seriously, she would be steered toward different books. History books make their predecessors obsolete. So that if she wanted to study the Harding era, her father's copy of *This Was Normalcy,* copyright 1948, would be useless. The books needed him.

She thought of all the knowledge he'd accumulated, all the years of ripened understanding. All gone.

The days went by, but his death was still fresh. Every step she took brought fresh news of it. Sally and Ben drove to the dry cleaner to pick up some things he'd left there. In the parking lot Ben said, "Maybe I should go by myself."

"No. I want to."

She handed the receipt to the woman behind the counter who worked the big machine, the merry-go-round of clothing, until his clothes arrived, and she unhooked two suits and his winter overcoat. Sally paid, took the clothes, pressed them against her body, and, in the parking lot, started to cry.

Because of the overcoat. Because all the nonsense about premonitions was just nonsense. He was planning to live into the winter. He was planning to live.

She'd stopped smoking, but now she started again. In honor of him. She smoked on the sly: it would have grieved her mother if she'd known. On Saturday afternoon she said she was going to the library, and she drove to a place she knew, a big brown grassless field on a hill, and she stood near the playground looking out over the little town, smoking two or three cigarettes, the harshness of them troubling her lungs and making her dizzy. November had turned cooler; a few days of rain and then a sudden cold had made the turf hard and crackly underfoot. She stood on the crest of the field, smoking the cigarettes, which gave no pleasure, watching the cars pass meaninglessly below.

She was glad she had no life to go back to.

All the things of the world had been swept out of her circle of care. Even the children in her classroom. She didn't care whether she ever saw them again. And it wouldn't matter to them either. Who remembers their first-grade teacher?

At the memorial service speaker after speaker had said that Burke's acts would outlive him. Following the rhetorical expectations of such occasions, several had said that his contributions would give him a kind of immortality.

Sally knew it wasn't true. She knew that her father had had an influence—on his family, on the people he'd worked with. But his influence would no more live forever than the ripples of a rock tossed in a pool would radiate forever. There comes a point where the ripples die. His influence would live in her, as long as she lived. If she had children, they would know him as the subject of a few anecdotes, a colorful figure from the distant past. If she had grandchildren, they probably wouldn't even know his name.

She felt uneasy, having been away from Hannah for so long. But just a little longer. With her denim jacket providing just a little less than enough warmth, she stood blue-lipped in the grassless field.

She couldn't blot out the picture of him lying before her on the table. The moment had finally come: the moment she'd been dreaming about with dread for years. Sometimes, in those last years, when death was clearly doing its work inside him, she had watched him, in one of his heavy living-room slumbers, with his long, shuddering breaths, his monumentally lined face, and wondered how his face as she saw it then differed from the way it would look after he died. It had turned out that the difference was greater than she'd ever guessed it might be. But that wasn't the point. The point was that she had obscurely felt, during all those years, that by thinking about the worst she was somehow warding it off.

But the worst had come.

And now, smoking a fifth cigarette on the jagged field, feeling nauseated and dizzy, she felt that the worst had not been the worst at all. When she had stood beside him for the last time, she'd at least been standing beside him. He was still near. And when she remembered how she hadn't had the courage to kiss him, she felt ashamed. In their last moment together, she had failed him. She could have kissed her father one last time, but she'd lacked the courage.

Or she could have spoken to him. She knew that it was stupid, but she'd been thinking, these last few days, that there might have been a chance—the slimmest, most infinitesimal of chances, but still a chance—that if she had leaned down and whispered in his ear, "I love you, my father" . . . he might have heard.

Who knows how long it takes for the soul to be fully and finally wrested from the body? Who can know for sure that it's impossible that for a few hours after the heart has stopped beating, a slim hint of consciousness might remain? She was Burke's daughter, so she was a lifelong atheist, an enemy of

God; but she was human, and therefore unable to suppress the hope that something . . . something might have lived on. If only for a day. If only for an hour.

She thought of her mother, "screaming like a banshee" the morning she'd found him. Of course she'd gone mad; how could she have done otherwise? But if Sally could have rewritten the script, then her mother, after seeing that Burke had died, would have come close to him on the bed, and kissed his lips, and whispered into his ears that she loved him, she loved him eternally.

It might have eased his passage into oblivion.

It was turning dark. After seven cigarettes she felt thoroughly sick. She walked back to the car, spinning with nausea in the cold dusk.

It was Saturday. Meaningless. Except that Daniel and Penelope were going back to Vermont on Sunday. Leaving Sally to take care of Hannah by herself.

Today there had been only two or three visitors. The quiet was welcome, but she could see that the hardest part was starting only now. Most of the people who had seen them through so far would go back to their own lives now. They'd become less patient with your mourning, less solicitous. And you'd find that his death had been easier to live with in its freshness than in the complicated permutations of the weeks and months ahead.

The four of them sat around the TV. No communion. She was finding out that everything you'd want to believe about the consolations of bereavement—the deepening of insight into life, the deepening of love within the family—it was all horseshit. With her brother she shared nothing: their com-

munion had begun and ended with their strange embrace. He
was shielded at all times by his Dark Lady; he was unreach-
able. Penelope was so thin that when she put herself at a right
angle, she could move through walls; yet Daniel was able to
hide behind her. He was obviously suffering, as much as Sally
was; but even his way of suffering set her off. He would occasionally make a smug remark to the effect that she wouldn't
be able to understand the special poignancy of how this loss
affects a son.

She didn't want to be left to take care of Hannah by herself.

For the first time in her life, she wished she came from a
large family. She would have liked to have six or seven brothers and sisters, filling up the house with hearty voices.

Without quite knowing how it happened, Sally found herself staying at her mother's house four or five nights a week.
She'd decided to do this for a while, but she hadn't thought
out what "a while" meant.

She thought it was her mother's call. She waited for Hannah to suggest that she stop staying there so often. But Hannah never would. At the end of the night Hannah would head
upstairs and blow her daughter a kiss and say, "You don't
mind staying with your momaleh? My bubaleh is a good
girl. . . ."

What the bubaleh found impossible was to sort out her
mother's needs. Some of the needs were the old needs, which
Sally had learned to reject in order to grow. When Sally had
left Owen and moved back to New York, Hannah had suggested that she move "back home"; she was outraged when
Sally's only response was to smile. Even when she was happy,
Hannah had thought it perfectly natural to expect Sally to
live there.

But some of Hannah's needs were new needs, the needs of

a woman in misery. She exuded her suffering as an aura, almost an odor. Sally suffered also, but she knew that her suffering was different. The death of your father, even if it's sudden, is something your entire life has prepared you for. It's finally a part of your life. The death of your husband is something closer to your own death. Sally spent New Year's Eve at Hannah's, eating cheese and crackers and sitting in front of the tube. As the ball climbed up toward 1985, she looked at her mother. Hannah was crying. The last year that had held him fell into the past.

The cat had a stroke, or something resembling a stroke. He slept in his litter box; he walked, cautiously, into walls. Sally sat down at the kitchen table; Napoleon unsteadily approached her, let himself down heavily at her feet, and put his paw on her shoe.

"I think it's time to put him to sleep," Hannah said. "Or maybe he'll just die in his sleep one night. Maybe it'll be a family tradition."

Hannah led herself carefully to her sorrow, as one leads an animal to water. She nurtured it; she cultivated it; she suckled it at her breast.

At least this was how Sally saw it. But she knew she wasn't thinking straight. She was just tired of staying there four nights a week.

Napoleon had been eating less and less; now he stopped entirely. They tried to coax him with his favorite foods, but he wasn't interested. Finally they decided it was time to take him to the vet. Sally put his pillow into a cardboard box, lifted him carefully, and placed him on the pillow. He was a tiny thing, all bones. Sally took him by herself, in Hannah's car; she steered with one hand, touching him with the other. She sang to him as she drove.

The vet was a squat man with a smock and a nosecold. He put Napoleon on a gray table. "Can I hold him?" Sally said. He nodded sternly as he filled his syringe.

He left the room for a moment. She whispered into Napoleon's ear: "My dear little man." She held him as the vet gave him the injection. She felt his little body quiver. He died.

At work, the children, sensing her pain, were gentle with Sally; they seemed to want to heal her. Wouldn't that have been sweet, if they'd acted like that? In fact, the children were horrible: they scented her weakness and homed in on it. They were ungovernable. She felt like a colonial overseer in British India, trying to subdue the natives. A young man on winter break from college came to help in her classroom: puffy-faced, uncertain, pale, he was always nervously licking his lips, so that even the skin above his lips was chapped and red. One day he showed up with a silly haircut, and one of the more inventive students started calling him "Fruitcup." All the kids in the class picked up on the nickname, in a mocking croon. The poor guy didn't know how to deal with it: whenever one of the kids called him Fruitcup, he looked as if he was going to cry. Sally didn't know how to deal with it either. Two days later, when she was still trying to figure out how to suppress this latest revolt, she learned that he'd called the principal's office, pleading illness, and that he wouldn't be back.

She meant to call him, to tell him not to take it too hard. It probably would have meant a lot to him. But she was too absorbed in her own sadness, and she never did.

Ben was a better daughter to Hannah than Sally was. He'd show up at the house with a potful of soup—bland soup, usually; and he'd laugh as Hannah, after tasting it, scolded him for not adding any spices. Then she'd add them herself, congratulating herself for having turned a ho-hum soup into something delicious. Sally sometimes wondered if he made it bland on purpose.

"She never turns off the fucking tube." Sally was bitching to Ben, in a little bar in the West Village. "You wake up in the morning and Elie Wiesel is on the 'Today Show.' Before you leave the house she sets the VCR so she won't miss 'Donahue.' Sometimes we sit there watching the Weather Channel. When we eat we watch in the kitchen, and when she goes to bed she has a little tube for her room. And she's talking about buying a Watchman. So she can keep it on in the car."

Ben was about to take a drink of beer; now he put down the glass. "What do you want from her, Sally? It's self-medication. Some people do it with liquor; she does it with the TV. What do you expect her to be doing, filling her life with self-improvement projects? Taking a course in the philosophy of science at the New School? Attending a seminar at the Learning Annex—'How to Flirt'?"

But she couldn't help but be hard on her mother. It was self-medication. She'd discovered a great defect in Hannah. She'd discovered that Hannah wasn't Burke.

Hannah looked up from the *Bergen Record* and said to Sally, "Do you look both ways before you cross the street?" Apparently some unlucky local had been run over by a Mister Softee truck, and it occurred to her that Sally was all too likely to meet the same fate. Hannah seemed to believe that her loved ones were slightly retarded. She was forever hectoring Sally about Vitamin C, umbrellas, the eternal problem of Sally's thinness ("Doctors now believe you need a little fat, so if you get sick your body has something to nourish you"), muggers, unwashed fruit, bodily moles that should have been removed long ago, the subway, and the perils of venturing out on winter days without a hat.

Burke had had the gift of distance. When he was alive

she'd sometimes thought of it as coldness. But it wasn't coldness—or it wasn't coldness alone. It was the knowledge that people need room. It was the knowledge that you can't control people, even if you might want to. In the open spaces of his detachment you could find room for yourself, you could breathe.

He'd had a certain class. He was personally rigid, but he didn't get upset about what other people did. Hannah was always narrowing her eyes and saying, "You see those two in the corner booth? If those two aren't lesbians I'll eat my hat."

"You're a true suburbanite, Ma," Sally would say, and then she'd be mad at herself for saying it. She knew that if she was so annoyed at her mother for these suburban vulgarities, it was only because she wasn't grown-up enough to let them pass.

She walked around feeling perpetually suffocated, perpetually hemmed in. It grieved her that it had come to this. It was hard to remember Hannah's goodness, her generosity. In Sally's state of sourness, her mother's generosity seemed like nothing but a way to put you in her debt.

When Sally was little she used to come down with high fevers at least once a year. They could last for a week; sometimes they were so bad they brought hallucinations; but even at the worst moments she always felt safe, because her mother always knew exactly what to do. Ministering with toast and tea, changing her sheets and her pillowcase every day, caring for her attentively but not so attentively that it chafed. She would touch her lips to Sally's forehead to check the fever, which could never be considered broken until Hannah made it official by giving her forehead one last kiss, nodding in satisfaction, and pronouncing it "as cool as a cucumber."

She tried to keep things like this in mind. Hannah had put herself out for Sally for twenty-seven years—couldn't she repay her, for just a few months, without whining about it? Nope. Couldn't be done.

On a Friday night Hannah lay facedown on the carpet as Sally straddled her, massaging her back. J. R. Ewing grinned like a snake as he hatched a new plot against his brother. Hannah had had back problems for as long as Sally could remember—she claimed they'd begun with Sally's birth; so Sally had to give regular massages as a lifelong penance. When Sally was a tiny thing she used to walk up and down on Hannah's back. That she enjoyed; she didn't enjoy this. Taking in her hands the loose soft flesh of her back; then down to the hard platy hips; then, skipping the prime assiness of the buttocks, down to the globular thighs and the strangely slender calves, tapering to the delicate bones of the ankles.

"Now the feet," Hannah said.

"Not the feets!"

"You can wash your hands right after!"

The worst part, the perpetually smelly feet. Hannah's feet exuded an oily unpleasantness, which in Sally's mind was a sign of a character flaw.

Working her hands over the greasiness of her mother's feet, Sally was too aware of the unwanted intimacy of family.

Of course, if Burke had outlived Hannah, life would have been strange in another way. Hannah drove Sally crazy sometimes, but they talked, they gossiped, they laughed, they ranted at each other—they were comfortable together. If Burke had outlived Hannah, Sally might have seen him once a month or once a year—she had no idea—but she knew that when she saw him they would have been unable to speak.

One day Sally had lunch with an old teacher from college; they spent two hours talking about her father. Later it occurred to her that she'd never talked with her father for that long.

Burke without Hannah, Hannah without Burke. The simple fact was this: together her parents had made a magnificent person.

Hannah and Sally spent a Friday night in front of the tube. On Saturday afternoon they went shopping.

"What would you like for dinner tonight?" Hannah said.

"I'm not staying over tonight. I have plans."

"What plans?" Hannah sounded hurt.

Sally had no plans whatsoever.

"I'm staying over at Ben's."

Hannah's face relaxed into an expression of something close to acceptance. "You're back together?" She didn't like the thought of losing Sally, but she did like Ben, and she liked the idea of a grandchild. Ben was her best shot.

Sally wondered why she had said it. Because she wanted to stay with Ben? Or because she knew this was the only excuse she could have come up with that Hannah would accept without complaining . . . ?

And so she went to Ben's. To see what she had meant.

She still had his key. She let herself into his apartment. She walked from room to room, with the lights off. Remembering the first time she'd been there, impressed with what a grown-up he was. Impressed with his refrigerator. A man who could take care of me. She remembered the first time she'd met him, at that party, when she was still with Owen.

She'd never heard from Owen, never told him. Owen seemed like another life. Throwing his watch into the river. You live one life after another, and all of them disappear.

She sat on Ben's couch. She didn't know what she was doing there. But it was blissful to be back in his apartment. In contrast to the wild disorder of her mother's house and the absentminded minimalism of her own. Ben's place was filled with plants, books, quiet wood surfaces. On the coffee table was a chessboard with a few pieces on it, the white king top-pled in disgrace; next to the board was an ashtray with a pipe. Ben played chess once a week with a friend, and when he played he smoked a pipe.

It wouldn't be an honest bargain. She didn't know if she loved him. She thought he loved her.

So why was she here? To have time with him again in this apartment, with this man who miraculously kept plants alive . . . to sit beside him in the subway late at night and feel completely safe . . . to feel like a better person herself, because she was cared for by someone so good . . . she could have all that.

She waited for him.

About an hour later, he let himself in. He closed the door and took off his overcoat. As he was opening his closet door, he saw her. She was sitting on the couch, in the light of one small lamp. He didn't say anything. He took out a hanger, hung up the coat carefully, and closed the closet door.

She had to admit he had a certain style, this union guy.

He came into the living room. "The eternal wanderer," he said.

"I'm not really much of a wanderer," she said. "Did you know I've never been further west than St. Louis?"

Deflect an emotional situation with a witless irrelevancy: a formula she had always found helpful.

"Would you like something to drink?"

She said no. He poured a glass of bourbon for himself. She'd never seen him drink bourbon before. She felt a crazy shot of jealousy: he'd been living a life without her.

He sat on the couch. On the other side of the couch.

"I'm glad to see you. But . . . why are you here?"

"I missed you."

When she had formulated the sentence, in her mind, it had

seemed like half a lie. But when she said it, it felt like the truth.

"I'm glad." She could feel him relaxing. It was so easy to make him happy, really. But she'd done so little to make him happy, during all the time they were together.

"Why do you even *like* me?" she said.

He laughed. "That's a good question. Requires some thought."

As he sat there, thinking, she was afraid he might realize that, actually, he didn't like her.

"I like you for a lot of reasons, Sally. But maybe the thing I like most is that you're still searching for the meaning of life. I think you'll always be searching for the meaning of life. It makes you a bit of a jerk, in a way, and it makes it very frustrating to be with you sometimes. But next to you, most other people I know seem so . . . earthbound."

She felt herself turning red.

"Maybe I like you for selfish reasons," he said. "I think my greatest fear in life is that I'm going to turn into this pompous . . . what did you once call me? Mr. Good. I feel like I'm in danger of disappearing into this Mother Teresa act. I like the way you don't quite buy it. I like the way you make fun of me."

She wasn't good enough for him. She remembered that night in the hotel in Sag Harbor, when the mutterings of the man in the next room had spooked her, and she'd felt so estranged from Ben—she remembered how she'd wished she could find a way to knock down the wall around herself. She had finally given up that fight. She didn't know if she could take it up again now. She felt too battered. All she wanted was comfort.

They went to bed together, and she was sure she gave him no pleasure. She barely touched him, she barely did anything to please him. She couldn't. All she wanted was to lie still and be caressed by him. Forgive me.

Winter. They went to the movies in Paramus and when they came out the parking lot was covered with snow. They were spending the night at Hannah's. Instead of driving on the highway they drove through the empty narrow quiet white streets. For no particular reason, in some unknown suburb, Ben stopped the car; they walked the unfamiliar streets, streets without sidewalks, as the snow caught in their hair, falling so hard they could hardly keep their eyes open.

Life made her dizzy. She lofted a snowball his way; they engaged in brief combat; but instead of ending the battle by coming together with kisses and laughter, which is the script they would have followed in the TV movie version of their lives, they drifted apart, walking aimlessly, thinking. She looked at Ben, half a block away. She had him in her life again, but it had only reminded her that loneliness is a much more complicated thing than she usually imagined. He was the perfect helper: mostly because he understood how little he could help. Often, in his apartment, in the middle of the night, she'd get out of bed and go to the living room and lie on the couch in the dark and cry. For one or two nights he had followed her there and tried to comfort her, but he'd learned that there was nothing he could do. Finally she'd come back to bed and he would hold her. She was grateful for that, but the mourning was deeper than his comfort could reach. Walking through the thick snow she had to keep her eyes half-closed; she could hardly see him. The loneliness of life was insane. This mourning was the deepest connection she had ever felt. It was incredible to think that if Burke were still alive she wouldn't be embracing him, wouldn't be telling him that she loved him. She hadn't told Hannah that she loved her, not since the first week. Fear is stronger than death. The street was so quiet it made her ears ring. Ben was walking through the snow.

She walked slowly, scraping the snow off the parked cars with her bare hand. Each car after she passed it had a thin snowless band. A human lives in a shell. On the morning of November first, before the phone rang, she had awakened for a moment around seven, checked the alarm, and, reveling in the pleasure of having another half-hour to spend in bed, she'd gone happily back to sleep. Without the faintest intuition that the man who'd made her was gone.

They walked in silence, twenty feet apart. When they finally decided to go back to the car, they decided without speaking; Ben was attuned to her somehow. He drove slowly through the snow. When they reached Teaneck he took his foot off the gas, cut the lights and the windshield wipers, and let the car go drifting, like a large, silent ship, through the snow.

They reached the house. When they got out of the car Sally passed the window and saw the light of the inevitable television.

As she put the key in the lock she was surprised to feel a certain sense of freedom. She stood in the doorway, appalled by her own mind. Whenever she'd visited her parents, she'd knotted up slightly, at the prospect of facing the test of her father's scrutiny. For years she'd lived with the feeling that she wasn't measuring up to his standards. And now there was nothing to measure up to. It was appalling, but, pushing open the inner door, she felt a strange, giddy ease.

"How was the movie?" Hannah said, in a toneless voice. She was watching HBO.

"It was a little arty for my taste. Ben loved it."

"That's true. I did."

"Ben loves all those foreign movies."

"I'm lucky it *was* a foreign movie. Your daughter was snorting so much, and sighing, and wheezing through that deviated septum, that I was just happy to be watching something with subtitles."

Hannah smiled. "The apple doesn't fall far from the tree," she said. Sally felt proud to be carrying on the great Burkean tradition.

Ben went upstairs to bed and Sally stayed up with her mother. They watched the last part of *The King of Comedy,* and then they sat through something by Neil Simon. Hannah looked old. Sally had an impulse to walk over to her mother and embrace her. The impulse passed. Fear is stronger than death.

Months. Spring. The world turned green. She didn't feel the traditional renewal . . . or at any rate, she didn't feel it simply. Everything that was newly born, each tender shoot springing from every tree, had the seed of its death within it. Caitlin had another baby, three weeks premature. Sally went to see them in the hospital. The baby was in intensive care; Caitlin, wasted from her C-section, couldn't leave her bed; Sally stood before a partition as a nurse on the other side held the baby up to the glass. Sally felt something go loose in her throat as she stared at the little shriveled face.

The world was in bloom again, in sadness. Hannah let her backyard grow wild. The swimming pool, untended, was full of stagnant life. Hannah wasn't old—she was sixty—but in her own mind she was too old to begin again. She had decided to take early retirement: she wouldn't be teaching next year. In the library Sally came upon the memoirs of Dylan Thomas's widow: *Leftover Life to Kill.*

If Sally left the room for a moment, Hannah would look up and say, "Where are you going?"

Sally stood in the kitchen, two rooms away from her, and she could feel her, clutching, clutching, clutching. Hannah wasn't sure what room Sally was in; Sally could feel her mother's long invisible tentacles searching through the house for her—gropingly, stumblingly, inexorably searching through the house.

Every room in Hannah's house was a cry for aid. For the first month or two Sally had been perpetually cleaning, but after a while she slackened off: she'd lost the energy or the sense of selflessness or the freshness of the wound. And soon the two of them sat in the living room nearly lost to each other, separated by huge piles of newspapers and magazines. None of them could be thrown out; they all contained articles Hannah hadn't gotten around to reading yet. On top of her native squalor she added the squalor of being a child of the Depression: before Napoleon died, when the price of a bag of cat litter went up by fifteen cents, she took to scooping out his shit with a rusty spatula. Now, as her latest economy measure, she no longer flushed the toilet when she urinated. There were four toilets in the house, and each of them was filled with misty yellow piss and a tissue.

It was easy for Sally to see how much Hannah's grief had deranged her: the evidence was all around. She was only intermittently aware that her own derangement was equally evident, in her pitiless accounting of her mother's sins.

Ben and Sally took a weekend in the mountains. They went to a little inn near Woodstock. They sat outside at a picnic table with a glass of wine; bees zipped around past their heads; Ben kept shifting and squirming on the bench. "I never knew you were such a coward, McMahon."

"I'm allergic to these guys."

A bee came swooping and Ben jumped to his feet, quickly duckwalking away. Sally laughed at him.

"I'm serious, woman. If he bites me I'm done for."

They took a walk up the mountain trail. They were accompanied by the inn's resident dog, a plump old mutt named

Tina. Old leaves were mulching beneath their feet. Tina walked ahead of them, ignoring them, as if she was perfectly comfortable to be venturing up here on her own; but whenever the two of them stopped for a moment, Tina, glancing behind her, would stop as well.

The sun began to set; the evening began to grow cool. Ben was allergic to bees. Spring in the mountains is bleaker than fall.

Sally reached over to a thin branch and with a quick delicate movement pinched off a young leaf. She held it out to Ben. "Thank you," he said.

They had a big dinner, read in the public room of the hotel, went to their room, undressed, made love. Bodies.

Ben fell asleep. The wind made a racket outside; the night was cold. She was glad that Ben was asleep; she'd looked forward to this all day. Now she could be alone with her father. She lay in the dark as Ben breathed evenly beside her, and her father, her feeling for her father, which was like a secret she hoarded in a small place during the day, was now allowed to emerge. Lying in the cold and the dark, she could feel his spirit rising out of her body, filling the room. Not his spirit, but the spirit of her love for him. She turned in bed. She felt as if she had been beaten over every inch of her body. Everything was tender.

Her father had never been up to this area. She didn't like to think about things like this. She didn't like to think about his limitations, not even the most trivial. She didn't like to think that the list of his limitations would grow.

She lay in bed, thinking of the things she'd have to tell him if he came back. Gorbachev had replaced Chernenko; he'd be interested in that. Reagan had been reelected. Dave's—the diner on Canal Street that made the greatest egg creams in the world—had closed down. She saw her father's ghost, still dazed and bewildered by the passage to death, wandering the streets of New York in search of an egg cream; looking for Dave's, and being disoriented when he couldn't find it.

Ben snored. He'd been as sympathetic as he could be; but his own period of mourning had long been over. She couldn't rationally blame him for this—but she did blame him. For the first month, her grief had been his grief; Ben had loved Burke, in a way. But of course he hadn't loved him as Sally loved him; and there had been a day when, after Ben came home from work, though he'd still ministered to Sally tenderly, she'd noticed a certain quickness in his movements and his voice, and a certain absorption in his recounting of his work-day, and it was as clear as if someone had drawn a thick black line on the calendar. He was still sad about Burke; he was still infinitely tender to Sally; but he could no longer share her grief. His work of mourning—the little he'd had to do of it— was over.

It made her feel alone; it made her feel betrayed. She felt betrayed by the quickness of his motions; betrayed by the casualness of his appetites, as standing in front of the open refrigerator he drank from a carton of milk and wiped the whiteness off his lip with the back of his hand. He was back in a world of simple need and simple taking. Sally maneu-vered through a world in which the objects called out to remind her of her loss.

What made it worse was that in his story she saw her own. For her it would take much longer, but no matter how long it took, the work of mourning would be done: she would finally no longer grieve for him. It was six months since his death, and she'd cried every day. Finally she would stop crying. Hannah had loved her own father desperately; yet she said she didn't really miss him keenly anymore. Burke would fade.

The next day they took the train back to New York. There was a story about Lech Walesa in the *Times*. Ben was going on about how wonderful Solidarity was. It made her unhappy. Her father could never accept Solidarity, not fully. He was a union man, so he appreciated what they'd done; but he was a Leninist also, a believer in the guiding role of the party; it was a belief he could never shake. He was formed in a Leninist moment and he bore the stamp of that moment till he died. It bothered her to hear Ben going on about Solidarity so glibly—because she agreed with everything he said. It seemed to push Burke further into the past.

At two in the morning she left the bed and went to lie on the couch. For the first time in months, he followed her. He sat across from her in the dark, in his rocking chair. He was wearing a robe. "You look like Bruno Samartino," she said.

He didn't smile.

"What are you thinking?" he said.

"You'll think less of me if I tell you."

He didn't say anything. She could hear the creaking of his rocking chair.

"I know this is insanely selfish . . . but sometimes I think what hurts the most is the *way* he died. I never got a chance to say goodbye to him. I never told him I loved him. Sometimes I think I could accept it if I could just talk to him for five more minutes."

At this he did smile. "A tender deathbed scene? I think Burke would have been happy to skip that." More quietly: "He knew you loved him."

"You want to hear something even stupider? Sometimes, with the way he died, I feel like I was cheated out of a lesson. I always thought he'd teach me how to die."

"He did teach you how to die. He taught you how to live."

"Oh, bullshit."

"It isn't bullshit." He leaned forward with a sudden intensity. "I think he did teach you how to live. I'm just not sure you were paying attention. Whatever else Burke was, he was a fighter. But I don't see you fighting at all. I understand how much it hurts for you to lose him. I don't understand why you're letting it knock you out. For a couple of months I thought my role was just to not put any pressure on you, help you heal. But . . . I don't know. I feel like I've been taking care of a sleepwalker for the last two months, just trying to make sure you don't wander off a cliff."

Leave me alone, she thought. Let me wander off a cliff.

She didn't say anything. He went back to bed.

But a few nights later, in her dream, she received testimony in support of Ben's point of view. She came to a house in the woods and met Burke there. She told him how terrible life had been since he'd died; she said she couldn't go on without him. He looked at her with a touch of impatience and quoted Samuel Johnson: "Grief," he said, "is a species of idleness." It was just what he would've told her.

A booksale at the Mid-Manhattan library. Thousands of volumes. She noticed a few books that might have come from Burke's shelves: *Giant in Chains. The Big Strike. The Many and the Few. The Wind in the Olive Trees*. She picked up *The Wind in the Olive Trees* . . . it felt light in her hand. She could feel a faint, faint tremor. It didn't come from her. She knew what it was. It was the tremor in the hands of the bereaved one, the person who had packed the book not long ago. The meaning of the presence of these books was obvious. Another old Communist had died.

She took a few of the books to a table and sat down. "Dialectical materialism, the one scientific philosophy of our time." "The coming victory of the world proletariat." "The proletariat is becoming enlightened and educated by waging its class struggle . . . it is learning to gauge the measure of its success." Sentiments of utter confidence about the future, on flaking paper.

The hopes of her parents. Their hopes for the victory of the world proletariat had died long ago, before she was born. But they'd held on to some sort of faith—it had kept them alive. It was strange how the hopes they lived for meant nothing to her. Strange how quickly things are lost.

She left the library, opening her bag to the guard at the door, and started walking downtown. It was a muggy Monday in early July. Fifth Avenue was bleak in the hot afternoon.

Lost . . . but not completely. Her parents had believed that the world needed mending, and they'd given themselves to the task. Sally didn't believe the mending was possible: not the kind of deep mending they'd believed in. But somehow she still felt it was necessary.

She would never find a home, as they had, in the effort to transfigure the world. But in her belief that she lived in a world that needed to be transfigured, she'd probably always feel homeless. A feeling of homelessness was not what her parents might have wanted to pass on to their daughter. But to have passed on anything at all was rare enough.

She went down into Penn Station to catch a train back to Brooklyn. In a long dark filthy passageway, where the smell of urine was sharp in the heavy air, five or ten of the truly homeless were sitting on sheets of flattened cardboard. Learning to gauge the measure of their success.

To Sally's surprise, Hannah volunteered to supervise a summer day-care program sponsored by the Board of Education.

Sally dropped in on her there one afternoon. Among the children, her mother looked younger. Chinese checkers was all the rage among the kids, and Hannah was taking on all comers. She sat cross-legged on the floor in front of the checkerboard, tossing a marble from hand to hand. "You think you can beat *me* at Chinese checkers? *You* have the ever-lovin' nerve to think you can challenge *me?!*" Lining up to play against her, the little kids hopped around with delight.

Among these children, Hannah could forget her sorrow. Sally had almost forgotten what a pleasure her mother's company could be.

Hannah was more at ease with children than Sally was. Sally was much more *serious* with them—as if she were trying to touch the developed, rational being, the philosopher within each child. Hannah was more comfortable with children's sheer childishness. Sally studied her mother, wondering how she could learn from her style. Can you learn to be more spontaneous?

Later that evening, Sally received another surprise. Hannah told her that she'd booked a place on a tour-group to China. Sally was impressed. It was a big step. She was going with two friends, two other widows. They were leaving in October; they'd be away for a month.

Hannah was terrified of flying. "I'll have to make sure I have a lot of Valium with me when I go." She sat in the den, in the middle of huge piles of paper. "I'll never be able to clean this place by then. If I crash, don't bother cleaning it yourself. Hire a maid service. Better yet, just rent a dump truck and get rid of all this junk with a shovel."

Ben spent most of the summer in Georgia for his union, coming home on weekends when he could. One Friday, when he was getting back in around six, they arranged to meet at a restaurant. On an evening so humid that it was difficult to breathe, she made her way through the crowd on Sixth Avenue. Joggers, roller skaters, businesspeople racing for the bus—everyone was pushing each other, and her thoughts were pushing each other also, in a discontented buzz.

She turned the corner and saw him in front of the restaurant. He was in a blue suit, leafing through the paper, half a head taller than everyone else. He seemed like the one calm, steady person in the crowd. As she approached him, she took a deep, calm breath, the first deep breath she'd been able to take all day. He still hadn't seen her. She was surprised by the simplicity of her feelings. For that moment, at least, there were no complications: knowing that she was the one he was waiting for, she felt proud.

School began again. She sat with the kids in a circle and read them a story. A girl named Melissa, daydreaming, put her thumb in her mouth and twirled a strand of Sally's hair, leaning heavily against her.

Her first few weeks of school were pleasurable in an almost physical way. The freedom with which these children touched you; the constant pressure of their scrutiny, the constant pressure of their needs—it gave her a pleasure that was almost like the pleasure of loving and being loved. Sometimes she wondered how people in other jobs, where you have to wear a stiff skirt and act like an adult all day—she wondered how they survived.

The job had other benefits, less metaphysical. One of the good things about being with six-year-olds is that they think you're a genius. There was a rabbit named Waldo in the classroom. When one of the kids shouted out a swearword and then denied having done it, Sally said, "Well, who did— Waldo?" This was received as the wittiest remark ever made. The children laughed about it for half an hour.

Autumn was in the air now; the weather crisp and cool, as it had been on the days after he died; and sometimes she felt as if the seasons were a wheel, leading her back to the time of her father's death. On one such afternoon, little Touissant Thompson, annoyed by her strange remoteness, sank his teeth into her wrist. Harder, she thought. Harder.

She missed her period. Her breasts were aching, and she had a taste of metal in her mouth. She made an appointment with her doctor. Yes. It was true.

She left the doctor's office and walked up Central Park West. It was a chilly October afternoon. Burke had been dead almost a year. The buildings near the park were copper brown in the afternoon light. She drew her jacket collar close around her throat and walked alongside the park, near the long stone wall.

Hannah had left for China that morning. Her fear of flying had reached hysterical proportions as the day approached. She'd been crying for a week. Maybe it wasn't only the terror of flying. This was her first major undertaking since Burke died. Maybe for Hannah too, new undertakings pushed Burke further into the past. Maybe she was feeling her loss all over again.

Sally wandered over to the Museum of Natural History. She walked up the great stone steps and paid her two dollars at the door, and she was given a pin with a picture of a homey-looking dinosaur. She went into the great central room with the enormous dinosaur skeletons. The noble dinosaurs. The most impressive of them were a two-legged tyrannosaurus and a four-legged stegosaurus, with an armored skull. Years ago, when they used to visit the museum, her brother would speculate endlessly about which one would prevail in a fair fight. Sally had never much cared. She stood beneath the enormous tyrannosaurus, conscious that this was a suitable occasion for awe. This giant had actually walked the earth, a million years ago. She was aware that the scale of time should blow her away—should reduce her own concerns, the life she was trapped in, the mourning she was trapped in—reduce it all to insignificance. But it did no such thing. The dinosaurs did not impress her. They'd had their day. It was gone.

She wandered around the museum for another hour, looking at birds, beasts, and flowers. Nothing spoke to her. Finally, just as she was about to leave, she came upon an exhibit that did.

The stages of conception: the growth of the fetus inside the womb. The last few panels were models made of wood or plastic or whatever. But as you walked back toward the beginning of the exhibit, life in its earliest stages was represented not by sculpted models but by fetuses that had been preserved after spontaneous abortions. There were four of these. Tiny; tinier; astonishingly tiny; tiniest. Sally walked slowly back along the trail of life until she came to the first and smallest. It was a month old, about the same age as the being that was taking form within her. It was about the size of an aspirin.

She stayed in front of it for a long time.

She left the museum and walked into Central Park. On a bench near the Great Lawn she sat and watched the runners, with their muscular legs. Everyone in New York had muscular legs. They all looked splendid; determined and fierce; their bodies were taut, tight, intimidating; each of them, man and woman, ran alone. Each of them dedicated to the perfection of the body, in proud singleness. With a regard for their own bodies so extreme it seemed doubtful they could ever really love anyone else. And for the first time in her life, she found herself in a situation in which she didn't think herself the most isolated person there, the most alone. Each of the runners was dedicated to an idea of self-creation, of solitary perfection, that she couldn't believe in any longer. Most of them were older than she was; but as she watched them she felt as if she were watching children at play. Their dream of self-creation seemed the naivest delusion in the world. She felt old; she felt tethered by a thousand commitments. She had never in her life entered into a commitment without trying to make sure it had an escape clause, but nevertheless she'd been committed. She was committed to her own past. Committed to her people, the living and the dead. She carried them inside her. She lived with them.

She wondered if she was still what Ben would call a Dylanist. She probably was, and she'd probably always be one: restless; not really political, yet edgily intent against selling out; putting her feelings first. Dylan himself, with his restless honesty, would probably always mean a lot to her. But lately, when she'd looked at his records, she could never find anything she wanted to hear. His concerns weren't her concerns. His work contained nothing about loss; nothing about aging—his own, or that of the people he loved; nothing about being a father, or being a son. Nothing about the complexities of relationships that last.

She wandered out of the park, took a subway to the bus terminal, took a bus to Jersey. She thought she'd spend the weekend at her parents' house, watching cable TV, reading, taking in the quiet.

She sat in the back of the bus with her hands folded over her stomach. Cradling her baby, the size of an aspirin.

Since Burke had died the thought of having a child had begun to seem attractive to her, for the first time in her life. But she hadn't been looking to have one so soon. She didn't see how she *could* have one now. She didn't feel ready.

But you can't plan everything. Maybe this was her chance. Life serves up its chances, and you take them or you lose them.

Ben would be a good father.

She could see the look of delight on his face if she told him that she was pregnant. Scenes from their married life unrolled before her: she saw him reading Dickens to their child before a fire.

The bus, a local, making all stops, wound its way through the dreariest parts of New Jersey. Maybe the dreariest parts of the world.

She turned away from the window; most of the people on the bus looked bleached out, worn down from work. The difficulties of it were insurmountable. Did she want to bring up a baby on her own? No. Did she want to marry Ben? It was hard to imagine.

The bus disgorged its passengers in Hoboken, Union City, Weehawken. It climbed up finally toward Boulevard East, from which you could see all of New York.

She didn't see how she could keep this baby. This baby who needed her. This baby the size of an aspirin. Maybe someday, maybe another child . . . but how could she keep this baby? She was still so young herself, so confused, so weighed down by her grief. It would be best to tell no one, not even Ben. Especially not Ben. Just make the appointment, get it done, and go on as if nothing had ever happened.

. . . but why should she *defend* her grief? Was that what she wanted—to choose the grief, and send this new life back into the dark?

The bus had reached the top of the hill. With her sleeve she cleaned off the window: the city was before her, in all its glory. The spire of the Empire State Building was lit with a soft pink light. The city looked new. There was a tiny being within her, a tiny boy . . . why was she so certain that it would be a boy? He was drawing nourishment from her, drawing life from her life. He needed her. He was asking her a question. He was asking a question of her life. She didn't know how to answer.

When she reached her mother's house, instead of going inside, she sat on a folding chair on the cool dark lawn. So quiet. In the dark her eyes played tricks on her. She thought she saw Napoleon trotting up. It was just the play of the high unkept grass in the wind; but once she had imagined it she wanted to keep the image, and she blurred her vision a little to see him as he'd been for so many years, trotting up in his trusting way, nose lifted hopefully into the wind, searching the air for harbingers of friendship.

Near the swimming pool was the picnic table where she had sat with her parents that wonderful summer two years ago. Burke finally relaxing. It had looked as if her parents were really going to achieve the impossible: were going to enjoy their old age. When she was little, she was told in science class that sound waves, vibrations of all sorts, are never lost. They disperse and disperse until they can't be perceived by the senses, but they're never entirely lost. And if this is so, then wasn't it true that the sounds of two summers ago—not that loud to begin with—were still, however faintly, in the air? Without straining, just letting herself go, she thought she could hear the click of cups as Burke poured out his famous coffee. In what was one of the few gestures of warmth they could ever share.

She felt the cold nose of the cat in her hand. She looked down, but the cat wasn't there.

It was dark; the last mosquitoes of the year were starting to gather. She got up and let herself into the house. Into its quietness. The den was like a portrait of her mother's distress. Newspapers, cups, orange peels, mounds of coupons, piles of recipes, diet plans cut out from *Prevention* and *Woman's Day*. Hannah was miles above the ocean now, taking a Valium with her martini, chattering with nervousness to a stewardess, forcing herself forward into a future she had no desire to live.

She turned on the TV. She sat with the sound off. Fred Astaire was gliding lightly across the screen.

Ben was away somewhere. She called his number so she could hear his voice on his answering machine. She hung up without leaving a message.

This was serious. This was serious life. He had given of himself to her, so freely, for so long. The being that was taking shape within her was his as well. He should have a part in the decision. It was her decision, in the end: she wouldn't necessarily do what he wanted her to do. But she would talk to him.

She found Hannah's car keys, threw on an old denim jacket, and took a slow drive, through back streets, to the Hudson River, to the little park near the George Washington Bridge, where she used to come after school, day after day, with Beth.

She sat in the car, taking in the brilliance of the skyline. She remembered how she felt when she came here, day after day, as a young girl: she'd been awed by the majesty and the vastness of the city, but she'd felt that the city was no more majestic, no more vast, than she was.

Now she felt that the city was more vast than she was.

She got out of the car and walked to the river. There was a huge wind blowing toward the south. She stood, shivering, with her hands in her pockets, under the great bright bridge.

The city, Burke's city, was radiant. It didn't need him to tell its stories. It glittered vastly. It went on.

She fished around in her jacket, hoping a cigarette would turn up. She found something in the breast pocket. It was the photograph she'd come across a year ago: her father as a little boy.

His lips were slightly parted. He looked innocent. He looked expectant. He looked eager for the life to come.